HEART OF FIRE

Dragon's Mate 2

Hope Bennett

Copyright © 2021 Hope Bennett

All rights reserved

The characters and events portrayed in this book are fictitious. Any similarity to real persons, living or dead, is coincidental and not intended by the author.

No part of this book may be reproduced, or stored in a retrieval system, or transmitted in any form or by any means, electronic, mechanical, photocopying, recording, or otherwise, without express written permission of the publisher.

CONTENTS

Title Page	1
Copyright	2
Chapter 1: Seren	5
Chapter 2: Dane	16
Chapter 3: Seren	32
Chapter 4: Seren	41
Chapter 5: Seren	48
Chapter 6: Dane	59
Chapter 7: Seren	70
Chapter 8: Seren	80
Chapter 9: Seren	89
Chapter 10: Dane	98
Chapter 11: Seren	112
Chapter 12: Dane	122
Chapter 13: Seren	129
Chapter 14: Dane	136

Chapter 15: Dane	149
Chapter 16: Seren	157
Chapter 17: Dane	167
Chapter 18: Dane	179
Chapter 19: Dane	187
Chapter 20: Seren	197
Chapter 21: Seren	211
Chapter 22: Dane	220
Chapter 23: Seren	231
Chapter 24: Dane	239
Chapter 25: Seren	248
Chapter 26: Dane	259
Chapter 27: Seren	273
Chapter 28: Dane	284
Chapter 29: Seren	299
Chapter 30: Dane	310
Chapter 31: Seren	320
Chapter 32: Dane	330
Chapter 33: Dane	338
Next in Series	350
Other books by Hope	351
About Hope	356

CHAPTER 1: SEREN

The Hoskins clan had come to our castle to escort my cousin Morgan home. I had been sent to my room and told to stay there. I knew why: I was an embarrassment to Lord Somerville. I was weak and he didn't want anyone to know there was any weakness in his clan.

But I couldn't stay there. I felt like my skin was crawling all over my body, creeping and unnatural. I'd watched the Hoskinses arrive, peeking out from the window, and I hadn't seen Dane. I told myself that I hadn't expected him to come, but the sinking disappointment called me a liar.

I waited a moment for them to get inside the castle and then I crept out of my room. It was stupid, since Lord Somerville had ordered me to stay in there, but I was not being my most rational. I crept down the stairs and managed to avoid one of my aunts who was walking along the corridor and it was lucky that I had learned to be stealthy years ago, and all dragons habitually concealed their scent; she had no idea I was there, holding my breath in the shadow of a doorway.

I thought my luck had changed when I saw Morgan standing there alone. It was the best chance I'd get, and I took it. My sole focus was getting him upstairs to my room so Lord Somerville would never know that I'd left it. Morgan was being guarded by a stocky *curaidh*, tall and broad and dark-haired, just like most *curaidh*. He wasn't a patch on some I'd seen, though. When I tried to politely tell him to get lost, he didn't take the hint and I was too desperate to ask my question to bother with him. I led Morgan to my room and asked.

I managed to retain enough of my grasp of social etiquette not to just blurt out the question I wanted. Instead, I asked Morgan how he was and tried to listen to the answer. I might have asked something else, too, about whether he'd enjoyed himself. I didn't care. He looked healthy – in fact he looked much fitter than when he'd left, and there was a lightness to him that hadn't been there before, too – so I wasn't worried about him.

Eventually, after what felt like several excruciating minutes, I managed to ask the question I wanted. I nearly flung myself at Morgan and begged to know whether Dane was fit and healthy, what he was doing these days, whether he had a partner or a lover. Shit, I was going to drive myself completely mad thinking about that possibility.

My voice was tight as I asked, and I tried to keep it casual. I don't think I was fooling anyone, but I tried.

"And, oh, what is his name? The other warrior, the big one? Dane, is it? Was he an adequate instructor?"

Adequate? If I knew anything about Dane, it was that he was more than *adequate* in everything he did. I was trying *way* too hard there.

Morgan had the same features of most *uasal* – the noble dragons – of blonde hair and silver eyes, though his were tinged with blue. He had inherited Lord Somerville's particular expression, though, a cold disdain that kept his face immobile and stopped people asking questions. I couldn't remember seeing Morgan smile, ever. And he answered then like I was the most boring person on the planet and he was being forced to pass the time of day with me. "I wasn't taught by him."

I lost my cool a bit at that. He had delivered his answer in the same monotone that Lord Somerville used when he wanted to show something was beneath him, and my fickle imagination filled in a hundred explanations, each worse than the last. I snapped, "Why not? Was he not there?"

Morgan's cool voice took on a little feeling. "No, he was there. He just… didn't teach me. I get the feeling he doesn't like *uasal* much."

That didn't make sense.

"Dane likes *uasal*. We- he worked for Lord Somerville."

"Well, he didn't like me."

"You didn't see him at all?" I was getting desperate, practically begging for information like a dog.

"Not much."

"Did he come here with you today?"

"No."

Something inside me deflated. The space where my dragon had been was suddenly more empty and I felt the familiar search inside for the part of me that should be there and wasn't. I'd never known anyone lose their dragon before – there were no records of it and nobody could explain it – but mine had vanished from me one day, sinking down, down inside me until it was so low and still that I couldn't feel it any more. I'd felt it retreat. I'd *felt* it. It was unnatural. My dragon was part of me, it shouldn't just... leave. But it had, and I'd felt empty ever since. That yawning empty space inside me seemed suddenly bigger than ever, big enough to swallow me up, and I wanted to sink down into oblivion.

"Seren, are you ok?"

I drew myself up, forcing my back straight and my chin up. Lord Somerville had instilled that into me. Always stand proud. Never look weak.

"Yes. It's none of my concern what the *curaidh* do. If you don't mind, I'm going to rest now."

Unfortunately, Morgan didn't take the

hint and shove off. No, he asked about Alfie, his brother, and didn't look like he was in a hurry to leave me in peace. Then the *curaidh* guarding him began to sneer. He was talking to Morgan, not me, and began to walk steadily towards my cousin, who had crossed to the window. I didn't like that. He was moving steadily, focused on Morgan, totally dismissing me, and it made me focus on him for the first time. He was stalking towards Morgan like he was a hunter.

They were arguing over Lew, who was the Hoskins man who'd been Morgan's instructor. I didn't give a shit about Lew. But when I saw the *curaidh* reach behind him and pull a knife out from its sheath, I got a very bad feeling. My stomach seemed to clamp down around the emptiness in my centre, and I didn't think. If I'd thought about it, I'd have done anything other than what I actually did, which was to launch myself across the room and tackle the *curaidh* to the floor.

He was much heavier than me, taller than me, and he was a dragon. Me, I was slim and had no dragon. I was about as weak as it was possible to get. I was surprised I even managed to knock him over, but then he was so focused on Morgan that he'd totally forgotten about me. I didn't particularly mind that, since I'd grown used to being forgotten, but it just served him right all the same.

The problem came about when Morgan gave a shriek of pain and the *curaidh* twisted beneath me and managed to grapple with me, shoving me off him and onto my back, and I felt the snap of something inside me and the crack against my head. We were a tangle of limbs and I began to calculate the odds of me surviving. Weak. No dragon. No magic. No back-up. Ok, so the odds weren't in my favour.

Just as the *curaidh* raised the knife above my throat, Morgan flung himself forward, doing barely any better than I had. The *curaidh* was knocked off me, which was enough for me to wriggle away. Morgan and I were both alive, but neither of us was in a position to fight the bulky brute before us. We'd lost the element of surprise and that was our only advantage.

As I tried to climb to my feet, I was suddenly aware of the sharp pain in the front of my thigh where that knife had sliced through my flesh. It felt like he'd cut to my very bone. Red blood poured from me, and I felt sick, weak, ill. When Morgan got his arms around me and began to drag me backwards, away from the *curaidh*, I began to search desperately inside me for my dragon. If ever there was a time for it to come back, it was then.

Dragons were protective. It was their instinct to protect us from any danger. It was unnatural in the extreme for it to leave me to die, refusing to heal me. If it didn't come back, if it didn't heal me and grant me my magic again, we'd both die. We were the same bloody person, for fuck sake – why wasn't it here?

I tried to tell it that, inside me, tried to reach down to my core and drag my dragon up to the surface again. Shift, heal, magic. I couldn't do any of it.

Without my dragon, I stood no chance at all of protecting Morgan. Even if my dragon didn't think *I* was worth protecting, it should surface again to protect Morgan. He was my cousin. My family. Lord Somerville's son, no less. I needed to protect him. But my dragon refused, staying low and untraceable.

"I can't help you, Morgan."

"What do you mean?" Morgan was dragging me across the room and my leg was completely useless. *I* was completely useless and the *curaidh* was standing up again, clutching that knife in his hand.

"I can't- just run, Morgan. Get out. Get downstairs."

"I don't—"

"Get downstairs! They'll protect you." What part of this was he not getting? I couldn't protect him – he needed to get to someone else who could! I shoved him, but I was much weaker than I thought. I nearly toppled over and only Morgan grabbing me under my arms kept me upright. This was not going well.

The *curaidh* snarled and his teeth lengthened.

"Run," I said again, but I heard my own

voice like it was somebody else's. I was slurring and the room was rotating slowly like a carousel, which did not help with my coordination.

Blue light burst across the room and for a second I thought the magic was mine, but I'd never had blue lightning. My leg went numb, everywhere but where the cut was, and all I had was a throbbing wound below the waist.

I was dragged, and had to choke down the bile that rose up my throat at the movement, and I wasn't standing on my own legs any more and that *curaidh* was getting nearer and nearer and I wanted to tell Morgan to get out but maybe I didn't because he stayed beside me.

When there was a crash that deafened me and I felt pinpricks of glass rain down across my skin, I thought I'd died.

Dane was there.

Dane.

He was in dragon form, larger than any other dragon I've seen, dark grey, snarling, and absolutely beautiful. My heart stopped beating for a second, and I was sure it was the end, but then I felt it thud in my chest again and the blood that spilled over my hand, where it clutched at my leg, was pouring in bursts, throbbing in time with my heart.

I was still alive, then, and Dane was really there.

His head shot forward, his mouth open

wide, his teeth glinting in the white light of the room, and he closed his jaws around the *curaidh*'s torso and bit down. I heard the squelch and the crunch, and then the body slipped from his mouth.

I tried to say his name – I wanted to talk to him – but my mouth wasn't working and I barely managed to force out the word. "Dane?"

He shifted back, like I'd seen him do a hundred times, and he stood before me as large as life, huge and muscled and beautiful. His dark grey eyes were locked on me, and my stomach clenched. Then I saw it.

"You're hurt!"

There was a slashing wound on his neck and red blood cascaded down his shoulder and chest.

He reached up to touch the wound and shrugged. "It's already healing."

"What are you doing here?" I asked.

"Sent as security."

"Oh, right," I said. I wanted my dragon. I wanted to be able to stand, to look at Dane properly, but my head kept lolling and things were not staying in focus.

Dane nudged the body of the *curaidh* with his foot and it flopped around. He must have been checking they were dead.

I fell. I hadn't been aware that I was standing, but suddenly I wasn't. Instinct had me scramble to sit up and I found myself leaning back against something, propped up. It was far too early for the sun to set but the room was definitely getting darker.

All I could see was Dane's face, glaring down at me. "Why isn't that wound healing?"

I looked down at my leg. My leg wasn't what was making it hard to breathe.

"I think he broke my rib."

Dane's eyes were angry and locked on me. "Why aren't you healing?"

That was the question, wasn't it? And I couldn't tell him the answer. No way could I do that. "It's none of your business."

I don't know what happened then. Dane stood, retreating from me, and my chest clenched and the pain inside me stabbed down again. Someone else burst into the room and then Dane was fighting and then he wasn't fighting any more. I suppose he must have won. Someone else might have been in the room, but it was too dark to tell. I thought I heard voices. The room seemed empty except for me, and then a hand on my cheek.

Ok, so I wasn't very clear about what had just happened. That was because I'd hit my head hard when I'd first tackled the *curaidh* to the ground, and I felt like I was viewing everything from under murky water. I could feel the hand on my cheek, though.

It was warm. It spread the warmth all down my body and, even without opening my eyes, I knew it was Dane touching me. I couldn't work out what he was saying, though. His voice was incredibly far away and snatched away by the wind.

"Dane?"

I was still warm. I didn't know if that was good or bad. But I felt less hollow. I felt awful still, but awful in a different way. Then I caught a snatch of Dane's words.

"Why weren't you healing, Seren?"

He was speaking softly, and I thought I felt the warm sweetness of his breath across my cheek, but I might have imagined it.

"… with me when I leave…"

I wanted to ask him to repeat himself, but I couldn't open my mouth. My whole body was heavy and sore, and the hard thump of my heart was a warning.

"… could have lost…"

Well duh. Of course I could have lost that fight. It was almost guaranteed that I'd lose any fight with anybody, at the moment, especially a dragon, and double-especially if they were a *curaidh*.

"… go."

I became cold again. My body felt hollow, like I was nothing but skin and raw, gaping wound, and then I felt nothing at all.

CHAPTER 2: DANE

I was in trouble. Again.

Nana had been chewing my ear off for five minutes, which might not sound like a lot but Nana isn't prone to talking endlessly, not like some I could mention – Gramps, for example – and so five minutes was a long time. It also seemed longer because I had to look Nana in the eyes for that whole time and doing that always made my insides turn thin and watery. I have no idea why, since I couldn't see Nana's dragon in her eyes, but she gave off an aura of power. She was the head of the family. She could take me out without even standing up, despite the fact she was well over a thousand years old and absolutely tiny and delicate, like a sparrow. A sparrow that could blast me into a thousand charred pieces from the pretty little sofa she was sitting on.

"Are you listening to me?"

"Yes, Nana."

I hadn't been, not for the past minute, but no way was I going to tell her that. I'd get the lecture all over again and then some.

She looked at me steadily and my stomach slipped around uneasily. I'd had officers in the army threaten me with actual decapitation and still had never been as in awe of them as I was of Nana.

"Dane, you're not to leave the castle grounds."

"Yes, Nana."

She narrowed her eyes.

"I won't Nana," I said. I was starting to get antsy and shifted around, wishing the sofa I was on was about a foot higher than it was.

She jutted her chin at the door. "Go on, get out of here, then."

I left, glad to have been let off. I thought I'd go and find Gramps. He always made my insides stop squirming after I'd had a run-in with Nana. He was downstairs and, normally, it might have been difficult to find him, since we lived in a castle and a great big castle at that. The corridors were long and wide and high-ceilinged, big enough for any of us to get through in dragon form. I knew where he was at that moment, though; I could hear him half way across the castle.

"No, no, put that here. Have you made that sign yet? Yes? Let me see it! Oh, that's wonderful, you did such a good job."

I walked round the corner into the dining room and said, "Please tell me you haven't written 'Happy Mating' on that sign."

Gramps looked to be about in his early sixties, with silver-grey hair and a few wrinkles lining his face, but obviously he was much, much older than that. He was full of energy, though. He stood, putting his hands on his hips, and frowned at me. I wasn't in the least intimidated by Gramps. He was human, he was a softie and I was his favourite grandchild.

"No, I have not put 'Happy Mating' on the sign. They're already mated."

He said that like it was the only reason he hadn't done that.

"Besides, this isn't just a Mating Party."

I turned my lip up slightly, to show what I thought of that. "I wish you wouldn't call it that, Gramps. You make it sound like we're all going to stand around and watch them mate."

And coyness might be a thing of the past for our family but I really did not want to see my cousin fucking his little *uasal* lover. Ever.

Even Gramps looked a little disconcerted about that. He cringed. "Well, it's a good job we didn't put that on the sign then, isn't it? We went for something else. It's a Welcome to the Family party as well, for Morgan."

I shrugged.

Gramps cocked his head to the side. "Don't you like Morgan?"

"I don't care either way, Gramps."

He sighed. "Try not to say that in front of the kid, will you, Dane?"

"Of course I won't, Gramps. Morgan's alright. I've got nothing against him. And he sav—"

I stopped, realising what I was about to say: he saved Seren. I bit down on my tongue. I didn't care whether he'd saved Seren or not. Or whether Seren had saved Morgan first. Or whether it was my own family who had tried to stab them. No, that wasn't going to give me vivid nightmares at all.

I felt my dragon push at my skin, wanting out, wanting to go and check on Seren. Damn him! Why did my dragon care one way or the other?

I must have looked like I was going to shift because Gramps' voice took on a warning tone. "Dane, your Nana wants you to stay here."

It looked like I'd got myself a reputation for shifting and flying off. Which, to be fair, I did an alarming number of times. But my dragon only seemed to settle when it had eyes on Seren.

"I'm fine, Gramps." I kept my voice neutral. I'd learned years ago that I had to strive for neutral, project nothing into my face or voice, or I'd scare the children. "Morgan's alright for a *uasal*."

Gramps opened his mouth to reply, probably to tell me I was being a bigoted idiot, which I was, so I cut him off. "What do you want done?"

His face lit up. I might even have clawed back some favourite grandchild points with my offer. Gramps loved a party, especially if he could get all his family together for it.

"I'm glad you asked. We have a lot to get done, and you can do the heavy lifting." He bent forward a little and placed a hand on the small of his back. "My poor old back, you know."

I gave him a shove. Not too hard, because he might be mated to Nana and have drawn some of her healing ability, but he was still human and still very breakable.

"Don't try to con me, you fraud."

He sniffed. "Gramps to you."

I shrugged. "So what do you want done?"

He kept me working for about an hour. I felt like a donkey, dragging huge mahogany tables and overstuffed sofas across the room while Gramps gently chided, "Mind the floor."

Once we got to the stage of actual decoration, Gramps passed me over to Jill, a stern woman who enjoyed bossing me around for a further half an hour. I have no idea why she got so much pleasure out of it, but I swear I saw her lips twitch like she was trying not to laugh as she instructed me to tie a bunch of balloons together and hang them above the window. Maybe it was because I didn't normally go in for home décor. Normally I stayed well out of it.

By the time everything was ready, and the family began to gather, I excused myself to go to my room and take a shower. It wasn't like I'd been sweating loads, since I was pretty strong, but I thought it would be polite to freshen up and make an effort for Lew. The party was to celebrate him finding his fated mate. That was a big deal.

As I climbed into the shower and began to scrub my skin, I tried to scrub away the envy I felt. I'd never been jealous of other people. I'd never needed to be. I was a dragon, for a start, which basically meant I was awesome. That's not bragging, it's just fact. And I was big and strong, I spent years training and was now one of the best fighters in the family. Even Lew – who'd been in the Fife Army – thought I could fight well enough. And I enjoyed what I did: training people to fight, to defend themselves, to learn to use their own skills to the best advantage. Everyone has their talents and mine was finding out what other people's talents were. Or, if I were being honest, it *had been* my talent. I hadn't done anything like that in five years.

I turned the temperature of the water up,

wanting to burn the itch off my skin. My dragon moved inside me, threatening to come out and I felt like, if I could just burn that itch off me, it would settle.

It didn't. It never did.

For just a fraction of a second, I considered shifting and flying over to the Somerville's castle. I wanted to check on Seren, to make sure he was healed. Just to check.

Quickly, I clamped down on that urge. I knew better than that. Just to think about it would bring it about. My dragon had been near the surface for years, and I couldn't push it down again, couldn't get it to settle, put it in that sweet place inside where we worked in tandem. I was in a constant battle with it as my dragon tried to break out and fly to the Somervilles, and I tried to stop it. I lost more often than I would like. And I knew that, if I considered it for even a few seconds, my dragon would take advantage of my weakness and push through my skin.

Realising I wasn't helping myself, I turned the water to cold. I'd freeze the bastard.

My dragon grumbled inside me, but freezing it never worked either. I felt a rumble in my chest and realised I was growling. Shit, I'd have to get a grip before I went to Lew's party. I needed to be there to celebrate with him – he'd found his *mate* – and he was happy. I needed to show him that I was glad for him. And I should congratulate

Morgan, too, since he'd found *his* mate in Lew. They would be good for each other, I could tell. They loved each other the way everyone wishes they could be loved.

I climbed out of the shower and dried off, swallowing my growls back down my throat. My dragon wanted to fly. I wanted to stay. I wanted to show Lew and Morgan I was happy for them, because I really was. And Nana had told me to stay. I couldn't go now.

It was a close thing. I went to the party, joined in the cheering when Lew led Morgan into the room like he was presenting us all with the most wonderous gift, I congratulated myself on not freaking out because Morgan looked so like Seren, I waited for them to talk to a few people and kept my expression forcibly in neutral, I went over and congratulated them myself and saw Morgan shuffle uncomfortably like he didn't want to be near someone who could bite a man in half (which I could and had), and then I left. I had to leave. My dragon was being a real dick and I was struggling not to shift.

Morgan looked healed. He wasn't fully recovered, though, anyone could see that. Just a little bit weak, just a little bit pale. It had only been a few hours since he'd gone back to his family castle to see Lord Somerville and had been disowned for falling in love with Lew. Not only that, he'd been stabbed by one of my own clan.

I was angry with myself that I hadn't seen that coming. Years of training, years of learning, and I hadn't foreseen that one of my own would turn on him. Morgan had bled for my stupidity. Just like Seren had bled. My dragon rippled across my skin, half-shifting, and I forced it back inside. Seren had been stabbed, too. Seren had bled. Seren had fallen.

The memory of the hot, fresh blood made me feel sick. I could still smell the iron tang of it, just like I had earlier, for long, long minutes, while I waited for the wound to close. I still didn't know why the wound had taken so long to close. Dragons could heal so quickly that it should have stopped bleeding. My own wound had healed. Why had Seren been almost unconscious by the time it even started to knit back together? I hadn't been able to stay long enough to see the skin completely close back up, but it had at least begun to heal.

I rushed outside. That might have been a mistake, since my dragon might take it as permission to break free and fly to check on Seren, but I couldn't stay cooped up a moment longer.

I began to run out across the large expanse of grass that surrounded our castle. I wasn't wearing the right shoes for that but it didn't matter, all that mattered was I kept moving and stopped my thoughts from bending towards Seren.

I ran for miles, wishing I could exhaust myself, but I couldn't. I'd taken to running and working out as a way to drain off some of my anger over the past five years, and it took a lot to tire me out these days. Ironic.

Stopping on the cliff to the west of our castle, I pulled my phone out of my pocket and dialled the one number that might stop me shifting and disobeying Nana.

"You got some nerve ringing me, after the stunt you lot pulled today."

"Is he healed?"

His voice was heavy with sarcasm as he said, "Hello, Glimmer, nice to talk to you. How are you? I'm interested in you as a person and not just as a machine to illicitly relay family business."

"Is he healed?" I asked again. I couldn't concentrate until I knew.

"He's mostly healed."

I breathed out, for some reason more relieved than I expected. I'd been holding myself tight all evening and I flopped down onto the ground, not worried that it was damp.

"Thanks, Glimmer."

I knew better than to ask for more. Glimmer had rules about telling family business to other people. To be fair, dragons were pretty protective of their own. I have no idea why he put up with my calls, actually.

Taking a deep breath, I tried to remember what I'd been like before I lost my mind; what would a reasonable person say then?

"How are you?"

He snorted. "You sound like you're reading that off a cue card, Dane."

I shrugged, not that he would see me.

"You haven't had any backlash?"

"No. But that was quite some stunt you pulled."

Reading between the lines, Glimmer meant Lord Somerville was furious and there would be hell to pay at some point. That's what happened when you went to someone's house to return them home, let one of your own fucking family stab them and their cousin, and then flew off with that same person you were meant to be returning. That's the kind of bullshit that starts clan feuds that last generations.

On the other hand, Morgan had been mated to Lew at the time, so it wasn't like we'd kidnapped him. He'd *wanted* to come home with us. I tried to speak lightly. "Just taking what's ours."

Glimmer snorted again. "Somerville might have disowned him, but Morgan's still mine, Dane, and I guard the treasure. Just you remember that."

"Will do. I'd have to be having a better fucking day than this to think of challenging you,

G."

"Long as we understand each other. I'd hate to kill you for hurting my baby cousin."

There had been a time when Glimmer had been a very average fighter. Strong enough, for a *uasal*, but not as strong as a *curaidh*. *Curaidh* were warriors. *Uasal* were nobles. But being a dragon meant he was strong, and Lord Somerville had wanted him to guard the treasure – and, yes, dragons still had treasure, especially the *uasal* who'd hoarded it for generations – and I'd been hired to train him. I'd been hired to train both him and Seren and I'd more than done that.

It had taken me weeks to realise what Glimmer was capable of. Everyone thought Seren would be the guardian of the treasure, and Glimmer just a back-up, but he'd had power hidden away inside him. I blame the fact that I wasn't used to working with magic for why I didn't see that sooner, but it was probably because I'd had my eyes on Seren most of the time. He was beautiful in a way that I've never seen before or since. Perfect.

Anyway, once I'd realised what Glimmer could do, all I'd had to do was draw it out and help him control it. We'd almost finished our training when I'd been unceremoniously removed from the premises and told never to return, and Seren had looked me in the eye and said he never wanted to see me again.

My chest clenched. I never got used to that feeling, the sharp pain and the spasm that stopped me from breathing for seconds and seconds. I got it every time I thought of that moment.

Whatever. Seren didn't want me, I was relieved of duty, and Glimmer had become the guardian.

"You ok Dane?"

I'd been silent too long.

"Yes, I'm fine."

"Either you've hurt Morgan and are trying to work out how to make it so that I never find out, or you're building up to something."

"Did you clear Brendan's body?"

"Yes. Burned it in the incinerator. If you wanted to do it yourself, you should have taken him with you."

I hissed with anger. "Traitor. We don't want him."

"I gathered that from the fact that he was bitten in half. There's only one dragon I know who's big enough to do that. Even I could only take a chunk out of him, not cut him clean in two."

"He attacked— He attacked me. I just reacted."

"You'll get no blame from me. A dragon shouldn't turn against his own. We protect our treasure."

That was the thing with Glimmer, he was obsessed with treasure and his duty to protect it. Most people assumed he meant gold, because that's what most people thought of when they thought of dragons. And I'm not saying he doesn't like gold, he does. He *really* does. But that's not what he means when he says treasure. He means his family. Glimmer would do anything to protect the people he loves. That's why I ring him when my dragon is too close to breaking out, because I know he'll tell me what I want to hear.

"Is he healed?" I asked again.

"Yes, he's healed."

"He wasn't healing, G."

"It was one of your fancy *curaidh* daggers that cut him, Dane."

"He should still have healed. I healed."

"Seren is healing, Dane. He's just taking it slow."

"He lost a lot of blood."

"He did, and Glenwise gave him a transfusion. He's fine. He'll be fine."

"Sorry," I said. I don't know why I kept asking.

"Don't be an idiot, Dane, what else am I going to do with my evening if I'm not talking to you?"

Glimmer was the only person I knew would give up his time to repeat himself to me over and over again. I loved him for it, as much as I loved any of my family. And he did it because he loved me. To him, I was family, and he was the guardian.

I made a decision then.

"G? You want to know how I get into your territory?"

"You know I do."

He wanted to know, but he'd never asked. I'd seen him over the years plugging up all of the weak areas, all the holes, all the ways he could find of sneaking in. He was good. I had been lucky to get in last time I'd visited. Telling Glimmer how I got in would mean he'd plug that hole and I'd never get in again. But it would mean nobody else could get in, either, and I needed to make sure they were both safe more than I needed to get in.

My dragon gave a whine inside me. It was torn. It wanted to make sure nobody else could get to Seren, but it also wanted to be able to get inside and keep its eyes on him. It didn't trust anyone else to protect him.

I told Glimmer how I got in. I described the place where I could squeeze through, if I were in human form, and the protections I used and the route I took to the castle that avoided all the eyes that should have been scanning the area. I gave him everything.

"Thanks, Dane. Can I call you back?"

"Sure. Call me tomorrow. Let me know how you've plugged it up."

He laughed. "No way am I telling you that. You'll just find a way to get in around my added security."

Damn, he was good. My dragon stirred in my chest.

"Is he safe?"

"He's safe. We've got guards all over the castle tonight. I'm about to send two down to the fence where you got in, and it'll be secure by tomorrow morning."

"Thanks, G."

"Good night, Dane."

CHAPTER 3: SEREN

"How are you feeling?"

"Fine," I said.

Glenwise nodded and took my blood pressure. I'm almost positive he did it just to look like a proper doctor. Not that he needed to do that – Glenwise *was* a proper doctor, it's just that he also was the family medic and he didn't normally have much to do. Dragons didn't really get sick. The only time any of us really needed to see Glenwise was when we were bleeding or we'd broken a bone and needed it to be set properly. It would heal quickly – in just a few hours – but if it healed at the wrong angle, Glenwise had to break it again and re-set it. I'd done that once. It had hurt.

On this particular occasion, though, I was in for bleeding. Because I'd been stabbed by a bastard Hoskins dragon who'd attacked my defenceless little cousin. Not that I was bitter.

"You're still healing," said Glenwise. "Does this hurt?"

I yelped as he pressed against my chest, right above the rib that was broken.

"Yes, it still hurts."

Glenwise didn't look sorry for his prodding. He just typed a note into my file on his tablet.

Apparently, somewhere in the scuffle, I'd cracked my rib. At least I hadn't broken it like I'd thought. Glenwise had studied the x-ray for a long time and then said, "No, it's only cracked. It might have been broken but if it was, it's healing nicely."

I didn't understand that, since I hadn't had my dragon's healing ability for five years. Why it chose to come out and heal one broken bone when I was unconscious, I don't know. If it had surfaced, without me knowing, it might have healed my leg as well, which was still throbbing with pain and had tested Glenwise's sewing skills, since he'd had to stitch it up and he hadn't done anything like that since he'd been at medical school – like I said, dragons didn't generally need any doctors. And if my dragon *had* surfaced at all, why had it vanished again? I couldn't feel it at all. Couldn't smell, couldn't shift, couldn't bring up any magic. Perhaps I hadn't broken the rib after all, and had only cracked it like Glenwise said.

"When can I go?"

Glenwise gave me a stern look but I didn't drop my gaze. I wanted to get out.

He pursed his lips and asked, "Do you have somewhere you need to be?"

Damn, he had me there. "No."

"Then you can stay in overnight, like I said. I want to monitor you during the night."

"I'm fine."

There was a pause while Glenwise turned from where he'd been fussing with folding the blood-pressure cuff back up and panned his head round to look at me. Bit of a showman, was Glenwise.

"You're not even healing, Seren."

"I am."

He snorted. There was nothing I could say to that, since he was right. I wasn't healing properly. I certainly wasn't healing as quickly as a dragon should. For years, every scrape and cut and bruise and slice was healed by my dragon, the skin knitting back together again swiftly until there wasn't even a trace of a scar left. Not now.

Now, I was healing like a human. Slow and painful and laborious.

"I'll come back in an hour," said Glenwise, and he turned off the light he'd been using beside my bed. The room was plunged into darkness and it was only after a minute or so that I could work out the shape of things from the residual light through the window. The whole room was in gloom and the uniform beds and chairs and the medical equipment stacked on the sideboard created pale lumps that rose out of the darkness.

I'd had to get used to that strange existence. I hadn't even realised before that my dragon allowed me to see clearer in the dark, until it was gone and I was almost blind.

I wriggled to get comfortable and my leg gave a twinge of pain. I'd never really understood pain before, either. Before, it had been a transient thing, brief and fleeting. Now it was permanent. It was tiring and stretched out into the future and I wished my dragon would come back to me and heal me.

The night wore on and Glenwise came back to check on me. He prodded and poked, shone a light in my eyes, listened to my heart, took my pulse and my blood pressure, and told me to ring the bell if I needed him. I have no idea why he'd needed to do any of that if I looked the same as I had an hour before and said I was fine, just like I had the hour before. Probably because he never got to play doctor properly with anyone else.

He left me with the ominous promise, "Lord Somerville is coming to see you in the morning." If he meant that to be reassuring, I can assure him it wasn't. He turned the lights off again and left me in the dark.

I tried to change position but it was hard to move without twisting my leg and that pulled at the wound. Bloody Hoskins men, going around stabbing people. And one of his own, too! The man had stabbed Dane.

That moment was burned into my memory. Dane appearing, being stabbed, killing his attacker. And then he'd been there in his human form and I'd looked into his eyes. There was something in there that I couldn't quite recognise and it bugged me that I didn't know what he'd been thinking. There had been a time when I'd been able to read him better than anyone. Not any more, it seemed.

I spent the rest of the night uncomfortable, slipping in and out of sleep, replaying the day before when I'd been attacked, watching Dane be stabbed, watching my little cousin Morgan bleed. By the time morning came, I was more exhausted than ever and would have had the babies of anyone who could just knock me out and put me out of my misery for a week.

I suggested that to Glenwise but he just said, "You can't have babies," like that was his objection.

"I could adopt them and raise them like they were my own," I suggested.

"If I want children, I'll adopt my own,

Seren. Don't be an idiot."

"I'm not being an idiot, I'm just asking for a dose of Night Nurse or something."

"Night Nurse doesn't work on dragons."

There was another awkward pause. I was used to that. It was the pause when someone said something and then realised it didn't apply to me. I didn't have a dragon any more. A mild sedative would probably do it for me.

"Besides," said Glenwise, recovering. "Lord Somerville is coming to see you this morning."

"Any idea what that's about?"

"No."

I didn't believe him.

"Are you sure? Because you don't sound sure."

He looked me in the eyes, face sober, just like always – Glenwise doesn't have a sense of humour – and said, "I am sure. But he didn't sound happy when he told me, so your guess is as good as mine."

"You're such a comfort, Doc."

He patted me on the shoulder, which he probably meant to be more reassuring and less like a battering ram than it turned out to be.

I lay there and fretted half the morning. I didn't know when Lord Somerville would arrive, so I was kept in a state of constant anticipation. Eventually, I wished he would just turn up and get it over with, whatever it was.

When he did arrive, I took back that wish. I wanted to wait just a little longer.

"You'll live."

I chose to interpret that as 'I'm so glad you'll live, Seren.'

"Yes, sir."

"You're going to take Morgan's place."

"His place?"

"Cementing our alliance with the Scaldan clan."

He meant mating. Mating an ally. The thought made me feel nauseous.

"Um," I said. So articulate.

Lord Somerville was a tall, slim man with white-blonde hair and silver eyes. He had a cold, hard face and I'd never seen any warmth in it, even when he was looking at his own wife or his sons. As he looked at me then, his eyebrows went up and his voice was chilling.

"Do you have something to say?"

"Um, I'm not healed yet."

"Healed enough. And Leicester Scaldan won't be here for two days anyway."

"Don't we already have an alliance with the Scaldan clan?"

"We have an understanding. But our two clans have no bond. I have decided that we need such a bond."

"Does it need to be now?"

He looked at me and I tried not to squirm. I felt the irritation radiating out from him that he was having to deal with such a difficult person.

"Yes."

No explanation then, just a statement of fact. My uncle never went in for lengthy explanations. He made the decisions and he didn't see that he had to justify them.

"Does it have to be a mating bond?"

Our two clans already had an alliance – an understanding, as my uncle put it – and we'd been happily living with that for years. Decades even. I didn't see why he needed to change that now, just because we all knew that family bonds were stronger. Mating into someone's family meant you were part of their clan and it was typically how the strongest alliances were made. Still, I also didn't see how Lord Somerville could arrange it so calmly when it would have meant sending one of his own to live with the Scaldans.

Lord Somerville didn't reply. He just scanned his eyes down my body with a disapproving air and said, "You'd better hope he wants you," and then left.

That was it. My big speech. No 'sorry to see you go' or 'too bad Morgan found his fated mate and flew off to live happily ever after, you're going to have to do instead' or 'why don't you meet Scaldan and see whether you like him?' for me. No, Lord Somerville didn't go in for messing around and wasting breath. He was giving me to the Scaldan clan, and that was that.

CHAPTER 4: SEREN

I didn't even know Leicester Scaldan. I'd heard of him, and I wasn't sure if I was remembering properly because there were three Scaldan brothers who ran the clan together, but my memory nagged at me that Leicester was big for a *uasal* and was the clan's guardian. Made sense. Lord Scaldan himself wouldn't mate a broken dragon but his brother could, if the alliance was tempting enough, and Leicester's position meant Lord Somerville was satisfied that his clan (namely me) was not being dishonoured by the alliance. It seemed that Leicester was either gay, bi, or simply willing to mate a male in order to secure an alliance with the Somervilles.

As I looked in the mirror at my reflection and tried to get my image right for the evening, I tried to ignore the void inside me that had begun to press against my skin. I felt actively empty. My dragon had pressed against my skin before, wanting to be let out, filling me, but now it was the nothingness that made my skin feel too tight.

I buttoned up the shirt that I'd been given. On the basis that I'd been given a new room that afternoon, and that I only had one outfit hanging in the wardrobe, I assumed I was to wear that. It was black tie, which was unsurprising.

The room felt familiar and strange all at once. Each bedroom was so similar that moving from one to another hardly made any difference, really, but that wasn't the point. The other room had been *mine*. I had memories of that room. Glimmer and I had sparred in there and shared secrets in there, and Dane had been in there, too, once, not that Lord Somerville knew that.

I clamped down on the memory. Thinking about it made my chest hurt and it was already throbbing in a dull way from the healing rib.

I would focus on the future.

My future, in which I was mated off to Leicester Scaldan. It felt surreal. I'd never really considered the possibility. I knew that Lord Somerville had wanted to mate Morgan off, and I hadn't exactly been pleased about it but, since I was powerless, there hadn't been anything I could do. I'd never considered the possibility that he'd mate *me* off. I'd always had power, unlike Morgan. I'd been a fighter. I'd been in line to be the Guardian. I'd been useful. Now, it seemed, my only use was to be a virgin bride to an old ally.

I was dressed and ready far too quickly. Checking myself in the mirror one last time, I saw that I was still pale, looking a bit sickly. I kind of hoped this Leicester would take one look at me, curl his lip in disgust and ask Lord Somerville if they couldn't come to some other arrangement. Perhaps they could invest in a nice little business together or something instead.

Unlikely. What I looked like probably wouldn't even matter. I had other attractions for the Scaldan clan. Namely the centuries of Somerville blood in my veins. The power wielded by Lord Somerville himself was *very* attractive to potential allies. And our treasure. I knew a little about that, too. Even if the Scaldans guessed wildly, they couldn't imagine what we really had.

Damn. If Lord Somerville was offering me as a way to unite our clans, the Scaldans must be pretty desperate for an alliance. Accepting a broken dragon? If they knew I had no dragon and still accepted, I didn't think there was anything I could do to put them off.

I went downstairs and waited. I'd become very good at that, over the years. I'd tried to blend in with the furniture as much as possible for the past five years, and that had been quite the change in me – blending in hadn't been what I was good at before that. In fact, arguably the least Seren thing in the world. Still, times change, people change, and being ignored was infinitely preferable to being out on my ear.

Nobody spoke to me. I might as well have been a cheque they were going to hand over at the end of the night for all the notice they took. The only time anyone even looked at me was when Lady Somerville swept her eyes over my form from top to bottom and gave an approving nod, but since she did that to the dining table and the flower arrangements, too, it didn't boost my confidence.

And then the Scaldans arrived.

Lord Somerville turned to me for the first time that day, and said, "Wait in the lounge. I shall have you summoned when we want you."

"Yes, sir."

"And don't speak unless I say so."

I nodded, not sure whether he meant I was to start straight away or not, and went into the lounge, where I stood on my own for nearly fifty minutes. I was too nervous to sit down but I didn't want to make any noise, so I couldn't pace. I just stood there, waiting to be summoned. How had I become this person?

When I was eventually summoned by a maid, I entered the drawing room where the Scaldans were sitting.

Robert Scaldan was the head of the family. He was slightly bigger than Lord Somerville, slightly darker in skin tone, and he smiled a lot. His brother, Leicester, was bigger than him. Nowhere near as tall as Dane, who towered over everyone, even other *curaidh*, but still much taller than me. His eyes landed on me as soon as I stepped into the room. They locked on me, and I felt like I was being tested. That annoyed me. I held his gaze until it became awkward and Lord Somerville said, "This is my nephew, Seren."

I dropped my eyes. I wasn't sure whether I was comforted or not that Leicester wasn't interested in my body – he hadn't bothered checking me out, which meant what I looked like wasn't important. It seemed unlikely that the deciding factor was going to be my personality, either.

There were five Scaldans there in total, all male, all pure blood-line. The third brother wasn't there, though, so I assumed he'd been left behind to run things. Two of the extra ones looked sour and mean-eyed and the third looked irritable, like we'd rudely interrupted his weekend. I couldn't get much information from them. Lord Scaldan was talking animatedly, a stark contrast to Lord Somerville, who was like an ice statue in comparison, and Leicester Scaldan glowered.

His eyes were silver, like all *uasal*, and it might have been a trick of the light but they looked a tiny bit yellow, just a faint trace of yellow among the silver, like a sheen on a pearl. He was classically handsome in the way that most noble dragons were. High cheekbones, slim face, delicate features, long fingers. I couldn't get over the impression, though, that there was something ugly about him. I couldn't trace it to any particular thing. I put it down to my imagination.

I was introduced to all of them. I nodded my head at each of them in turn and stayed quiet. As I felt the watchful eyes of Leicester on me, though, I began to feel more and more vulnerable. I was weak. I was powerless. I was prey.

After just five minutes, I no longer believed it was my imagination. He was mean. It was in his eyes, his yellow, yellow eyes. The more I looked at them, the more I saw the yellow sheen to them. That, in itself, wasn't a problem – all dragons had a variety of colours mixed with their silver irises – but this yellow was sickly, venomous.

His mouth was pinched into a straight line, and his lip really did curl into an ugly sneer whenever anyone mentioned something of which he disapproved.

Was I judging him too harshly?

No. No, I wasn't.

Every instinct in me rebelled against being in the same room with Leicester and, even though my dragon wasn't the one to guide me any longer, I trusted my instincts. Going anywhere with Leicester Scaldan would be a mistake. Mat-

ing him would be the biggest mistake of my life.
    The only problem was, refusing to mate him might *also* be the biggest mistake of my life.
    I was screwed.

CHAPTER 5: SEREN

The morning after I'd met Leicester Scaldan, I found myself in my new room, listening to Lord Somerville. He was telling me about my mating like my only concern could have been whether I'd get to take my belongings with me.

"You will leave with the Scaldans tomorrow. Feel free to pack an overnight bag. The rest of your personal belongings will be sent after you next week."

Firstly, I didn't have any personal belongings; I had whatever the family bought for me, usually impractical suits, jewellery and technology wired in to the family system. Not that I wasn't grateful for everything I'd had access to, it's just it didn't count as 'personal', that's all.

Secondly, I was leaving tomorrow?

"But- I only met him for five minutes," I

said.

I actually cringed when Lord Somerville looked at me, and I hated myself for it, but I had flinched away instinctively from his eyes. There had been a flash of dragon in them and, even before, I'd never been able to look his dragon in the eyes.

"It is your duty to the family to mate Leicester Scaldan."

I told myself not to speak but found my mouth opening anyway.

"Does he know I don't have a dragon?"

I'd never learned to read Lord Somerville's icy expression. He could have been thinking anything. "You are a Somerville. Your blood is pure and you once possessed powerful magic. The Scaldans are aware of your current circumstances."

It didn't sound like they did, not really. If Lord Somerville had sold me as temporarily not able to use magic, they might end up pretty pissed off when they realised it was permanent.

He continued. "Be ready to leave with them at noon."

"I—"

Lord Somerville had actually started to turn away from me, dismissing me. At my aborted sentence, he froze, and turned round slowly. At least I knew where Glenwise had got his theatrics from. Only, with Lord Somerville, it filled that hollow place inside me with ice.

"Yes?"

"I- I don't want to mate Leicester Scaldan."

"You cannot mate Lord Scaldan and his other brother is already mated. Leicester is the only one who can have you."

Jeez, thanks. Misunderstand much?

"I mean," I said, swallowing the cold fear that had begun to expand out from my stomach, "I don't want to mate anyone."

He blinked at me. "What else will you do?"

He had me there. I wasn't good for anything now.

"Um, I- I was hoping…" I trailed off. I was hoping you'd just keep me here even though I wasn't any use to you at all? That didn't sound like a sensible thing to say to Lord Somerville.

"Forging a mating bond with the Scaldans will benefit the family, Seren. Are you saying you don't want to do your duty?"

I thought about that. I really, really didn't want to anger Lord Somerville and I had nowhere else to go, but I pictured Leicester Scaldan on top of me, his bigger body pinning me down and his sharp teeth piercing my skin to claim me and my stomach clenched and rolled so hard that I nearly threw up. I swallowed the bit of sick that had burned its way up my throat.

"I don't want to mate him."

The thing about Lord Somerville was he was a very efficient head of the family. He didn't waste energy and he was highly organised and logical. I almost saw him follow the flow-chart in his head: *will this dragon be useful? No. Can he be persuaded to change his mind? No. Conclusion: this is a dragon you don't want in your family.*

"I expect all members of my family to perform their duties, Seren."

Ok, that was a threat. If you're a member of the family, you perform your duty. If you don't, you're not in the family.

I nearly faltered but the nausea in my stomach at the thought of that dragon sinking his teeth into my neck to claim me still lingered and I took a deep breath.

"I won't mate him."

The dragon flashed in his eyes again and I actually stepped back. When I blinked and looked again, his eyes were the pale, pale silver they always were.

He didn't say anything. That was more nerve-wracking than if he'd yelled at me, but Lord Somerville never yelled. He simply spun on his heels and walked away.

I took another deep breath, feeling my lungs expand against my cracked rib, and, strangely, wanted to laugh.

The feeling danced inside me. It wasn't a happy feeling, it was more... elation and strangeness and fear and hysteria. I knew what I'd done. I'd practically signed my death warrant. I'd be thrown out. Even now, Lord Somerville would be snapping at his PA to have me escorted from the castle grounds and I'd have until midnight to make it clear of the whole territory before the hunters came out to kill anyone there who wasn't meant to be there, aka. Me.

I rushed back to my own room and began to pack a bag. I didn't bother with a suitcase but I grabbed a rucksack I'd once used for hiking and then threw things into it, crushing them down. Ok, so packing wasn't my skill but I also kind of wanted to get out as quickly as possible.

That wasn't to be.

I heard the door open and jumped back, relieved when it was only Rhod, Lord Somerville's PA. Rhod was also highly efficient and the posterboy for a good, dutiful Somerville. Even before I'd lost my dragon, I'd disliked Rhod. He'd never had any ambition except to serve, never did anything Lord Somerville wouldn't approve of, and went about his life as though there was nothing in his head except his duty. I grabbed another shirt and stuffed it inside my rucksack.

The door closed.

"Seren, look at me."

I did, looking over my shoulder. He was standing just inside the door and his face was serious. Big deal. He was *always* serious.

"What?"

"I'm here to inform you that you are being disowned."

"Yeah, I got that, thanks."

I turned back to my packing and jumped when I felt the brush of his hand against my arm.

When he spoke, it was quiet, so quiet that I had to lean in to hear him. If I'd had my dragon hearing, I'd have heard him just fine but it looked like Rhod didn't want anyone else listening in.

"Seren, you know what this means?"

"Yes."

"You're being disowned."

He said that like it was the worst thing he could think of.

"I know."

"Seren, you're weak. Who will protect you?"

"I don't need protecting."

"You're a dragon, of course you need protecting. You know there are *ridire* out there, right? And if they hear about a dragon all on his own, they'll come for you."

Yeah, that wouldn't be good. Like I said, I'd signed my death warrant.

Rhod must have seen my fear because he carried on. "Go to Lord Somerville. Apologise. Beg. Do anything but don't let him disown you, we both know you'll be killed out there. Even a real dragon—"

He paused. "Sorry. But even someone who can shift," he clarified, obviously meaning a 'real' dragon, "needs protection. That's why we have clans, Seren. Don't leave your clan."

I pictured being on the streets outside the castle, alone, and watching a *ridire* knight slip out of the darkness with their sword drawn. Even at full strength, I wasn't convinced I could take a dragon-hunter out. Rhod was right. I'd be killed.

Then I pictured getting into a car with the Scaldans, pictured Leicester on top of me, his teeth about to break my skin, and my stomach heaved.

"No!"

"Seren—"

"No. Just no."

He finally got the message. Rhod stood back from me a bit and, when he next spoke, he used his normal voice. It looked like we were done with the secret conference.

"Seren, Lord Somerville has declared you disowned. It is my duty to inform you that the Somervilles protect their territory fiercely and, if you are found within the bounds of our land after midnight tonight, we will deem it to be a deliberate threat to the safety of our clan."

He was reciting this from memory, a list of things to tell the banished before they left. His face was blank and he didn't look me in the eyes any more.

"You will leave here at once. You will leave all Somerville property here."

His gaze strayed down to the shirt in my hand and the rucksack I was about to shove it into.

"Are you kidding? You're not going to let me take anything with me?"

"It is Somerville property. You are no longer entitled to use it."

I dropped the rucksack. "Fuck!"

"I'll need your mobile."

I looked at the hand he held out. "Seriously?"

"It's Somerville property and has access to the Somerville system. We can't let you take it."

Shit, that had everything on it. Everyone's numbers. Although, actually, since the only person I would ever have called for help anyway was Glimmer, and since he was the Guardian and therefore the last person who was allowed to help me once I was disowned, it probably didn't matter. Shit, Glimmer!

"Can I see Glimmer before I go?"

Rhod's jaw ticked and I wasn't sure whether it was irritation or sympathy.

"I'm sorry, Seren, but no. I'm to escort you out of the castle grounds immediately. No detours. And you really need to be off Somerville territory by tonight. You're going to need all the time you can get, since you can't, you know, fly," he said, trailing off at the end. Maybe it was sympathy in his face, if I looked really, really hard.

My voice had become much less certain and I sounded dazed when I spoke. "Yeah, sure."

It was just starting to hit me. Disowned? I was disowned.

I felt the brush of his fingertips along my palm and realised he was taking my mobile from me and sliding it into his pocket.

As he looked at me, I got the awful impression that he wasn't done yet.

"I'm really sorry, but your clothes... they're Somerville property too."

"You want my clothes?"

"Not all of them. Lord Somerville was going to have you stripped – it's, you know, tradition. To be sent out with nothing."

I did know that. And I couldn't believe that hadn't occurred to me.

"But I persuaded him to let you keep your trousers and shirt. Most dragons shift and fly off once they've been disowned, to get out of our territory faster. Since you can't do that, I- I'll need your jacket and tie and everything, but you can keep the shirt and trousers."

For the first time, it occurred to me that Rhod did have some good points after all. He'd thought about this when I hadn't. And he'd actually asked Lord Somerville for something, to spare me the humiliation of walking through human towns in the nude. That was sweet. Totally pointless if I was going to have my throat slit by dragon-hunters within a day, but still, sweet of him to care.

"Thanks," I croaked.

In a trance, I slipped my jacket off my shoulders and undid my tie, laying them both on the bed.

"My shoes?" I asked.

"You can keep them."

"Thanks."

I didn't even bother to look around me as I walked out of the bedroom. That urge to laugh filled me again, and I tamped down on it. A few hours ago, I'd been whining about being in a different room while mine was being repaired after the fight. The window had been ripped completely out of the wall and there was so much blood on the carpet that no amount of scrubbing would save it. At least my leg had healed enough for me to walk on it. Sure, it hurt, but it could have been a whole lot worse.

Rhod followed me along the corridor and down the stairs to the front door. There, almost the whole family was gathered in two neat rows, forming a guard of... dishonour? They looked at me dispassionately and I didn't bother searching among their faces for sympathy. I had definitely bought his upon myself.

At the door, Lord Somerville looked me in

the eyes and said, "Traitor."

That was it. Man of few words. And that word was more than enough to do what he wanted. I heard the hiss of anger and disapproval from the surrounding dragons. I don't know whether they knew exactly what I'd done, but any dragon who betrayed their family was an outcast. If a dragon didn't have loyalty, they had nothing.

As I walked out the front door and down the sweeping white stone steps, I felt the laughter bubble up again. And, finally, I let it out. I didn't need to hold anything back any more, didn't need to repress any part of me. What would they do? Disown me again? I laughed as I walked down the drive, long and loud, finding the whole situation absolutely hilarious as I marched out to my inevitable death. Yes, I was probably hysterical.

CHAPTER 6: DANE

I was going to fight Lew. He was outside on the lawn and had the mats out so he could 'train' Morgan. That's what he called it. To me, it looked much more like they were dry humping with Morgan's lean little body pressed back against Lew's as he held him in place and Morgan tried to break free. I didn't know as much about fighting as Lew did – he was the best fighter in the whole family, hands down, and even Nana admitted that – but it did seem to me that Morgan would be better off trying to get out of Lew's hold by stamping on his foot or headbutting him or something, rather than grinding his ass back against Lew's crotch. Of course, that was only an opinion.

As I drew nearer, I studied them. Morgan looked scarily like Seren and it made me cranky, even though I didn't want to be cranky. Morgan and Lew looked beautiful together. Lew was big and tanned and muscular, with dark hair and dark grey eyes, while Morgan was slim and lean and fair and blonde with the light-grey eyes of the *uasal*. Before I could stop myself, I'd wondered if that's what Seren and I would have looked like together. Seren was taller and broader than Morgan, stronger, more confident, louder; but then I was bigger than Lew, so maybe that is exactly what we'd have looked like together: perfect.

My dragon stirred inside me and pressed against my skin. Fuck, my dragon was a dick these days. Why couldn't it just stay inside me where it was meant to be?

Morgan was the first of them to spot me, which just went to show how distracted Lew got by his mate. Normally, he'd have spotted the first sign of movement. As it was, I was almost at the mats. Morgan's eyes met mine and I was glad they were so blue, not the beautiful silver that Seren had, since it would have been beyond creepy to have Seren's eyes looking at me like that.

Morgan gave a small gasp and pushed back instinctively against Lew. Great. He was still scared of me. I stopped a little way away, not wanting to make him more afraid. I might be an asshole, but I wasn't that much of an asshole. Maybe.

"Dane," said Lew, finally looking up from Morgan.

"Lew," I said, nodding. "Morgan."

Morgan gave a nod but didn't speak. That was probably for the best. Normally, he got snooty with me, which wasn't a great tactic to take, and then he looked at me out of that cold, proud face that looked just like his father's, and my dragon began to snort inside my head. Lord Somerville had never been my favourite person and Morgan was the spitting image of him.

"Dane," said Lew, and I heard the warning in his voice. I blinked. Oops. I'd been staring at Morgan.

"Came to fight," I said, which was about as articulate as I got these days. If I opened my mouth to say anything more, I was sure I'd roar. I felt it throbbing low in my throat, a thick swell of sound that wanted to push up and out of my mouth, to scream at everyone and breathe fire and fly and fight. I swallowed the feeling down. Fuck, I needed to fight.

Lew looked down at Morgan, asking permission to cut their training short. I was meant to train Morgan too, actually, but firstly, I didn't think Lew would appreciate anyone else putting their hands on his mate, and secondly, I couldn't be sure I wouldn't break him. He looked so like Lord Somerville and my dragon hated it. I had to remind myself constantly that he was not his father, he was not his father, he was different, he was innocent… I chanted it in my head, willing myself not to lash out.

"Go ahead," said Morgan and pushed away from Lew, who watched him walk to the edge of the mats. "Can I watch?"

Lew's gaze turned to me. I nodded.

"Yes, you can. Stand further back, though. This is going to get rough."

I grunted, so fucking grateful that Lew understood what I needed. I needed to fight, to feel pain, to lash out. I needed to do it now, in a controlled way, or it would come out later when I didn't want it to, and I might hurt somebody.

Morgan frowned, which was one of the first times I'd seen any expression on his face. So like his father.

Lew smiled softly at his mate. "It's fine. Dane and I have done this for years."

He was right. We'd done it for four years, since he'd come back to the family castle. He was the best fighter in the family. He was the only one who could stop me if I lost control. I needed it to be him I fought.

Morgan was still frowning and Lew walked over to him and dropped a kiss on his forehead. "I want to fight him, Morgan. Don't interfere. Dane and I know our limits." He winked. "He's one of the few people I can beat the shit out of without feeling bad about it."

Amen to that.

Morgan blinked and I chanted to myself,

he's Morgan, he's not Lord Somerville, he's not his father, he's Lew's mate, he's innocent, until I thought I had myself under control.

Lew was back on the mats and he said, "At least my boner's gone down."

I grunted. I wasn't in the mood for jokes.

"You ready, Dane?"

A nod.

"No shifting."

I nodded again.

"Safe-word is red."

"Mmm."

My dragon was so fucking close to the surface and I could feel the scales of it breaking out over my skin. It wanted to fight. It wanted to fly. It wanted to go straight to the Somerville castle and tear its way in and set its eyes on Seren, just to make sure, just to see if he'd really healed.

Lew came at me fast and his fist slammed into my jaw hard enough to send me spinning to the ground. He wasn't holding back today. Good. I needed this.

I was up before he could land another blow and I balled my fists and went at him with all the force in my body, confident he'd block me. And he did. I kept my eyes on him, focusing all my attention on him, narrowing my world so that Seren wasn't in it and Morgan wasn't standing there; it was just me and Lew, and I had to fight to survive. For the first time in weeks, my dragon wasn't trying to break out of me and I lost myself in the moment.

It hurt, I would admit, but most of the blows Lew landed were throbbing pain for a few minutes and then nothing as my dragon healed them. We didn't have weapons that would draw blood, except our teeth and claws and we weren't shifting, so we had nothing but fists and kicks and tussling. It meant my whole body was bruised but I never bled.

The first blood came when I slammed my fist into Lew's face and his nose exploded with a fountain of blood. Shit! Why the fuck hadn't he blocked that?

I moved forward to see what damage I'd done and then, out of nowhere, I felt a bolt of lightning strike me, tearing through my body and wracking me with the pain that only magic can bring. My vision became nothing but blue sparks of light and my dragon reared up inside me, angry and hurt and confused. It pushed at my skin and began to take over. It was instinct, when under attack; my dragon was stronger and the thick scales would protect me.

Lew's voice was distant as he shouted, "No, Morgan, stop!"

The pain stopped, the magic stopped, but my dragon was coming out now, it was angry. Fuck, I was so fucking angry all the fucking time. When my vision cleared, I was looking through my dragon's eyes. My vision was sharper, coming to me in shades of red, and I saw the heat from Morgan's body as he stood there with his hand raised to attack me and his cold grey eyes.

"Somerville." It was an accusation. It was a threat. My mouth was filling with teeth and I was going to kill him.

Then Lew was in front of me. His nose was broken badly and his whole face was covered in blood. He spoke clearly, though. "Dane! Dane, I need you to calm down. He didn't mean to do it. Dane, stop, please."

I felt his hands on my shoulders but the touch was light and even though he pushed me back, I was bigger and I was stronger and his fingers stood no chance of hurting me where they were pressing into my thick scales.

"Dane, stop. Dane, Dane! Dane, I need you to shift back. Seren needs you to shift back."

I'd heard the words, but they were faint and there was a ringing in my ears that blocked them out. The only word I was sure I heard was *Seren*. Turning my head to look at the man while he was speaking, I tried to listen. What was that about Seren?

"Seren needs you to shift back, Dane."

Seren needed me? I began to force my dragon back inside me. It didn't want to go. It wanted to fight, it wanted to tear Lord Somerville to pieces, it wanted to fly as fast as it could to see Seren.

"Seren needs you to shift back, Dane. He needs you human."

It was a struggle to shift back and my dragon was strong. That had always been a bonus, having a strong dragon, and mine was – objectively speaking – one of the strongest, but it meant it was a real pain when we disagreed. It was why I'd been like a zombie for five years because I was half in my head all the time, trying to force my dragon back.

"That's right, Dane, this is what Seren needs. He needs you human. He needs you to listen to me. Seren needs you to listen to me, Dane."

As I gradually wrestled control of my body from my dragon and shifted back to human, I managed to concentrate more on what Lew was saying.

"Seren needs you human, Dane."

He was repeating it, over and over. He was tricking me.

"Welcome back, Dane," he said as I glared at him. "I had to. It was the only name you responded to."

I swallowed. I wasn't ready to speak yet. My dragon was too close to the surface and that roar was still desperate to be let out.

It was only then that I realised we were surrounded by people. Not all of them were people, either. There were six dragons around me

– six of the strongest. My dragon saw their stance, ready to attack, and it hummed in appreciation of the fight they promised.

"Shift back," I said, barely getting the words out. If they stayed like that, my dragon would take it as a challenge and it would be more than happy to oblige.

Nana was in front of them all, a tiny old lady with a dragon in her eyes. I didn't flinch. My dragon wanted to challenge her. What the fuck? It was fucking suicidal if it wanted that.

"Shift back," said Nana. "Go away, all of you."

She didn't take her eyes off me while she spoke. I kept my eyes on her, trying to make my dragon afraid of what it had done. In my peripheral vision, I saw the people walk away, glancing over their shoulders, and the six dragons shift back and walk inside.

"What is it, Lew?"

I held Nana's gaze. I was certain that she was the only one who could stop me if I lost it and I needed her there. God bless Nana.

"It was my fault, Nana." I'd never heard Lew's voice sound so small before.

"No, it wasn't," she said. She was right. It was mine.

"I—"

Nana snapped, "I know what happened, Lew. You're not to blame."

"It's not Dane's fault, Nana," insisted Lew.

She tore her gaze from mine and met Lew's eyes and he actually flinched back. Then her eyes were back on me and I held her gaze, comforted by the power I saw in them.

"You can't look me in the eyes, Lew. He can. What does that tell you?"

"Um…"

I didn't bother trying to think of an explanation. Nana would tell me or not. She'd kill me or not. She'd banish me or not.

"There's more to this than either of you understand. Neither of you are ready to hear it. I'll tell you when you are."

We stood there I don't know how long. I just looked into Nana's eyes, the head of my family, and let that ground me. Until, at last, I felt more myself, pushed my dragon down where I might be able to keep it there, and then I found the sheer power in those eyes disturbing and couldn't meet them any longer. I dropped my gaze.

Nana stepped towards me and laid her tiny hand on my arm. "Come with me, Dane. Lew, go get your face looked at. And keep Morgan away from Dane for a while."

I noted that I'd probably have to apologise to Morgan at some point soon, but I didn't trust myself to do it just yet.

Lew tried to speak only to Nana, as though

I couldn't hear him. Not that I cared what he said. "Nana, did you hear...?"

"I heard. I understand."

At least one of us did. I allowed myself to be led inside by Nana, following her like a lamb. It was nice, to feel nothing for a change.

CHAPTER 7: SEREN

I no longer had a phone to check the time, but I could tell it was getting late. It had been dark for a couple of hours and I was finding it difficult to make my way. I still hadn't got used to my human sight. Or maybe it was that I was used to it but there was no light and therefore couldn't see where I was putting my feet. That was probably it, actually. The ground was a black pool and no matter how hard I stared at it, I couldn't tell what was ground and what was shadow. There could be anything lurking in that darkness.

I didn't want to think about that. Fearing it wouldn't stop it happening. I'd literally just learned that: I'd feared being disowned for five years, since I'd not been able to shift or use magic, and it had still happened. Being afraid of *ridire* wouldn't stop them finding me and definitely wouldn't stop them slaying me. At least a death dealt by *ridire* was meant to be quick. I had that to look forward to. If I lasted long enough for them to even find me, since I wasn't even out of Somerville territory yet.

Hurrying didn't help. I had the mud-stains to prove it. All that happened was I missed my step or slipped on the slick ground and fell, and then it took me time to scramble up and it made my knees and ass ache where I'd landed on them, and it made my healing leg throb. I was already limping. I really didn't need to do any more damage that would slow me down further.

As it drew nearer to midnight, I felt the swirling anxiety in me rise up. No matter what I told myself about being resigned to my fate, the fact remained that I didn't actually want to die. I was walking as fast as I could without falling, keeping my leg straight so as not to stress it more than I had to, but I needed to get out of the territory before midnight.

Time passed in a blur, and I was straining my human ears to listen for the sound of anyone approaching. I thought it would give me some advantage if I heard them coming. It didn't.

The first shriek was distant, but I knew that sound. It was a dragon, far behind me, but it had spotted me and was summoning the others who'd been fanned out all over the territory looking for me. I spun around to see but there was only the inky blackness of the sky and some patches of silvery light where the moon shone through the clouds.

I began to hurry, slipping and sliding on the mud underfoot, and I tumbled, jarring my leg and groaning as the pain blinded me for a moment. I didn't have time to recover. I hobbled along, panting loudly in the night air, focusing entirely on making my way forward. I was long out of the castle grounds, but the Somerville territory stretched for miles around it. I'd headed out in the direction where the territory stretched for ten miles. I'd considered going another way, even out the other side where it stretched for twenty miles, on the basis they might not look that way, since I'd have to be stupid to go there but, in the end, I'd decided I really would have to be stupid to go there. Instead, I'd set out to cover ten miles before midnight. I'd actually done quite well, being human, being cold, being injured. At least I had tried.

Behind me, I heard another shriek. It was nearer. I kept my face forward and just ploughed on. I didn't know who it was behind me – I couldn't see their dragon form against the sky – and I did spare enough energy to worry that I'd be found by someone vindictive who'd enjoy tearing me to pieces slowly. That wasn't impossible.

A dragon dropped to the ground in front of me. They were about twelve metres long, snout to tail, and needless to say, I felt entirely too small and vulnerable. If I'd been able to shift, I'd have out-matched them. Even if I couldn't shift but had my magic, I'd probably be able to keep them at bay long enough to escape. But, as it was, I had nothing and so I stood and looked at them. They were completely blocking my path.

Another two thumps behind me cemented my fate as two more dragons landed.

The dragon before me hissed, snaking its head forward. I was so small and those teeth were so large.

Behind me, a voice spoke. "Conley, stop."

The dragon – it was hard for me to be sure it *was* Conley, in the darkness – raised its head and looked over my shoulder.

The voice spoke again and it was Rhod. Of course it was.

He walked up to me and stood almost beside me, naked after shifting back to human. The low growl behind me made it more than clear I was not to try and do anything while Rhod was vulnerable, not that I'd consider him particularly weak if he still had his dragon.

"He's out of the territory, Conley. There's nothing we can do."

The dragon hissed in anger and then began to shrink, changing back to human.

"He's still inside the territory," he said. Yep, that was Conley's voice alright. Deep and rough, but not in a nice way. More in a he's-definitely-thinking-about-what-it-would-be-like-to-feel-my-blood-pour-over-his-teeth kind of way.

"He's not. The territory ended fifty metres back, where the oak tree was fallen," said Rhod. He sounded patient and calm, and I hated it. I just got to stand there while they discussed the edge of the territory like it was an academic problem and not like my life depended on where they drew the line.

"It's not back there, it's here." Conley gestured behind him, at a large oak about thirty metres in front of me. Damn, I'd nearly made it, too.

"I'm afraid that's a misconception. If you look at the official maps, you'll see that we are, in fact, out of the territory right now. There are residual protections around the place where we are, which is why you can feel magic at work."

They could feel it. I couldn't.

"If it's protected, it's our territory," Conley insisted.

"I'm afraid not. It's merely our protections leaked over the boundary and into the surrounding area. Of course, if you look at the spells that have been placed in this area, you'll see why many of them were needed on the outside of the boundary, since they're warnings and deterrents; they, by necessity, must be laid down to take effect before an intruder can even attempt to cross the line."

He sounded like he was settling down into a lecture, getting into the swing of it. That was Rhod. We were all about to get a history lesson on exactly what protections were in place.

Behind me – and yes, having three dragons surrounding me *was* making my skin break out in goosebumps, thank you very much – another voice joined in. This one belonged to Glenwise. I was surprised he'd been sent out on the hunt, being a doctor, but then he was also young (for a dragon) and fit and Lord Somerville must have wanted everyone who could hunt to try and catch me.

"For the love of mercy, Rhod, don't start giving us a lecture on the bloody boundary."

Rhod spun round and I saw the flash of anger on his face. "Just because I pay attention to details, don't blame me when you get them wrong."

"I wasn't saying you were wrong, I was saying that we don't want to hear you drone on about it."

Conley stepped towards me, and I backed up. It put me nearer to Glenwise but that was probably better than Conley right then.

Rhod huffed. "Alright, I didn't realise I was so *boring*."

Conley's voice was rough when he said, "You are. So shut up."

"You can't talk to me like that."

"Shut up, Rhod. I don't care if you're Somerville's favourite. We're not in the castle now."

I stifled a groan. How was it that when I was about to be killed, I *still* managed to get in the middle of a family argument? This was exactly why I'd volunteered like a shot to be the Guardian. At least they were kept away from the rest of the family. Too bad Glimmer turned out to be better suited to it than me. And, you know, a dragon and all.

The three of them were talking over each other and I was basically being ignored.

"... the treeline is in all the old documents..."

"... so touchy about everything, we were just saying..."

"... inside the territory or not, we still found him..."

"... not how it works, Conley, and you know it."

Conley huffed and the other two fell silent. "It's not like anyone will know. He's barely fifty metres out, we can just say we caught him."

"No." Rhod folded his arms. "That's not in the rules."

"Don't be so anal about your bloody rules for a change. He's a traitor!"

"And if Lord Somerville wanted him dead,

he could have killed him no problem. He wanted him banished, and there are rules to follow."

"Nobody will even know! He's so close."

Glenwise stepped up to me. "I'll know, Conley. I hate to agree with Rhod on anything but that's not what our instructions were. If Lord Somerville wanted us to hunt him down, I'd do it, but he didn't. We only have permission to kill him if he's inside the territory."

Conley gave a snarl and then his face lengthened into a snout and he turned away, taking to the air as his wings burst from his back and then he was lost to my sight against the blackness of the sky.

Glenwise frowned. "Now see what you've done, Rhod. You couldn't have just pretended that the boundary was at that tree instead?"

Rhod's voice was tart. "No, I couldn't. It's not right."

Well, gee, thanks for all your help, guys.

Glenwise turned away without even looking at me. I searched his face and it was blank. He didn't care. I guess I'd just interrupted his evening, that's all.

Rhod did look at me. He opened his mouth like he was about to say something but then shook his head and turned away. "I'd keep walking, if I were you, Seren," he said, and then he shifted and took flight after Conley and Glenwise.

Wow, what a goodbye that was. Not that it

was a surprise. We weren't exactly a hugging and kissing family to begin with, and I was a traitor so, actually, I'd come out alright in that encounter.

It was a depressing thought and I began to trudge forward, my leg protesting at every step.

I had no idea where I would go. There was nobody I could go to. I wasn't close to anyone. The only people I'd really cared about in my life were Dane and Glimmer. I'd burned my bridges with Dane, and for good reason. And Glimmer was the Guardian.

As I trudged, I thought. Dragons out on their own didn't last long. That was a documented fact. We were powerful and that made us valuable. There were known cases of dragons being killed to harvest them for their blood and bones. There were cases of other people – shifters, witches, sprites and gargoyles – forcing a claiming on a dragon if they could, to tie them to their pack or coven or family or whatever. I tried to tell myself that was unlikely in my case, since I didn't have any magic and couldn't shift, so it was unlikely anyone would find me a worthwhile mate. It wasn't like I could use my powers for their advantage.

That left being killed by mercenaries to harvest for my organs, or being killed by *ridire*, the dragon-hunters.

Neither was appealing.

Dragons alone didn't survive long. They were killed or taken in by another clan. I couldn't think of another clan who would take me in. I hadn't even been any use to my *own* clan. Nobody would take me in for nothing.

I walked into the darkness and thought. And thought. The only way I could even hope to survive was by getting my dragon back. That way, I might be able to protect myself, or I could convince another clan that I would be useful to them.

I needed to find a way to get my dragon back.

I needed to find a witch.

Stiff from cold and pain, I focused on moving forward. I had a plan. I had a chance.

CHAPTER 8: SEREN

I was standing in front of a little café called the Honey Pot and studying it. It looked to be just like any other café you might expect to find, but there was an air about it that made me sure it was more than that. I couldn't see what exactly was giving me that feeling and, since I didn't have any magic any more and my dragon wasn't telling me anything, I knew there had to be an actual explanation for why I got that feeling.

It had a cute little awning over two tables outside, and there was one old man sitting there, wrapped up in a thick coat and scarf, determinedly enjoying his morning coffee and pastry despite the chill. The reason he was sitting there was obvious. He had a little dog at his feet which was being incredibly good but also incredibly hopeful, if the way it watched him bite into the pastry was anything to go by. I was there long enough to see the man eat most of the pastry and then feed the dog the last little bit before draining his cup and leaving.

The building was brick and wooden window frames, painted a welcoming shade of green. There were flowers in the window, as well as teapots of all shapes and sizes. Not a honey pot in sight, despite the name.

I stayed where I was, across the street, just staring at the place, trying to work out if there was magic going on in there or not. I wasn't sure whether I wanted there to be. If it was somehow connected to magical beings, then I might be safer going in and being surrounded by them. On the other hand, if they knew I was a Somerville, or they worked out I was a dragon, I could be sold out to dragon-hunters within a day.

A fat tabby cat came ambling towards me from the end of the street. It looked like it was going to ignore me, in the way that cats do, but it stopped by my feet and deigned to let me scratch its head. When I went to stand up again, it nudged me, demanding more. That's what I got for petting it; I was now its slave.

As I continued to stroke my fingers over the ears of the cat, my leg began to cripple in pain. It was nowhere near healed and walking on it all night had split the skin open again; I could see the dark blood spreading a stain down my thigh and could feel it trickle over my knee and down my shin. I needed to rest.

The trouble was, I had nowhere to go that was safe. I wanted to go into the café but I couldn't be sure it was safe. And I had no money to buy anything. And it wasn't like I could just go in and ask if there was a witch in the house.

I needed to move. I felt a chill across my skin and shivered. It was pointless to wish I'd been allowed to keep my jacket; it wouldn't have done much to keep out the cold and I was lucky I'd been left any clothes at all. I was actually comforted by that thought, which just went to show how low my expectations had become.

Standing stiffly, I turned away from the café and began to walk down the street. It was an old-fashioned high-street in the little village of Lower Dipton, looking all kinds of postcard-perfect. There were barely twenty shops but I wanted to get a good look at all of them. I knew there was a witch in the village somewhere; we'd all known that for years. All I had to do was find them.

I shambled along, studying the front windows of each new building as I came to them. I was looking for any sign that there might be a magic-practitioner inside. I was so focused on studying the displays that I didn't pay enough attention to my surroundings. When I came across a small alleyway, barely wide enough for two people, leading between two of the shops so they could cart the bins out to the front or wheel deliveries round the back, I felt strong hands on me and I was dragged off my feet.

My whole body was disconnected from my mind by cold and pain, and so I did absolutely nothing to stop myself being dragged right to the end of the alley. When we got there, I was punched hard in the stomach and doubled over.

Before I'd lost my dragon, I'd actually liked to spar with people. I'd loved to spar with Dane, because he was a real challenge and I only won once every three or four rounds, but I liked the excitement of it, and the physicality. Glimmer had become great to spar with, too, once Dane had found the power inside him. To this day, I have no idea how our whole family had missed that for decades, but Dane had seen it after just a few weeks and had taught Glimmer to draw on a power that left me speechless. The reality was, though, that I'd liked to fight because I stood a chance of winning. That was not the case now.

I felt another blow land on my side and grunted in pain because it was just below my cracked rib and it felt like I'd cracked it all over again.

"He's not a dragon, you idiot," said a voice over me. I was on the ground, on my hands and knees in the dirt that lined the alley. Great.

"He is, I tell you. He's faking."

My chin was gripped in a firm pinch and my head dragged up so I was looking into the face of a burly man, like a bear.

"He's got no smell. He must be a dragon."

"So why hasn't he burned us, then?"

"You want to be burned?"

"Of course not, idiot. But he's not even fighting."

"We'll bag him. If he's not a dragon, we'll just dump the body."

No need to fill in the blanks there. If I *was* a dragon, they'd cut up my corpse for parts. I sighed heavily, annoyed that I'd lasted less than a day. I would have thought I'd have lasted at least 24 hours. Maybe even a little longer.

"What you sighing for?" asked the bear-man.

I didn't answer that. I knew from experience with Lord Somerville that questions like that were rhetorical. Instead, I drew myself up, fighting to keep the pain off my face, and looked directly into the man's eyes. It was a pathetic attempt to make him think I wasn't afraid. If he'd been able to smell me, I'd have reeked of fear. It was lucky I somehow still concealed my scent. Or maybe it was unlucky, since that's what had given me away.

We were pressed close together, in the tight confines of the alley. That was a disadvantage in a fight. I was outnumbered. Also a disadvantage. The bear-man was probably some kind of shifter, if he relied on scent, which, in my current state, was *also* a disadvantage.

My brain frantically sought some kind of solution. I needed an escape. Running was out. Fighting was out. Bargaining was out, since I had nothing and couldn't hope to match the price they'd get for my corpse anyway. Intimidation it was, then.

"Tell me, do you know anything about dragons?" I asked. I kept my voice low and soft, since I'd been told on more than one occasion that I sounded creepy as hell when I did that.

"You what?"

"I asked if you knew anything about dragons," I repeated slowly.

Both men looked at each other over my head, which wasn't hard, since I was still on my knees. What a sight I must have looked, filthy and bruised and trying to hold it together.

"What's it to you?"

I let the hint of a smile tug at my lips. It was cold and humourless. "It's nothing to *me*."

They shared that look again. I had caught their attention. Good.

"We know enough."

"Yeah, we know what you're worth."

"If you can take me," I corrected lightly. They could take me. They already had me. One of their hands was fisted in the back of my shirt, tugging at the collar and pulling it around my neck, and the other had wrapped his beefy hand around my upper arm.

The shifter leaned down so his face was close to mine. "You don't look so good. I don't think you got any fight left in you, dragon."

I looked him in the eyes. "Dragons never fight alone."

That was a lie, I admit it. Dragons fought alone plenty of times. Still, I wanted to make this guy scared and then maybe he'd leave me alone. Then I could find this witch, get my dragon back, get myself a clan and be safe again. I *did* have a plan.

The two of them began to move uneasily, looking around them, and then one started violently.

"Get out of here, Marcia. This is no place for you."

I tried to look around them but the strangle-hold they had on my collar wasn't helping, so all I heard was a pleasant female voice.

"Now, boys, you know my rule: no fighting."

"We're not in your café now. And we just bagged ourselves a fortune."

Her voice became a little harder. "I'm not going to stand by and watch you take him, boys."

"You don't need to watch."

"Yeah, turn around and walk away. We're

not letting this opportunity pass us by."

They had a point. It's not like they'd ever stumble across another dragon who couldn't burn them to a crisp again. I was a one-in-a-million chance. They'd have to be stupid not to take it.

"Don't you recognise him?" she asked.

Both men looked down at me and I tried my damnedest to stare back as though I hadn't a care in the world. I wanted to project confidence. I'd been confident once. I'd had buckets of it. I tried to remember what it was like to look like I could take out anyone who got on my nerves.

She continued. "Look at his eyes."

They looked. I blinked slowly and let that smile tip at my lips again, smirking. Now was my time.

I sounded cool and calm, even to my own ears. "Something wrong, boys?"

They dropped me and I saw the fear on their faces. Yep, they'd seen my silver eyes, which meant I was a *uasal*, and there was only one *uasal* clan around here. They scarpered pretty quickly and I watched them go from my place on the ground. It had taken everything in me not to tip over when they released me, since they'd actually been holding me up. It meant I couldn't move.

I just stayed there as Marcia walked into the alley. She'd approached from the back, behind the shops. Only when she came into my line of sight did I get a good look at her. She was small and plump, with a round face and a pixie haircut. I was fairly sure she wasn't actually a pixie, though.

"Come into my café, hon. We'll go in through the back."

I stayed where I was. I wasn't going to be able to move, I knew that.

"Aren't you coming?" she asked.

In answer, I collapsed. My whole body went limp and I sprawled on the ground, my cheek pressed against the rough stone and the layer of dirt. I could smell it, and I wanted to gag, but I didn't have the energy. I couldn't feel my body at all, except for the throb of my rib, and that was all I had to tell me I was alive.

Ok, so when I made my plan, it seemed I had underestimated just how weak I was.

Shit.

My vision was blurring and my last panicked thought was that I really stood no chance at all if I passed out, and then I passed out.

CHAPTER 9: SEREN

I woke up suddenly, with a crash of adrenaline and fear, and bolted upright.

The dagger-pain of my chest told me that had been a bad idea, and, anyway, I came face-to-face with a troll. He was big, in the way that trolls were; average height but broad and thick from top to bottom. Trolls were strong. And they could be mean.

This one, though, stepped back when my eyes landed on him and held up his hands.

His voice was gravelly, like his vocal-cords were made out of tarmac.

"Marcia? He's woken up."

I was in a small office with a large table pushed against one wall and absolutely covered in papers and mugs and food wrappers. It took up nearly half of the room. The other half was taken up with the camp-bed I was lying on. It sagged in the middle a bit and there were blankets piled around me like a nest. The remaining space was taken up by the troll.

"Where am I?"

"You're in the Honey Pot," said the troll, his gravel-voice making it hard to tell whether he was happy about that or not.

The door opened, knocking into the desk with a *thunk*. Marcia squeezed into the room, pressing the troll harder against the wall. She ignored him and focused on me.

"Ah, you're awake! Excellent. Here, drink this."

She held out a mug of something and I could see it gently steaming. I didn't take it, though.

"Who are you?"

"Ah yes, introductions! I'm Marcia, and I own the Honey Pot. This is Broadmire. He works a couple of doors down from me and I asked him to carry you inside. You're too big for me to lift and you were completely out of it."

"Thanks."

"You're welcome, honey. You're in a pretty bad way. Did you know you were bleeding?"

"Yes."

"And you didn't think to, like, stop and get help?"

"Um," I said, not sure what to tell her. I eyed Broadmire.

"I'm staying," he said, and leaned back against the wall. "I'm not leaving her alone with a dragon. No offence."

Narrowing my eyes, I studied him. "Not sure there's any way I can take that *except* as an insult."

To my surprise, he grinned. "Marcia's got a soft heart. She always takes in strays, just because they go around passing out round the back of her shop. Doesn't mean I trust you. What's a dragon doing here alone, anyway?"

Marcia used her free hand to smack Broadmire on the arm. "Don't be rude. And use his name."

"He hasn't told us his name."

"Seren," I said. It wasn't like I needed to hide my name. I deliberately didn't give my surname, though. I wasn't sure whether I was allowed to still use it, now that I'd been disowned. It was the sort of thing Rhod would know and I should have asked him before I left.

"Pleased to meet you, Seren. Now, drink this, it'll make you feel better."

She handed me the mug and I nearly spilled the lot down my front. The mug was heavier than it looked and my wrist wobbled. Or I was too weak to hold up a mug of tea. Either one.

Marcia held the cup and helped me bring it to my lips. I was actually desperate for any kind of help, enough to drink something a complete stranger gave me and hope it wasn't poison.

"What you get yourself beaten up for?" asked Broadmire conversationally.

I levelled a haughty glare at him. I was feeling a little better already, if I could do that.

"It was not intentional."

He grinned again. "No kidding. But those two! Marcia told me. They're not nice people. You shouldn't go down alleyways with them."

"Again, not what I had intended to do."

"Sure. You're lucky Marcia came along."

"Actually," she said, intervening, "it wasn't luck. Maud sent me."

I was starting to get a headache. This was a lot of information to take in. "Who's Maud?"

"My cat. You were petting her earlier. She's very fussy about who she lets touch her, so I knew you were a good person. She saw those two try to kidnap you and came to get me."

"Should've come to me," said Broadmire. "You can't fight them."

Marcia sniffed. "I think we managed quite well, didn't we, Seren?"

"You're lucky they were greedier than they were smart, or you'd be hanging up on a butcher's hook by now. What's a dragon doing out here on his own?"

We were back to that, were we? I still didn't know what to say. I needed help, that much was extremely apparent, but I didn't know who I could trust.

Marcia tutted at him and helped me raise the mug to my lips again. It was sweet tea, laced with something else. Magic.

"You're a witch," I said.

"That's right, hon. You'll feel better in a while, once you've drunk that. I'm afraid I don't do healing, though, so you're going to be a bit uncomfortable for a while. I wrapped your leg up again and the bleeding mostly stopped."

Broadmire's gravel-voice ground out yet another question, happy as can be. "How'd you manage to get yourself sliced up? That was a knife wound."

It seemed like they'd all had a good look at my thigh. Good job I wasn't bashful.

I ignored him and sipped at my tea. For some reason, that seemed to make him happier. He grinned hugely as he said, "Ok, I can see you're a chatterbox. No matter, Marcy'll have you talking in no time. She's got the knack."

I looked down at the tea and then up at Marcia. Was it a truth potion?

She saw my look, apparently, and smiled a soft smile that revealed a pair of cute dimples. "Nothing like that. I'm just nosey."

I nodded. Nosey was fine. Probably.

"You can stay here for the rest of the day. I think you need some sleep."

I *did* need sleep. However, I couldn't exactly sleep while I was in danger. Shit, I hadn't fully appreciated how vulnerable I would be once Lord Somerville threw me out. I literally had nothing but the clothes I was in.

As the full realisation hit me, it occurred to me to wonder whether I could ever go back. I'd never heard of it happening before – a clan taking back a dragon they'd banished – but it wasn't impossible, surely? I could go back to the territory, ask to speak to my uncle and tell him I'd...

I retched, my stomach clenching at the ghost of the feeling of being claimed. Leicester Scaldan on top of me, in me, sinking his teeth into my neck.

No.

I would much rather lay here, alone and vulnerable, ready to have my throat slit, thank you very much.

"You look weak," said Broadmire, suddenly.

"Thanks."

"Never seen a dragon look weak before."

I ignored that. It was obvious I *was* weak, but I wasn't going to tell him exactly *how* weak I was. I hadn't decided whether this was an elaborate ruse to sell me for parts. It seemed like a lot of effort to go to, considering either one of them could have just wrung my neck while I was unconscious, but still, it paid to be careful.

"Broadmire! Don't make personal remarks," scolded Marcia.

He shrugged.

"You're going to stay here and rest. I'll bring you some food in case you get hungry."

Only once she mentioned it did I realise that I hadn't eaten in nearly a whole day.

"And I'll come and check on you when I can. I'll leave Maud with you. She's an excellent foot-warmer and she'll keep her eye on you."

"I can't—" I began, but didn't quite know how to say it.

"What?" she asked, her face kind and her dimples dipping in and out of existence.

"I don't have any money to pay for the food, but thank you very much for the offer."

She stood up, looking offended, and huffed. "I didn't help you for money."

"You've gone and done it now," said Broadmire cheerfully. "She's going to get in a right snit about that."

The witch smacked his arm again, and he didn't move a muscle. Trolls were strong and, though they didn't exactly have thick scales like dragons, I was willing to bet he hadn't really felt that smack at all.

Marcia put her nose in the air and sniffed.

"You can stay here and pet my cat."

"Not a euphemism," added Broadmire.

I was a bit baffled by the time they left, leaving me laying on the little cot with blankets draped all over me and Maud eyeing my body like she couldn't decide where she would be most comfortable. I'd never met anyone like those two before. Helping someone just because? It certainly hadn't been something I'd seen before. My rational mind told me that they had to be after something, but I couldn't think what. If they knew I was a Somerville – and I was fairly certain they did, or at the very least they suspected – then they would expect either a horde of dragons to flock to the building and tear it down to get me out, or they knew I was disowned. If they knew I was disowned, they knew I had absolutely nothing to give them, and yet they were helping me anyway. I tried to puzzle it out as Maud decided that she'd be best off tucked into my side, curled into a little ball. I was glad she'd chosen the side away from my cracked rib and wasn't putting any weight on my chest, what with the lovely new bruise that was forming there from that punch.

As much as my rational brain tried to tell me it was dangerous to trust these people and sleep, my body overruled it and I found myself slipping in and out of consciousness.

There was something actually comforting in being there. I'd always felt the need to prove myself, like an itch just below my skin, wanting to show the family that I was worthwhile. I'd failed in that so spectacularly that I'd sunk as low as it was possible to go. It felt almost peaceful, knowing there was nothing else bad that could happen to me any more.

CHAPTER 10: DANE

Nana gave me something to make me sleep. It must have been strong to knock out a dragon but it did, and I slept like a baby for more than twenty-four hours. It was the best sleep I'd had in years. Normally, my dreams were plagued by nightmares that made my stomach roll and I tried to stay awake to avoid them or woke from them with my heart racing. Or, perhaps worse, were the good dreams. Sometimes I dreamed of Seren and then I woke hard and desperate and happy before it crashed down around me and I felt worse than before. I still went to sleep hoping to dream of him, though. Maybe one time in a hundred, I did. If I hadn't had that, I wouldn't have slept at all. I hated the nightmares.

When I woke, I didn't know where I was. I was used to starting awake, my body on high alert already, and it was strange to wake slowly with no adrenaline spike. It was nice.

I heard a scuff from the other side of the room and looked over. I was in the medical room and the constant light was dim but more than enough for me to see Prince sitting in a chair. He had taken out his phone and then looked up at me, saw me looking back, and dropped it.

"Ah, Dane, you're awake. I, um," he scrambled around under his seat for the phone. "I was wondering when you'd wake up. Nana said any time from noon, probably. You were supposed to be out of it until tonight but I guess you're pretty strong."

He was jabbing at his phone and then turned it around so it wasn't upside-down. That was Prince alright.

I didn't feel the need to answer him. I loved Prince, and I tried not to let my anger drive him away, too; he was one of the few people who still came to me. Before, people had come to be with me all the time, but now it was only a few of them, and mostly Prince and Lew. It looked like he'd been here, waiting for me to wake up.

"I didn't want you to wake up alone," he said, proving me right. That was pure Prince, too. He was the most thoughtful person I knew. It was a shame he was also the most destructive – purely by accident, of course. "It wasn't my phone that woke you, was it? I didn't mean to leave the sound on."

I shook my head.

"Good. Let me just…"

He trailed off and I lay in bed, just enjoying the feeling of *not* hurting. When had I got used to that constant ache anyway?

"Hello, Nana? It's me… oh, yes, I suppose you would know that. I guess my name came up on your screen, huh? Yes, I did ring you for a reason. What do you mean what is it? Oh, yes, Dane is awake. Yeah, he's looking at me now." Prince gave me a tiny wave and I raised my hand in return. "He just waved at me. No, I waved at him first. I don't know, I didn't ask him. Ok, but if he kills me, I'm coming back to haunt you."

He ended the call and stood up. When he approached, I was grateful that he didn't *actually* look afraid of me. I guess that last part had been a joke, then. Prince was family. I'd never actually hurt any of my family. Sure, I'd been a grumpy asshole for five years but that didn't mean they needed to be afraid of me.

"Nana wants to know if you can feel your feet."

I thought about it and wriggled my toes. All good. I nodded.

Prince smiled. "Great. She'll be pleased." He cringed. "Probably. Unless you weren't meant to feel your feet?"

I shrugged. With Nana it could go either way.

"Anyway, I guess you'll be thirsty?"

I nodded again and began to sit up. My limbs felt heavy. It wasn't unpleasant, it was just they were sleep-logged and I was still waking up, not trying to rush it at all. It had been years since I'd woken up feeling at ease.

Prince took the jug of water from the bedside cabinet and poured it into a cute pink plastic cup. He put the water jug down but he was already lifting the cup to give it to me and he wasn't looking at where he was putting the jug, so he missed the cabinet and it slipped off the end. There was a clatter and the definite sound of water splashing all over the floor.

"Ah, shit!" Prince was down on the floor, picking up the jug and holding it up to the light to see if it was cracked – it must have been plastic, too, to have survived that.

"Prince?"

He jumped when I spoke and dropped the cup, spilling the last of the water.

"What?"

"Never mind," I said. He was one of my favourite people but he was beyond clumsy. I suppose it was probably my fault that I wouldn't get any water now, since I'd been the one to scare him into dropping it.

"Um, just give me a minute, will you?"

He didn't look at me, so I didn't bother to respond. He grabbed a load of paper towels and dropped them on the tiled floor, but there was a whole jugful of water down there and they soaked through instantly. When he tried to pick them up, they were flimsy and dripping.

Trying not to sigh, I heaved myself out of the bed on the other side. My feet were bare and I felt a few splashes of water even from over here. I knew there had to be a mop around there somewhere.

When I found it in the cupboard, Prince looked at me like he didn't know what a mop was and I jerked my head to get him to move. He scrambled onto the bed and I hoped he'd stay there, since staying put was about the only thing Prince could do to guarantee he wouldn't cause any chaos. I mopped up the water, tipped the lot into the large sink in the bathroom and then filled the little plastic cup with tap water and drank deeply.

When I got back to the bed, Prince was still sitting in it, staring at me like he couldn't believe it.

I forced my voice to work. "What?"

"Nothing!" Yeah, he was subtle, was Prince. I raised an eyebrow. "Ok, well I was maybe wondering why you're not angry with me."

"About what?"

"For spilling all that water."

"No harm done."

"Yeah, but it was stupid."

"It was an accident."

"Yeah, but I seem to have more of them than other people do. Everyone gets angry with me when I'm such a disaster."

I waited for him to raise his eyes to me. I wasn't really in the mood to talk but I needed Prince to hear what I was going to say. I waited a full minute for him to look at me.

"I'm angry all the time, Prince, but never at you."

"Oh. Ok."

He beamed. When Prince smiled, it lit up his whole face. It occurred to me that I didn't see it much, and I'd seen his smile far less in the past few years than ever before, since I'd spent my time skulking out of the way so as not to snap at people or flying off to sneak into someone else's territory and get eyes on Seren. Did Prince even smile with the rest of the family?

I must have been feeling more myself because I was curious, something I also hadn't been in a long time.

"Who gets angry with you?"

"Oh, it's nothing. I just exasperate people, that's all. I don't blame them, not when I break their stuff all the time."

"Someone in particular?"

He shrugged. "Nope. I'm just a general disaster area."

He was, that was the trouble. I couldn't deny it. But I wanted to help him, another thing that had become far out of reach of me for years. I hadn't been able to help anyone in five years.

"Dane, do you think- never mind."

"What?"

"Do you think you can train me a bit? Then maybe I'd have more control over my limbs – they just seem to be everywhere without my permission." He raised his arms a bit and let them flop down to emphasise his point.

"Lew's the trainer," I said.

Prince dropped my gaze and said, "Yeah, sure, I didn't mean to bug you. I'll ask Lew."

I was being a real dickhead here if I was making Prince feel bad about himself.

"Hey, Prince. I just want you to have the best, alright? Lew's the trainer because he's the best. I haven't trained anyone in five years."

"But you used to train people?"

"Yes."

"Dimpy says you had a special power."

I raised my eyebrows again. "Really? News to me."

"He said you could find people's special talent. I thought maybe you could help me find mine."

He kind of looked hopeful, like I could pluck a gift out of thin air for him. But my only talent had been the ability to help other people find their talents, and I hadn't been able to do that in five years. I didn't think I was going to be much use at all to Prince. On the other hand, yesterday's debacle had proven that I needed to make some serious changes so maybe it was time to start trying.

"I'll speak to Nana."

"Yeah, about that…."

"What?"

"How can you look Nana in the eyes when she's like that?"

I thought about it. "Normally I can't."

"But you did. I saw it."

"I wasn't in my right mind."

Wasn't that the truth! I couldn't explain it, though. I could feel my dragon inside me, like normal, but it was skulking low. Maybe it was afraid of Nana after all.

"And you broke Lew's nose."

"Yeah, I didn't think he'd let me."

"Man, nobody beats Lew! He said you fought like—"

He broke off suddenly, lowering his head. I wasn't going to ask him. I didn't want to know. There were a lot of things Lew could compare me to – he'd fought a lot of different things in the Fife Army. I wasn't sure I wanted to know which unpleasant thing I reminded him of.

The ache that had accompanied me for years, deep inside my chest, began to return. I was starting to realise just how dangerous I was to the people I loved. If I could hurt Lew, I could hurt anyone.

"Is he ok?" I asked. I assumed he was. His nose should have healed within an hour.

"Yes, he's just- he wanted me to tell you it wasn't Morgan's fault, it was his."

"What do you mean?"

"For Morgan using his magic on you. It wasn't his fault. He thought you were really going to kill Lew and he reacted – Lew said he should have explained it better to Morgan, that you fight like that. That it'll look bad."

"Did it look bad?"

Prince cringed and I sighed. It had looked bad, then.

I suddenly wanted to get this over with. Whatever it was, I wanted it done. I couldn't go on like this.

"Were you supposed to tell me something, Prince?"

"Uh, no?"

"Like a message from Nana? Maybe that I wasn't allowed to leave the medical room?"

He frowned, which was kind of adorable, and said, "Aren't you allowed to leave?"

"No, are *you* supposed to tell me- never mind, I'll ask Nana."

I looked around for my clothes and didn't see them. I was wearing pyjama bottoms and no top.

"Um, your clothes ripped. When you, um, shifted."

"Right."

I'd go like this then.

Prince followed me as I walked up flights of stairs – the medical room was on the ground floor for easy access – to Nana's suite. As I walked, I saw a few people. They avoided me like I had the plague and was going to infect them if they breathed the same air as me. I'd never felt like a pariah in my own family before. I didn't like it. What made it worse was, they were right to avoid me. I'd lost control.

When I got to Nana's room, I knocked and Nana said, "Come in, Dane."

No surprise that she knew who it was.

I went in and looked directly into Nana's eyes, just to test myself. I felt the familiar squirming unease and dropped my eyes. Thank fuck for that.

"Thank you, Prince, you can go. I'll call you if I want you again."

His footsteps retreated down the hall and there was a thump and a clatter as he knocked into a table with a vase of flowers on it near the top of the stairs. We all waited to see if it would fall. It didn't. He must have caught it.

When Prince was out of earshot, Nana pointed at the couch. I sat down and looked around for Gramps. He was standing by the window and I thought for a second that he was going to stay over there because he was afraid of me, but then he crossed the room and sat next to me on the couch and took my hand.

"My sweet boy," he said, and I felt a lump swell in my throat.

It was hard to speak around, but I had something to say. "I'm sorry, Nana."

She studied me for a long time, her sharp black eyes raking over my skin, and Gramps' fragile human hand squeezed my huge hand tight.

"This can't go on, Dane."

"I know. I don't want to be a danger to anyone."

"You've never harmed anyone before. And Lew really should have blocked that punch. It might teach him to be on his guard a bit more."

I risked a glance up. Nana's face was serious – though I'd never seen it *not* serious, so it was hard to tell what her mood was – but she didn't look angry and I looked at Gramps, just to be sure. He was leaning his head against my shoulder, offering me comfort. No way would Nana let her precious mate near me if she thought I was a danger to him.

But.

"Nana, I lost control."

"Not in the fight, you didn't."

"I did. When Morgan used his magic, I lost

control."

"I won't blame Morgan, since he reacted instinctively. He saw his mate in danger and he attacked. It was natural. But if it weren't for that magic, would you have lost control?"

That was a difficult question. Made more difficult by the fact that I didn't want to admit the answer.

"Maybe. I can't say for certain."

There was silence and the three of us sat there unmoving except for when Gramps would tighten his hold on my massive paw, just to remind me he was there. He was the best Gramps.

"Nana?" I asked at last.

"Yes?"

"I didn't used to be like this."

"No, you didn't."

"Do you know how to change me back?"

She said nothing, and I took that as a 'no'. Until that moment, I hadn't realised I'd actually held out hope that she would be able to do just that. She was Nana. She was the head of the house. She could do anything.

"I can't change you back."

"Do you know why I feel—?"

It was so hard to describe what I felt that I couldn't pick the words I needed.

"Like your dragon is close to the surface?"

"Yes, that's it," I admitted.

"All the time?"

"Yes! What's wrong with my dragon? It never used to be like this."

"There's nothing wrong with your dragon."

I huffed in irritation, not daring to call her a liar to her face, but too irritable not to do something.

"Dane, I have a theory about why you feel like that. I can't be sure and I'm not willing to speculate until I am. Will you stay inside the castle for a while?"

I glanced up again, not sure whether this was a request or a polite way of telling me to stay the fuck inside. Her expression was hard to read.

"Is that an order?"

"It's... not an order. But I feel it will be best for you not to get too far from me right now."

I nodded. Nana didn't trust me outside. She needed to keep me in sight.

"Dane?" Her voice was strangely soft. It tricked me into looking at her. "You're not broken. You're struggling – there's a difference. You've been fighting to stay in control of your dragon for five years now. I trust you to hold on a little bit longer."

I would hold on. I held Gramps' hand as tight as I dared without crushing it and sat in that exact place for another hour, just letting the feeling of peace creep in at the edges of my mind. It was nice, to feel like Nana trusted me. And it was even better to sit there with her, knowing that, if I lost control, she could burn me to a crisp before I got to anybody.

CHAPTER 11: SEREN

I stayed in Marcia's office all day. I could hear the chatter and the clattering of plates and cups and so on from outside but it was faint and it soothed me as I drifted in and out of sleep. By the time Marcia came in with a tray of food, I was feeling much better. A little like I'd been slammed into a moving truck but less achingly tired than I had been. It was nice.

"I'm going to close the café soon," she said.

"Oh, I see." That burst my bubble. "I'll get a move on."

"No, no, honey, I didn't mean I was throwing you out. I want you to stay here tonight. It's at least going to be warm and you'll have plenty of food." She indicated the tray she'd set down on the desk by shoving papers and wrappers and a tub of baking soda across it, rucking up more papers.

"Why would you do that?"

"Why wouldn't I do that? It's not hurting me."

I thought about that. "You're not getting anything out of it, though."

"Maybe, maybe not. Did you know I found Maud out the back when she was a kitten, digging through my bins for scraps?"

"No."

"I took her in and fed her, not expecting to get anything from it, and now she stays. I've got myself a cat, just from one act of kindness."

"I hate to break it to you, but I'm not a cat."

"No, but you're not doing me any harm, either. From one stray to another, Seren, take a helping hand when it's offered to you."

At that point, I didn't have any pride left, so I nodded. She beamed and leaned across to take my hand. It was strange to feel her plump palm in mine, soft and smooth. I couldn't remember the last time I'd been touched, except when Glenwise took my blood pressure and sewed up my leg.

"How did you know I was a stray?"

She snorted. "If there's one thing I know, it's strays. Tomorrow, I want you to tell me all about it. Broadmire, too, if you can. Three heads are better than one. And we can work out how to find you your forever home."

"I don't know what to say."

"You don't need to say anything, you just need to rest. I'll leave Maud here and she'll look after you for tonight."

I had no idea what the cat was supposed to do to protect me from *ridire* if they showed up, but if it made her feel better, I didn't mind.

"Is there anyone you want to call? You're welcome to use the phone over there." She gestured at the desk and I assumed that, somewhere under there, there was a landline.

My throat was tight as I admitted, "I don't have anyone to call."

The only people I ever called were Somervilles and, even if I had wanted to call them, it would be pointless. It wasn't like they would help.

Glimmer was the only person who would even speak to me, and I didn't want to put him in that position: he would know by morning that I'd been disowned, and that meant no contact with the family. If I called him, he'd be torn between disobeying Lord Somerville and turning his back on me. It would be impossible for him. I loved him enough *not* to try and contact him.

All my contacts were on my phone, anyway.

Marcia gave me a sympathetic smile and her dimples flashed and then she jammed a hat down on her head and pulled on a puffy winter coat that made her look like a round bundle of clothing going for a walk.

"I'll see you tomorrow, hon."

"See you tomorrow, Marcia. Thank you."

She left me with a wave and I heard the doors locking at the back of the café. I was alone again.

Maud leapt onto the table and began to sniff around my tray of food, and so I decided that would be my first priority. I didn't want to find out if I was stronger than a hungry cat or not. Slowly, I dragged myself out of the camp-bed and across to the desk chair. It was all of half a metre and my legs felt like I'd just done a hundred-metre sprint. It reminded me that I wasn't fully healed yet. Even after so long, I hadn't got used to the way injuries lingered on me, how deep the aches went. When I'd had my dragon, even the worst wounds would heal within a day.

I sat at the desk and picked up the fork. Marcia had made me an omelette with mushrooms and peppers and cheese and ham. It was delicious. I found I was incredibly hungry.

Once I had cleared the plate, with just a little ham left over for Maud to nibble on, I sat back and put my hands carefully on my stomach. It was still tender to touch. That shifter packed quite the punch.

I sat there for a long time. The rest of the café was silent and empty, and it was only me and Maud in the place. The office was lit by one single desk-lamp, which had been thoughtfully switched on by Marcia when I'd blinked in the harsh glare of the main light, and it was strangely peaceful to sit there in the gloom. I was thinking.

Generally speaking, I tried not to think. When I did, I found that emptiness ached inside me and it actually made me short of breath, like the emptiness was swallowing up my lungs and I'd lose them and not be able to breathe at all. No, I had found that the best way to survive was to think as little as possible. That didn't seem to be the case now, though. Now, if I wanted to survive, I had to concentrate.

Every option I had – except dying horribly – was based on the fact that I needed to get to a witch who could heal me and return my dragon to me. They would have to be a powerful healer to do that, since our own Glenwise hadn't had the first clue how to go about it and, as much as I found his bedside manner lacking, I had to admit he was an excellent healer. But he wasn't a witch.

I knew no witches at all. I'd heard a few rumours, before people stopped talking to me. The only reason I'd known that there was a witch in Lower Dipton was that I'd become practically invisible to the household. They didn't like to look at me much, and I couldn't blame them. It must have freaked them out nearly as much as it did me, to learn that half my soul had suddenly vanished. At first, I'd been resentful of the averted eyes and the hushed voices, but then I had grown used to it and drifted about the house, listening to this and that. I heard quite a few things, but only gossip, never important things. A witch in the nearby village was exactly the sort of gossip I liked. It had led me here, anyway.

The trouble was, Marcia was not the sort of witch I needed. Not a healer. And, no matter how sweet and generous, she didn't exude power in the way I suspected I needed.

The more I thought about it, the more it became clear that I would need an incredible amount of power to fix me. There was no way I could get that on my own. I needed help.

It kept coming back to that.

And, unfortunately, for some reason whenever I thought it, my mind kept supplying the image of Dane.

There was no doubt that he *could* help. With the exception of Glimmer and Lord Somerville himself, there was no other dragon I thought was strong enough to protect me single-handed. He *could* do it, I was sure.

And he had a family, the Hoskins clan. They were powerful in their own *curaidh* way. If they extended their protection to someone, that person was safe as houses. I wasn't sure he could swing that, though. That seemed a bit much, to offer me the protection of his entire clan. Me, a weak man Dane once knew, years ago. It seemed unlikely they'd roll out the red carpet for me.

I didn't try to trick myself. I didn't consider that I might be able to walk up to the Hoskins' castle and knock on the front door and ask if Dane was in. I didn't think about throwing myself into his arms when he appeared. I definitely didn't wonder what it would be like to have him murmur, "I've been waiting for you," in my ear as he held me close.

No, I was entirely rational about the whole thing. I'd told Dane I never wanted to see him again, he had taken me at my word (which was a Good Thing) and we'd parted. He'd gone home to his family castle and I'd stayed in mine.

If I was lying about not imagining seeing him again, at least I knew it was impossible. These new dreams were fine, but they were just that. Dreams.

That didn't get me any nearer to solving my problem, though.

I sat there for hours, heedless of the way the clock ticked on the wall and Maud's warm, furry little body curled up in my lap. The fact was, I needed help. And there was only one person I could possibly even ask.

Dane.

I just couldn't think of a reason he would do it, that was all. I'd need to think of something so I could persuade him. There was no point in ringing him and asking him to do it as a favour.

I'd kind of lost the privileges that went with our friendship when I... I don't know, dumped him? That didn't sound right, since it wasn't like we'd even been together. But I'd cut him out of my life ruthlessly, I knew that. And I knew he'd been angry about it. I'd seen the dragon flash across his eyes when I'd told him I didn't want to see him again.

Still, he'd had five years to calm down. No way was he still angry about it. Right?

It had been for the best, too. Lord Somerville was *not* going to approve an alliance between the Somervilles and the Hoskins clan. Morgan getting himself mated off to one of them proved that – I'd seen the scars in the walls and the marble floor where my uncle had flung magic about in fury, something I'd *never* seen before. So my chances of ever mating Dane had been slim to begin with, even if I'd somehow managed to convince him to have me.

I didn't really feel bad about breaking off... whatever it was we'd had. I was sure it was for the best, to put a stop to it before he started to get too emotionally involved. More than anything, it was the *way* I'd done it that bothered me. I hadn't given him an explanation. I had just... ended it. Said I didn't want to see him again. Left him to assume I was bored with him and his services as an instructor were no longer required, as though all he'd been was someone there to train me and not the most important person in my life.

The memory left a bitter taste in my mouth. I could still feel Lord Somerville's hand on my wrist, the squeeze of it and the snapping of my bones. That had been when I knew beyond a doubt that my dragon was gone. My wrist had been broken in two places and Glenwise had frowned over the x-rays, saying, "It isn't healing," over and over again as though I defied medical science. I didn't. I was just human and healed slower, that was all. I'd worn a brace around that wrist under my jacket and had hoped Dane wouldn't notice it while I dumped him. He hadn't, and I'd been grateful.

It was getting cold sitting there in Marcia's little office and I was feeling empty and tired, despite the meal I'd just eaten. All my thinking had got me nowhere.

I began to push aside some of the papers on the desk, looking for the phone. I was never going to be able to think of a way to persuade Dane to help me because there wasn't a single good reason why he should. And I wasn't going to be able to think of anyone else to help, either. The magical community was tight-knit and secretive. The witches who stood a chance of healing me were powerful, expensive and required references. I needed help, exactly like I had two hours ago.

When I found the phone, I dug it out

and peeled off the sticky lollipop wrapper that flapped against the receiver, flicking it into the bin. I pulled the phone to me and took a breath. There was no point in dithering. I could ask. What harm could it do to ask?

Slowly, I dialled the only number I knew. I only had family numbers on my mobile, and the only person I would have wanted to ring now was Glimmer, and maybe Rhod to ask about my surname. Still, it didn't matter, since I'd had to give that mobile back and hadn't learned any of their numbers.

There was only one number I had learned, years ago. One number that I'd kept in my head because I'd been afraid of keeping it on my phone in case anyone saw it or someone deleted it from the family system.

Dane's.

CHAPTER 12: DANE

I stayed with Nana all afternoon and ate dinner sitting on her sofa, with my legs stretched out awkwardly in front of me so I could balance my plate on my lap. It was not ideal but the alternative was going downstairs with the rest of the family, and possibly Morgan, and I couldn't face that yet. I wanted to get more control of myself before I saw him again. I wasn't sure which was worse: that he looked like Lord Somerville or that he looked like Seren.

Nana and Gramps went down to dinner like normal and I tried not to wonder whether they would tell everyone about me, if they even knew what to say. Was Nana going to tell them I was dangerous?

A shuffling outside of the door drew my attention and I heard two little voices whispering. I stayed where I was; I didn't want to frighten them by opening the door and looming over them. I was the tallest dragon in the castle by a long way. I even towered over Lew, and I'd always been aware of my height and build – I was built like a tank – and had gone out of my way to make sure I didn't stand too close or intimidate. Not that it had mattered much recently. These days, I found it so hard to concentrate that people had generally stopped talking to me.

The door opened and two little heads peered round it.

"Uncle Dane," said Hannah, stepping into the room. She was young, though I forget exactly how old, probably about ten, and she was wearing a pair of bright pink dungarees and had her hair in bunches. She stepped into the room and looked around and, as always, was followed by Ed, her adoring shadow. He was only a year or so younger than her – nothing to a dragon – and he had some serious hero-worship going on.

"Gramps is downstairs," I told them. Everyone came here looking for Gramps unless they had an actual, serious problem and then they would be here for Nana. The children flocked to wherever he was, so I assumed they were after him.

"We know, he sent us upstairs to get ready for bed," said Hannah.

"He's going to read us a story," said Ed.

"We want the one about the Beheader,"

said Hannah.

"Or the one about the gargoyle who thought everyone had forgotten his Birthday but it was really a surprise party," corrected Ed.

"That's a good one," I assured them. It had been the most in-demand story about ten years ago, from the children, and I'd been forced to read it over and over again because, apparently, I 'sounded like a gargoyle' even though none of them had ever heard a gargoyle speak and I actually sounded nothing like them.

I stayed on the sofa and waited for them to go, but they came further into the room.

"Are you sick, Uncle Dane?"

I answered quickly and was surprised that it didn't feel like a lie. I certainly wasn't myself, I knew that, so saying, "Yes, I am," seemed natural.

Ed made an 'aw' sound and came over to the sofa quickly, scrambling up onto my lap and pressing his little hand against my forehead to feel my temperature.

"How did you get sick?"

"I just did."

"But dragons don't get sick."

"Not very often."

"What's wrong with you?"

Wasn't that the question? I faltered. "Um, Nana's going to find out," I assured them. She'd said she had a theory, after all.

Ed settled in my lap and nodded. "Nana

knows everything."

"Except where we keep our secret stash of sweets," said Hannah.

"Yes, except that. Hannah's the best at hiding things."

I nodded and Hannah climbed up onto my other leg and settled there, not wanting to be left out. I had spent so long angry that it was strange to me to feel something else. I felt… content. I sat absolutely still, as though the slightest movement would scare these two trusting little beings away, like frightened rabbits. I felt like a wolf with two innocent lambs curled up against me.

They didn't seem put off from talking at all. They chatted away and I nodded at whatever they said. Ed started to yawn loudly and his eyes began to droop closed.

Quietly, so as not to startle either of them, I said, "You need to go get ready for bed or you'll miss your story."

Ed yawned again and leaned heavily against me. "You take me," he murmured. That was right. These two had the whole household wrapped around their little fingers. I was sure Hannah just assumed we were all here as her personal servants.

"Alright," I said, and lifted them both, wrapping my arms around them as they leaned against my broad chest.

I carried them across the castle and down

the stairs to Ed's room, assuming they'd both be there for the story. When I was nearly at the door, I spotted Nadia come round the corner and stalk towards me. She was frowning at me, which wasn't great. Nadia was... difficult to get a handle on. There was something about her that called to me, some kind of power inside her that I could almost feel but not quite. Before I'd lost my ability to do anything useful, I'd been watching Nadia very closely. I remember I'd been sure there was a huge untapped power inside her, and I'd been waiting to see if she found it herself. I couldn't see it now. If she wanted to find it, she'd have to do it without me, that was for sure.

She raised an eyebrow slowly. I recognised it as a warning sign.

"So *you're* the one who's been hiding these two?"

I felt I should probably deny it automatically but I didn't. I didn't care.

"You realise I've been searching all over for them because Gramps is going to read them *Millie Learns to Fly* and you've been hiding them from me?"

"No."

Nadia stalked nearer. She was average height, but compared to me she was small. Everyone was. She craned her neck up at me and I wondered if she was drawing on that invisible power or not – I couldn't tell. She glared at me and prodded me hard in the chest, right in the middle, between the two children I was carrying. They were both fully awake by then and enjoying the sight of me being prodded, if their giggles were anything to go by.

"You are a cousin-stealer, Dane, and you need to put both of them back in their room now before Gramps gets here or he'll think I lost them."

"You *did* lose them."

"No," she said, and prodded me again. She had sharp fingers. She didn't take it easy on me, and, strangely, that settled me even more. I couldn't remember the last time anyone had done anything to confront me. It felt like people had been tiptoeing around me for years, afraid to anger me, and it felt natural and good to have Nadia pissed off with me. And, yes, that might be because we were a weird family and Nadia was especially odd but I was so glad to be treated like *me* again that I didn't even mind the prodding. "You *stole* them. Now put them back this instant."

I did as I was told, dumping them both on the bed hard so they bounced, and they giggled and rolled around. I was trying to keep both of them on the bed while they tried to roll off it when Gramps came in.

"You *still* haven't got into your pyjamas?" he asked, mock-affronted.

"Yes, we have," they said, blatantly lying, and scrambled to do just that.

Gramps looked at me and gave me a small smile. "You're a little more your old self now."

"Yes. Do you think Nana would give me some more stuff to help me sleep?"

"Yes, if you ask her."

I found Nana and she gave me a drink that tasted of blackberries and I fell into bed, settling into a deep sleep. I was more calm and content than I had been in years, and my last thought was that, if I could just do this forever, sleep deeply and not think of Seren, I might just survive.

CHAPTER 13: SEREN

I held my breath while the phone rang. I was going to speak to him again. It had been so long. I thought I remembered his voice from a few days ago, when he'd saved Morgan, but I'd been so out of it that I couldn't be sure I hadn't dreamed it. My whole body was tense, waiting for the first word in Dane's voice.

He didn't answer.

It got a robotic recording telling me to leave a message. Not even Dane's voice. It threw me. I'd been psyching myself up for talking to Dane, and I was completely unprepared to leave a message. Partly, the problem was that I'd been relying on hearing Dane's voice to gauge his response to me. I wanted to see whether it was a terrible idea to admit that I was unprotected, since that would be a stupid thing to admit to any other dragon, or whether he would offer me friendship when I had no right to expect it.

It meant I fluffed the whole thing.

I barely made sense.

"Dane?" I asked, like he was suddenly going to answer. It was a stupid start. "Dane, I wanted to talk to you. I know I'm not your favourite person, and I know I have no right to expect you to hear me out after the way I treated you, but I wondered if... you would ring me back. There are some things I need to tell you."

Wasn't that the truth! He deserved to hear me apologise, for a start. And he deserved to hear me explain why I'd ended... whatever it was we'd had. And, if it looked like he was even the slightest bit open to helping me (which would make him the most generous-hearted person in the world), I would ask him to help me get to a trustworthy witch so I could get my dragon back.

I suddenly realised that it had been five years since we'd seen each other, bar the fact that he'd smashed through the wall of my bedroom a few days ago to protect my little cousin from harm.

"Ah, it's Seren, by the way. I forgot to say that. I don't know if you... remember me."

He might not. My entire gut clenched and I felt sick. Dane might *not* remember me. We'd worked together. He'd trained me, but he'd trained me alongside Glimmer and even though I'd been a good fighter (at the time), I couldn't hold a candle to Glimmer. Maybe I was now just a face he vaguely recognised. It wasn't as though we'd even been lovers and, even if we had, *curaidh* were open to sexual experiences in a way that *uasal* weren't, so that would make me one of many. For all I knew, Dane had had a string of lovers over the past five years or, worse, he'd found a partner he loved and had settled down and mated. It wasn't like I knew. Somervilles might gossip about a lot of things when they thought nobody was listening, but they wouldn't stoop to gossiping about a *curaidh*, more's the pity. Then I might have some idea if Dane was happily mated.

That emptiness inside me seemed suddenly full of barbed wire and it stuck in my stomach and hurt like a bitch. It was getting hard to breathe.

"I'm in Lower Dipton, at a café called the Honey Pot, just outside of Somerville territory. If you *do* want to speak to me, call me there. Bye."

It was done. I'd asked for help. There was no point in being afraid of everything now: afraid of my uncle, afraid of being disowned, afraid of losing Dane, afraid of being rejected, afraid of being hunted, afraid I'd never be whole again.

I'd been afraid, and it hadn't saved me.

I was done with fear.

And then I heard the sound of glass shattering in the back of the café, in the kitchen, and it turned out I *wasn't* done with fear.

Maud was still on my lap, though she perked her head up at the sound. I really hoped Marcia had another cat she'd forgotten to tell me about; one who liked to smash glasses off the shelf or something.

My hopes were dashed when I heard a grunt and more smashing glass. I looked around me. There was nothing to use as a weapon except the tray with my plate on. I looked at the lamp, wondering whether to switch it off. If it was a regular burglar, turning the light off might mean they missed me completely. If it wasn't a regular burglar, turning it off would blind me and do nothing to stop whoever-it-was from attacking. I decided to keep the light.

There were whispered voices, it sounded like maybe two or three of them, and then the faintest pad of a footstep. If I could hear them with my human perception, they weren't being overly stealthy. Maybe they really were just a couple of human fools breaking into a witch's café. However, that seemed unlikely.

"You go that way," said one voice. "We'll go this way to check the back rooms."

I pushed Maud gently off my lap, not wanting her to get in the middle of something, and tried to retain the vague hope that the fact that I concealed my scent would be enough to conceal me. It didn't really come as a surprise, though, when that *wasn't* enough.

The door to the office opened and knocked against the desk, I saw the large body of one of the Scaldan clan who'd visited my uncle with Leicester and then he grinned. He was the evil, slimy one and his smile made my skin crawl.

"Got him," he called, and the other two began to move towards the office.

Now, logically it would appear that I was trapped and outnumbered and there was nothing I could do. But that had never stopped me before.

I grabbed the tray and rose from the chair, thrusting the thick plastic edge into the Scaldan's face. It wasn't like bashing him over the head with it would do anything, and at least this way I might break his nose. I didn't manage that but there was a cut on his cheek, right below his eye, and I brought the tray round again to do the same thing. He cheated by ducking out of the way.

Embarrassingly, he had restrained me in a matter of seconds. Still, I'd had the satisfaction of making him bleed, so that was something.

"What do you want?" I asked. Call me a cliché, but I wanted to know.

"Leicester wants you."

He did? That hadn't been the impression I'd got.

"You realise what you're doing?" I tried to sound like he wasn't putting pressure on my tender stomach and making me want to sob. I tried to sound like I was calm and in control even though I was neither.

He gave a nasty chuckle and I felt the warm, moist breath against my neck, which felt *way* too exposed with his teeth right there next to it.

"We know what we're doing. And don't try to pretend you're a Somerville any more, we know you're not."

I gathered my cool, low voice to me and breathed, "Is that what you think?"

He faltered. Interesting.

"Yes." He sounded like he was trying to convince himself. I pushed into that uncertainty.

"And you're willing to take that risk, are you?"

"You've been disowned."

Since it looked like their information was good, I couldn't deny it. Instead, I pushed in another direction.

"By the Somervilles, yes."

"Who else is there?"

Who else indeed?

"Do you really want to find out?"

He had his arms around me from behind, pressing my arms against my side and essentially immobilising me, but we were pressed so close together that I felt him shiver. It looked like my creepy voice was as good as ever. Strangely, I felt disproportionately pleased about that. It had been years since I'd had the confidence to use it – my whole family looked on me with a mixture of pity and revulsion, and I'd stayed as small and quiet as possible. It was nice to know that I still had some things.

Of course, it didn't stop him from clamping his awful hand over my mouth and dragging me out of the café. Apparently, he didn't believe I had a clan any more than I did.

CHAPTER 14: DANE

I woke slowly again, without the thumping anxiety of starting awake from my dreams. I could get used to it, the feeling of not constantly fighting for control of my body. My limbs were heavy and I felt sleep cling to me as I blinked awake.

I got out of bed slowly and stretched. I felt strong, after all my sleep, but not filled with the restless energy I usually felt, that need to move and fight my dragon. Whatever Nana had given me had pushed my dragon down inside me so it wasn't pushing at my skin in a constant pressure. I didn't even care what kind of magic was in it if it did that for me.

I showered and got dressed, ready to leave my room, and picked up my mobile. I couldn't remember when I'd last had it; before I went to fight Lew, maybe? I had stopped using it recently, not interested in anything except containing my dragon. I only used it to speak to Glimmer, when I couldn't fight my dragon alone any more.

Almost idly, I lit up the screen to see if I had any messages, and was surprised when there was a voicemail sitting there. I never got voicemails. Nobody rang me.

I left my room and began to walk down towards the kitchen where I could scavenge up some breakfast, casting my eye over the missed call. It wasn't from a number I recognised. At a guess, I'd have said it was a wrong number or someone cold-calling. It wasn't.

When I heard the first word, my heart jumped and began to pound in my chest. My dragon, which had been low and calm inside me, suddenly reared up, shrieking inside me. It recognised that voice. It wanted more of it.

"Dane?"

Seren's voice was as sweet as ever, smooth and calm, like always. Underneath, though, there was something out of place. It was a thin thread of unease. He'd never said my name in that tone before.

"Dane, I wanted to talk to you. I know I'm not your favourite person, and I know I have no right to expect you to hear me out after the way I treated you, but I wondered if… you would ring me back. There are some things I need to tell you."

There was a pause.

"Ah, it's Seren, by the way. I forgot to say that. I don't know if you... remember me. I'm in Lower Dipton, at a café called the Honey Pot, just outside of Somerville territory. If you *do* want to speak to me, call me there. Bye."

Why the fuck was Seren calling me from the Honey Pot? It was a café about eight miles out of Somerville territory and it was owned by a cute little witch named Marcia who made the best pasties and didn't ask awkward questions about why I kept turning up wearing the same dirty pair of jogging bottoms and hoodie and old trainers that smelled of mildew. The reason, of course, was that I'd stashed the clothes in the woods and only changed into them when I ended up at the Somerville estate in dragon form and needed to cover up. And, yes, it had reached the stage where I needed that contingency.

My dragon pushed at me, trying to get out. There was something wrong, I knew that. If I didn't know that Seren wasn't afraid of anything – seriously, I'd had words with him about it on more than one occasion when he put himself in danger and didn't think of the consequences – I'd have said that the ugly tone underneath his words was *fear*.

I turned around and ran back the way I'd come, along the corridor, up another flight of stairs, and straight towards Nana's rooms.

"Nana," I called, and my dragon slipped into my voice. I needed to get to the Honey Pot. Seren wanted to talk to me. He needed me. I needed to go. I needed to stop him being afraid. I needed to protect him. I *needed* to protect him.

It was all I could do not to shift in the middle of the castle and push my way out of the window and fly straight for the Honey Pot. I should have had a million questions in my mind, but I didn't. I had nothing except the driving need to get to Seren.

The door to Nana's suite flew open and she stood there in the doorway. Her dragon was in her eyes and I barely managed to lower my gaze as I skidded to a halt in front of her.

"I need to go," I said, and my voice was thick with teeth. I could feel the scales pushing up over my skin, breaking out of me.

"What happened?"

She stood back, gesturing me into the room. As I stepped in, she pointed at a place for me to stand, and I obediently walked over to it, struggling to control myself. I noted that Nana placed herself between me and Gramps, who was sitting in his dressing gown and looking worried.

"I need to go," I repeated.

Nana snapped, "I told you to tell me why."

I couldn't speak any more. I could only breathe, hauling my dragon back inside me by sheer strength of will. Instead of talking, I held up my phone and pressed play again.

At the sound of Seren's voice, I nearly lost it, and it was only a low growl from Nana that helped me stay still.

"Dane? Dane, I wanted to talk to you. I know I'm not your favourite person, and I know I have no right to expect you to hear me out after the way I treated you, but I wondered if... you would ring me back. There are some things I need to tell you. Ah, it's Seren, by the way. I forgot to say that. I don't know if you... remember me. I'm in Lower Dipton, at a café called the Honey Pot, just outside of Somerville territory. If you *do* want to speak to me, call me there. Bye."

Of course I wanted to speak to him. Of course I remembered him. How could he think that I wouldn't remember every little thing about him?

"Dane, stay where you are." Nana's voice was hard and commanding. "You are not to go alone."

I looked up, hopeful. Would she allow me to go? At that point, I wasn't sure I could stop myself anyway, certainly not for long. At least if she allowed me to go, I would be able to come back. Disobeying Nana was a no-no.

There was a knock on the door and Nana called, "Come in, Laura."

My cousin entered. She was instantly alert. Nana must have summoned her with the pull of her elder's magic.

"Laura, you're to go with Dane to a village near the Somerville's territory. He is looking for Seren Somerville. Help Dane find him and bring him back here. Don't let Dane near the Somervilles."

Laura nodded and began to strip. I looked away, back to Nana.

"Dane, you're not to go into Somerville territory." I nodded. "I am serious, Dane. Something has obviously happened and I don't want to start a war and it won't take much, especially not just after we took Morgan from them. You can bring Seren here. He is welcome here."

My heart almost broke at that simple kindness.

"Get ready," she said, and I began to strip as well. I bundled up my clothes into a ball, all wrapped up in my t-shirt. We learned early on how to make a bundle we could carry in dragon form. It was awkward to shift back and be naked. Particularly, though, I wanted to take my phone, in case Seren rang me again. I heard Nana speaking to Laura, though I missed bits of it. "Watch him, Laura, and protect yourself. I'd send Dee with him, but she's away. You need to be prepared to fight him, if you must."

It looked like Nana understood exactly how bad I'd got. I didn't know whether to feel bad that she thought I was that dangerous or pleased that she at least understood, though how she did I have no idea.

I moved over to the window, flung it open and stepped up onto the windowsill. I began my shift, and let my dragon roar out of me. Grabbing my bundle of clothes in my claw at the last moment, I leapt off the windowsill and out into the morning sunshine. Behind me, I heard Laura step onto the windowsill and Gramps' voice. "Good luck, son."

I flew swiftly and didn't look behind me to see if Laura was keeping up. My mind was blank, except for one focus: Seren.

Dragons can mask their dragon form from human eyes, as long as the humans don't look too closely or have any magic in them. It was a gift from evolution. Concealing our form from witches, shifters, goblins and such was another matter. I didn't care. I landed right outside the Honey Pot and barely had the intelligence to land round the back, where at least there was only the kitchen window and the bins, sheltered by a long wall that ran the length of the high street. I shifted back to my human form as I flew towards it, dropping the last few feet and rolling. I was scrambling into my clothes when Laura landed beside me, squeezing into the available space in dragon form. It was lucky she wasn't as big as I was or she'd never have fit.

I didn't wait for her. I leapt for the back

door. It was open.

I clattered into the kitchen, looking around for Seren. Marcia burst into the kitchen from the other side, brandishing a broom but, when she saw me, she lowered it.

"Oh, it's you. What are you doing here?"

"Where is he?"

"Where's who?"

From outside, I heard Laura's voice, loud and indignant, "Do you *mind*, I'm getting dressed."

A gravelly voice replied, "No, I don't mind."

"Well I do, so close your damned eyes or I'll burn you."

"Trolls don't burn."

"Then I'll claw your eyes out. Now look what you've done, I've lost Dane."

She rushed into the kitchen and almost barrelled into me. "Don't go running off like that," she said. She was still breathing heavily from the flight. I guess I'd gone fast.

Marcia blinked.

"Where is he?" I demanded again and began to move into the café beyond the door. I had to brush past Marcia to do it but I made sure I didn't hurt her. She just stared at Laura like she couldn't believe what she was seeing.

Laura said, "Oh, hi, sorry to barge in like this but we're looking for Seren Somerville?"

The café was only small and it was empty. I could see straight away that it was empty and I could smell the people who'd been in their recently, but no trace of Seren. I wouldn't smell him anyway, since dragons concealed their scent, so he could have been there. I went back into the kitchen.

"Where is he?"

The troll was the one to answer. "What makes you think Seren's here?"

I turned to him. He definitely knew where Seren was.

Laura got between me and the troll. "Ah, Dane, Nana said I was to stop you, um, you know, killing people."

The troll grinned. "Knew I liked you. You want to tell me why he's all worked up?"

"We got a message from Seren saying he was here."

"And you just got this message?"

"Why?"

Marcia stepped forward, right between me and the troll. "I think everyone needs to calm down."

I hadn't realised that I was growling until then.

Taking a deep breath, I said, "Is he safe?" If I knew that, I'd at least be able to concentrate.

"Seren was here last night. We need to know who you are before we tell you any more.

Safety first."

She had a point. If I was anyone other that me, I'd be pissed as hell if she went around telling people where Seren was. I had no idea what he was doing out of the Somerville territory but it sounded like he was alone, and that meant he was vulnerable, no matter how strong he was.

"Dane, was it?" asked Marcia.

I nodded.

"Why don't you take a seat?" She gestured at a stool by the large table in the middle of the kitchen and I sat. I felt she was working some kind of magic, filling the air with peace and calmness. "You too, Broadmire." The troll sat opposite me. "Now, what made you pop up out of nowhere?"

At first, I assumed she was talking to me but, since she had her back to me and was boiling the kettle, I wasn't sure and was surprised when Broadmire answered.

"When I see two dragons land outside your kitchen and charge in here, I'm going to come and see what the hell they want. Especially after last night."

"What about last night?"

"And you," said Marcia, ignoring me and looking at Laura. "Can I ask your name?"

"Laura Hoskins, and this is my cousin, Dane."

"What is it you're here for?"

"To find Seren. To make sure he's safe."

"You say you received a message from him?"

"That's right." Marcia waited for Laura to take the mug that she offered her and then she set one down in front of me, too, and Broadmire, and one for herself.

"When did you get this message?"

They all looked round at me.

"This morning. I got it this morning."

For some reason, Marcia and Broadmire exchanged a look at that. I didn't like it.

"Why? What's going on?"

"Are you sure he said he was here?"

I pulled my phone out of my pocket, found the missed call and pressed call back. Through a side door, presumably leading to an office or stock room, a phone rang.

"Ah, yes, it seems he did make a call after all."

"He was here, then."

"Yes."

"Do you know where he is now?"

I was already up and moving towards that door and neither Marcia nor Broadmire made any move to stop me.

It was a tiny office, filled half with a messy desk and half with a nest of blankets on an old cot. No Seren.

"Was he staying here?"

"Look, we appreciate that you're looking for your friend but we don't know who you are," began Marcia.

"You could be anybody," said Broadmire bluntly. "And you're *curaidh*. We don't know what history you have with the Somervilles."

I held up my phone and played the voicemail again. I wanted it to calm me, to hear his voice, but it didn't. That underlying thread of... fear kept me from being settled by his words. It had the desired effect on Marcia and Broadmire, though. Broadmire gave a shrug and said, "He was here, yes. Turned up yesterday in a right state. Weak as a kitten. Marcy took him in, like she does all the strays. Fixed him up, let him sleep in the office. Then she left him here overnight."

"And he left?" That didn't make sense.

"In a manner of speaking," said Broadmire.

"What do you mean?"

"We came in this morning to find the place broken into. Door forced, smashed glass, no Seren."

My brain refused to understand. "So where is he?"

"Don't know. Looks like he was taken."

"By who?"

"Don't know that, either."

"We're so sorry, Dane. I had no idea anyone would break in or I'd have taken him home with me, but he was tired and I thought it best to let him rest where he was."

I began to get a roaring in my ears. It drowned out what they were saying and I felt my dragon begin to take over me. It wasn't like normal, though, it was slow, and there was a finality to it.

"Dane! Dane! I'll get Nana here if you don't stop!"

Laura was shouting at me, though I had no idea why.

Marcia's voice was softer, but it caught my attention.

"Dane, we'll find Seren. He's only been gone a few hours and we know who took him. You'll get him back. You'll get Seren back."

I leaned into that voice, followed it, and traced it to its final word. "You know where he is?"

"No, but Maud saw the whole thing. She saw who took him. It was dragons. They didn't have any scent. She says they were *uasal*, so they must have been Somervilles."

It didn't make any sense for Seren to leave the protection of his family's territory, only to call me and wait around for them to come and get him back. Had they kidnapped him?

Grabbing my phone again, I rang the one number I'd called again and again.

"Glimmer? Tell me what happened to Seren."

CHAPTER 15: DANE

I knew it was bad when Glimmer didn't even crack a joke about being pleased to hear from me. He sounded wrecked when he said, "I'm so sorry, Dane, I didn't know."

"Didn't know what?"

"He's been disowned."

My world tilted and I had to ask, "Are you sure?" like Glimmer didn't know exactly what he was talking about.

"I'm sure. I only heard this morning. He was disowned two nights ago. He made it out of the territory alright, but I have no idea where he went. I'd never have let him go out unprotected if I'd known, but they didn't tell me. I wouldn't have allowed it."

He sounded as upset as I felt.

"But- why would Somerville disown Seren? He's- he's his nephew."

"That's family business," said Glimmer.

I roared. I didn't mean to, but I did. I roared down the phone and only stopped when I heard Glimmer saying, "Seriously, Dane? Deafen me much? It's family business. You know I tell you more than I should and, if it helps Seren, I will, but don't expect me to betray my clan for you."

When I looked around, I saw Marcia standing across the kitchen with Laura in front of her, her arm thrown out like she would protect her, and even Broadmire blinked at me in surprise.

"Sorry," I said, cringing.

Glimmer thought I was talking to him. "It's alright, Dane. Look, I can't tell you much. I can only say he's been disowned. It'll be common knowledge soon enough anyway."

"Would any of the Somervilles try to kidnap him? Take him back to the castle?"

There was a pause. It was the sort of dead moment in which the very air shifted, and then Glimmer spoke again, his voice colder than before, so sharp it felt like it might cut me.

"What?"

"Would any of your lot come after him? For revenge, or... as a challenge?" I was struggling to come up with reasons why anyone would be stupid enough to go after Seren. Or how Seren hadn't burned all of them to a crisp or at least done some hefty damage to the café before he was taken.

"No. Nobody would go after him; he's no longer family business. What do you know, Dane?"

"He was staying at the Honey Pot in Lower Dipton, with a witch. The café was broken into last night and Seren vanished. Would he go willingly?"

"No. No, he wouldn't. Dane, there's something you need to know. I couldn't tell you – it was family business, but Seren's not protected by Somerville any more, so I guess I can tell you now." He took a deep breath. "Seren isn't well. He's weak. Like, really weak. He wouldn't be able to protect himself, Dane."

We both knew what he meant. Protect himself from *ridire.*

"But he went with other dragons. Who else does he know?"

There was an answering growl from the other end of the phone. Glimmer knew who it was, then, or at least he was pretty sure.

"Scaldans. They knew he was disowned."

"But what would they want with him? They can't blackmail Lord Somerville if he's not one of the family any more."

Glimmer swallowed, and his voice was harsh and desperate. "Dane, do you have any idea where he is?"

"No."

"He's so weak, Dane – you don't understand how weak he is. We can't let them- we can't let them hurt him. You have to help me find him, Dane."

"I don't know how. Does he have a mobile we can track?"

"No, the Somervilles kept that."

"Or…" I was struggling for another option when Marcia spoke tentatively from behind Laura.

"I can track him, if I have something belonging to him. I was hoping to find some of his blood in my office, but it was clean. I could have used it before it lost its potency."

I deliberately ignored the implication that Seren had bled. I was not going there.

"I don't have anything."

Glimmer said, "I have something. I'll be there in ten minutes." And he hung up.

It was a long ten minutes. I sat still, concentrating on breathing, and Marcia cleared the table and wiped it down and then began to draw a chalk circle on it. She leaned over it and scrawled letters and symbols on but, even if I'd been interested, I couldn't concentrate on it. I was focused on the door, willing Glimmer to arrive.

Marcia suddenly stood upright. "Something's here."

I looked over to the door and saw nothing. With Glimmer, that didn't mean anything.

"That you?" I asked.

"It's me."

A few seconds later, Glimmer walked in, still yanking a t-shirt over his head. He was lean, like most *uasal*, and while he didn't exactly have any bulky muscles, he was wiry and strong. As he poked his head through the hole of his t-shirt, he showed us all what made him stand out from almost every other *uasal* out there. They were all pale, all fair-haired, all silver-eyed, but Glimmer had red hair. On a good day, it could be called strawberry-blonde. It was the most wonderful bright orange, and it matched his freckly face.

"What have you got?" I wasn't going to mess around with chit-chat until we found Seren.

"Hair," he said, and lifted the long, delicate gold chain from around his neck. It was long enough that, when he shifted, it didn't break against his dragon's larger neck. It was a locket and I'd seen it a thousand times. He opened it and brought out a lock of blonde hair.

I tried not to get angry that Glimmer had it.

"How did you get that?"

"He gave it to me. He's got a lock of mine, too. For emergencies like this. Or, you know, if we need to... remove each other for some reason."

Seren must have trusted Glimmer explicitly – literally with his life – to give him a lock of hair. He handed it over to Marcia and she placed it in the centre of the circle.

Glimmer stood next to me and eyed the others in the room. I watched him. He was tense. Far more tense than I would have thought. Generally speaking, Glimmer took life as it came and didn't worry.

"What are you worried about? You expecting one of the Somervilles to find you here?"

"No. They wouldn't come. I just need to find him."

Amen to that.

Laura was keeping close to Marcia but she looked up at that. "Why are you worried about finding Seren? He was disowned by your family. Sorry, Dane," she added when I growled, "But he *was* disowned. Aren't you disobeying Lord Somerville by helping him?"

It was a stupid question to anyone who knew Glimmer, but then Laura didn't know him, so she could ask. Glimmer looked at her out of blue-silver eyes, and said with the cold certainty he always spoke with when he spoke of his treasure.

"I'm the Guardian. Seren's mine to protect."

And if that didn't go to show that Seren was a true treasure, I didn't know what did.

Something about what Laura said nagged at me, though. Something was off.

"Glimmer? Why *are* you so worried about Seren? What do you know?"

"You don't understand how weak he is, Dane."

"Seren? Seriously?"

"Yes, seriously. He's not well. Trust me when I say he's vulnerable right now. And if those bastards want him—"

"What would the Scaldans want him for, anyway?"

I saw his jaw clench. "Leicester Scaldan wants to claim him."

My dragon had been pretty good for a while, now that we were actually doing something to find Seren, but at that, I felt my eyes shift and the rest of me following closely behind.

"He can't," I said, before I lost the power of speech. No way could Leicester claim Seren. No. No. No.

"That's why he was disowned: for refusing to mate him. Scaldan might have taken him to—"

"I've got him. Wait, that can't be right. He's in the middle of the ocean."

Glimmer moved close to the table. "Show me."

Marcia pointed at a faint image of a map, like a hologram over the table, and I could just make out a speck of light shining in the middle of nowhere in the North Sea.

"Glimmer," I growled, and my dragon

pushed out of me, cutting of my word with its dragon teeth and lengthening my jaw. It was a plea and a warning in one. Why was Seren in the middle of the ocean?

"It's an island. It's warded so it can't be traced, can't be seen by humans."

I'd heard of it but never been there. It had once been an outpost, used mainly by dragons – *uasal*-owned with *curaidh* guards – but it was long abandoned. If Seren was there, he'd either gone there to hide or he'd been taken by dragons.

He'd been taken by Scaldans.

With a rush of relief, I gave up all control to my dragon. I gave it everything. I was all in.

Laura was on her mobile, already talking. "Nana? Seren's been kidnapped but we're- oh, Dane is leaving. No, I *didn't* try to stop him."

It was good that she didn't. I would tear through anyone who got in my way.

I was out in the street, shifting already, letting my dragon lose. It felt good, to finally be doing what we'd wanted to do for years. We were going to get Seren back, and we'd kill anyone who got in our way. My dragon growled as I flew, warning anyone within hearing distance not to come near us, not to interfere. We had no mercy. We had no thought other than to reach Seren. Finally, my dragon was free.

CHAPTER 16: SEREN

I was leaning back against the wall of an abandoned, crumbling house, almost frozen from the cold air and the damp and the icy stone beneath me. I knew this island. All Somervilles did, since it had once been under Somerville control, during the Argyle War. It had been abandoned nearly a century ago and it was little more than a nearly-baren rock with stone buildings half-broken and decaying. The one I was in was missing half its roof and I had dragged myself across to the side of the room which was covered, with timbers stretching out and broken like cracked teeth above me.

The roof didn't help with the cold, but it did keep the drizzle off me. I had tried to leave when the Scaldans left me but, since I couldn't hear them or smell them or see them, I'd had no idea where they were and, it turned out, they weren't that far away at all. I'd stumbled out, my leg aching and making me limp, and they'd seen me and dragged me back. I had a lovely new bruise across my cheek to remind me of it. I actually might not have noticed it, a few hours later, since I was so cold that I couldn't even *feel* my face – which stopped the ache – but it was swelling and my eye was gradually closing.

So I sat, slumped back against the wall, and waited for my fate. I was so tired and it wasn't like I could get off the island anyway, since it was too far to swim to shore, especially in my condition, and I couldn't just shift and fly off.

How long I sat there, I don't know. The sky was a constant grey, as though sunrise and daylight and sunset were all one here. I just sat and waited.

Every now and again, a Scaldan head peered round the doorway to check I was still there and sneered at me when they saw me slumped there. It was always a different face, so I wasn't sure how many of them there were out there. Certainly more than the three who'd taken me from the Honey Pot.

I think I must have dosed off, surprisingly. It was probably a good thing that I woke when I did, since I was actually so cold that it was a genuine worry that I'd die of exposure. It wasn't like I had my dragon's healing to make me better again.

If I'd told the Scaldans that, they might have given me a blanket or something. Of course, if I told them that, they might do anything they liked to me without any fear, so it wasn't likely to happen. As far as I could make out, they were keeping their distance because they weren't quite sure what I was capable of.

I heard a disturbance in the sky and saw a sleek silver dragon sink down beyond the uneven top of the wall. Then there were voices, but I couldn't make out what they were saying. Finally, Leicester Scaldan came into view, wearing a remarkably smart pair of trousers and jumper. He didn't look like he'd dressed for the weather. Then again, he hadn't been there freezing his ass off for as long as I had.

"Seren," he said. I wanted to cover my ears so I wouldn't have to hear his horribly slimy voice. "I'm going to make you a very generous offer."

He waited then, as though he expected me to say something. Maybe it would have been polite but, since he'd *kidnapped* me, I felt social niceties were out the window.

"I see you're just as stubborn as Lord Somerville claimed. We know you have been disowned. You're alone in the world, Seren. My offer is this: let me claim you and become part of the Scaldan clan, and we will give you a place to live, protection, security. You will receive the comforts accorded to your station as my mate, and we ask only that you make your talents available to our clan in return."

There was a lot to digest there. The first thing was that Leicester still wanted to claim me, even without an alliance to the Somervilles, and the second was it looked like they didn't actually know I'd lost my dragon. Tricky.

I began to think it over. If I told him I was weak, that could go either way. Maybe he'd stop bothering with me – it was obvious that he wanted my power, not actually me – but he could also assume I wasn't telling the truth.

"No," I said. It was the simplest answer and it was heartfelt.

"No?"

"That's right. No."

"I don't think you fully appreciate the position you're in Seren." He was a patronising bastard, I could tell that. "You've been disowned."

"I am aware."

"You need to find another clan to take you in."

"No."

He moved towards me until he was barely two metres away, standing over me. I hadn't bothered to try and move. My limbs felt disconnected from me and it wouldn't have been graceful, not to mention totally pointless.

"Don't you understand what you're saying?"

"I understand."

"Then you're a fool!"

Glad we agreed on that.

Leicester stared at me for a while, his silver-yellow eyes looking sickly and tainting my vision. I just sat there, waiting to see what he would do, like it wasn't really me he was going to do it to. I was watching from the side-lines, looking at a thin man slumped against a wall and a powerfully-built *uasal* clenching his fists over him.

At last, he spoke, and he did it with an awful calmness.

"I do not think you are in a position to refuse me. Somerville said you were suffering from the effects of an illness, that your magic was weak. I don't think you can stop me from claiming you."

He was right.

I couldn't stop him. There would be no repercussions from my uncle for doing such a thing. The only chance I had was to persuade him not to, and I wasn't at my most eloquent right then. Still, I opened my mouth and formed the words using my numb lips.

"You don't want to mate a weak dragon."

"Somerville assures me that the effects of your illness will be negated by our mating."

"He lied."

Leicester tilted his head to the side. "That

would be foolish."

At that point, I had nothing left to lose – I had to tell Leicester the truth, if it would stop him claiming me. No way would he want to be mated to a useless dragon.

"I have no magic. If I did, I would have stopped your flunkies from kidnapping me, wouldn't I?"

"Or, if you were reluctant to be claimed, you would try to deceive me."

"I can't fake bruises. Can you stop your dragon healing you when you're hurt?"

He thought about it, which gave me the faintest trace of hope that he would be reasonable.

"No, I can't."

"Take a look at me. Do I look like I'm healing?"

He moved nearer and I wanted to flinch away but I didn't. I sat absolutely still as Leicester crouched down beside me and reached out a hand to touch my face. I couldn't feel his fingers through my numb cheeks. I didn't even feel him cut me but, when he withdrew his hand and there was fresh blood on his fingers, obscenely red against the white of his hand, I assumed he *had* cut me.

"You're not healing."

It was like watching the last five years play out over someone else's face. There was confusion, the keen watchful look as he waited for me to heal, expecting it, and then more confusion, anger, and finally acceptance.

"It's unnatural. Why aren't you healing?"

"I'm sick."

He studied me and I knew what he was thinking. Lord Somerville had assured him that whatever 'illness' I had would vanish with our mating. However, if he was wrong – or lying – then Leicester Scaldan would bind himself to a weak dragon with no talents. He wanted a strong mate who could fight and use magic and, if possible, ally him to one of the most powerful dragon clans in the world. He did not want what was in front of him.

"If you are deceiving me, you will be sorry."

"I'm not. I can't."

"We will see."

I didn't like the sound of that.

He stood and I looked up into his cold, angry face, wondering what he was going to do. He couldn't leave me here much longer, certainly not overnight. He would come back to find a corpse. The chill in the air had become almost painful, and there was a breeze blowing drops of rain round and round the room, even over to me, under the broken roof. Only a dragon could survive out in these open elements.

Leicester moved so quickly that I didn't

see it coming. One moment he was standing over me and the next, he had lashed out with his foot and I felt the blow to my chest. It punched the air out of my lungs and I felt a crack inside me. Shit. Another broken rib.

I didn't even have time to move before a clawed hand struck at me and ripped the shirt I was wearing. It was brown and grey from mud and grime, thin and soaked from the constant moisture in the air, and I looked down at it my chest, right over the place he'd kicked me, and saw the claw-marks there. I didn't feel them. I wasn't sure whether that was great – no pain! – or worrying – no pain? – but I did see the slices in my flesh and the blood that began to swell over them.

The red soaked the front of my shirt and I managed to lift one arm enough to press my hand against my chest. With my hand clumsy from cold, I pressed the heel of my palm against the deepest cut but still my blood ran between my fingers and, in under a minute, my entire front was crimson.

Leicester just stood there and watched. It was an experiment to him.

"You're still not healing," he said again.

"No shit," I snapped, and he smacked me with the back of his hand for that.

"Somerville said it was temporary."

"It's not. It's been years."

"I can't mate a weak man."

At that, I felt another flash of hope, but it was crushed.

"Either you'll begin to heal again, or you'll die."

It was a cold, hard threat.

"What do you mean?"

"You can't survive out here much longer unless you start to heal."

"Yeah, I got that."

I got another smack for that. I never learned.

"I will come back in the morning. If you are still alive, you might be useful to me after all."

With that, he turned and left. That was it.

I watched him leave, still trying to put pressure on the wound across my front, and saw Leicester talk to a gaggle of Scaldans just outside the doorway – there was no actual door there – and then he walked behind the wall and, a moment later, a large silver dragon took to the skies and flew away.

I was left behind. With several mean-eyed Scaldans glaring at me. I expect they didn't want to sit in the drizzle on a rock in the middle of the ocean, either.

Breathing hurt, and I concentrated on doing just that. In and out, in and out. My body didn't belong to me any more and my arm flopped back to my side and I couldn't convince it to lift back up to my chest.

My options were limited. That was the fact. I was alone and powerless and injured. If ever there was a good time for my dragon to come back to me, it was then. Of course, that also wouldn't go too well for me, if the Scaldans had any magic whatsoever. As far as I could see, my dragon could abandon me and then I would die either of exposure or blood loss before morning, or it could come back to me, in which case Leicester Scaldan would claim me against my will. It was an understatement to say that neither option was particularly appealing.

I reached inside myself, searching for my dragon. At least if I had my dragon, I could heal, I could fight. At least I would have a chance.

I searched and searched, looking for that place where I had once felt the magic thrum through me, but there was nothing at all.

As I sat there, it suddenly struck me as funny that, only twenty-four hours ago, I'd sat in Marcia's office, disowned and a bit bruised, feeling sorry for myself and naïvely assuring myself that I'd sunk as low as it was possible to get. I laughed at what a fool I'd been, and it came out wheezing and gurgling, and the Scaldans looked over at me and watched with curious distaste.

CHAPTER 17: DANE

I heard a growl behind me and recognised it. Glimmer was coming after me – or, rather, he was coming with me to get Seren back and tear apart anyone who'd dared to lay a fucking finger on him – but he was struggling to catch up. I was flying as fast as I had ever flown, my wings beating furiously, pounding at the air and propelling me forward. My neck was stretched out and I shot through the air like an arrow.

We went fast. It still took a while to reach the sea, though. I thought of nothing as I flew, except that I needed to keep going. Seren needed me. I let that thought play through my head, over and over, and it at once spurred me on and calmed me. Once, I let my mind take up the train of thought and begin to question: what state was Seren in? Had he been hurt? Had he been claimed?

I cut off those thoughts and it was harder than I'd imagined to force myself to block everything from my mind. My dragon was angry and it wanted to tear and kill and rage. I had to focus on getting to Seren and making sure that was the only thing in my mind. If I'd had time to think, I'd have been afraid of the feelings I had simmering inside the pit of my stomach. They were there, getting hotter and hotter, threatening to boil over. They were burning a hole in me and it was all I could do to focus just on getting to Seren and nothing else. I didn't need to think about anything else. If I did, those feelings bubbled harder and I could feel the abyss on just the other side of them, reaching out to me. I was certain that, if I allowed those feelings to take hold of my dragon, I'd never come back from them.

I kept flying and I kept thinking about getting to Seren. Just getting to him. Only reaching him.

Around me, the world became dark and the grey twilight filled the air around me, masking my form and making me shiver with worry that I'd taken too long. If I was too late—

No, I refused to think it. I just concentrated on reaching Seren.

When I finally reached the coast and the land beneath me fell away and I was flying across the surging grey waves, I heard another growl. I ignored that one, too. Glimmer growled again, more insistently, and I reluctantly looked round at him, twisting my neck to see him.

He dropped down to almost sea level and looked up at me expectantly and I followed suit, slipping down towards the ocean until I could feel the spray of the waves hitting my belly and coating my wings in a fine spray.

After that, Glimmer stayed silent and I just focused on getting to Seren. If I'd been able to think without the risk of that anger and desperation and panic and rage overwhelming me, then I might have come up with a better strategy than simply barrelling right up to the island and just fucking clawing everyone there to death. But I couldn't think and that really was my plan. It might have lacked finesse but I thought it was solid. My dragon loved it. It shimmered with excitement at the prospect of killing anyone who'd touched Seren. I didn't have the will to try and convince it that was wrong, either.

I saw the island in the distance and had to admit it was an excellent place to take someone you'd just kidnapped. Humans and many witches and other magical creatures couldn't even find it. Marcia hadn't been able to see it, even though she'd traced Seren there. Nobody would think to look there. If Seren was anywhere near as weak as Glimmer had indicated, he wouldn't be able to fly all the way across the ocean and if he tried to swim for it, he'd be bashed to death on the jagged rocks.

I only just stopped myself from shrieking out my challenge as I sped towards the island. My dragon wanted them to face me, to fight hard, but I thought of Seren and managed to stop myself. If they saw me coming, if they were warned, then they might hurt Seren before I got there. Surprise would be my friend.

As I reached the dark rocks, I swooped upwards, gaining height, and flew high over the rocks, over the dilapidated buildings that were in little clusters, flying high enough that I could see the whole place spread out below me, thick with shadows and strips of moonlight. Instantly, my eyes were drawn to movement.

Five men were standing in a cluster outside a long row of buildings that looked like a storm had ripped off any parts of it that weren't sunk into the foundations. Only scraps of roof remained and just shards of glass in the windows.

They were talking in low voices and hunched against the cold. Even from this distance, even over the sound of the wind tearing past me, I could have heard their conversation if I'd wanted to. But my dragon didn't care about talk. It didn't care who they were or why they had taken Seren. All it cared about was killing them so it could get to him.

I was flying fast and I swooped down on them, dropping like a boulder. I was in dragon form and they were in human, and I crushed one of them straight away, my huge claw clenching around his head and squeezing as I landed. The other four were knocked over.

I lashed out before they even responded, snapping my jaws around one of them and biting him in two. That was all I managed before they finally retaliated.

Thick black smoke began to billow around me and I felt it tighten like a boa constrictor around my chest. I hadn't known what kind of magic they had – if any – but I'd known they were *uasal*, so it stood to reason they'd have something. I still didn't slow down.

With the black smoke thickening and beginning to choke me, I snarled and went for the remaining three men. One was still in human form and the other two were shifting. I went for the human. He was the magic-worker.

The fight was not glorious. It was bloody and brutal. I barely knew what was happening, except that my dragon wanted to tear and rampage through the streets until it set eyes on Seren again. I became blind with that need and shrieked and roared my anger at the dragons as we clawed and bit and kicked and rolled.

They had magic and they were fighting for their lives, but I was stronger. I used my bulk and my muscles and my fury, and when more of them appeared out of nowhere, I turned my attention to them as well.

Some of them were in human form and they added their magic to the fight. I was shocked and struck and bound by thick green vines that multiplied as fast as I snapped them. I didn't care. My dragon felt great. It loved being out, being free, finally doing what it had wanted for so long. It didn't hold back and, with every attack that came, it felt a surge of renewed energy course through it. It was tireless. It would fight until it found Seren. Nothing could stop it.

I had no sense of time. All I knew was that I was fighting. I wasn't even aware of any injuries, though I must have had some. I couldn't feel them.

When I snaked my head around me to check, there were no Scaldans left alive outside. The last one lay dead in the shadow at my feet and with the last thud of him hitting the ground, there was a beat of silence.

"He's come for me."

That was Seren's voice. Quiet, weak, but still alive.

I tore through the building, knocking a whole section of wall down with my huge form, since I couldn't fit through the doorway, and surged forward when I saw a man standing over Seren. He was holding a gun, of all things, and I paused. He was holding it out and the barrel was pointing directly at Seren's head.

My dragon wanted to charge at him but I overruled it. This was not the time to take risks. I had to battle my dragon for a moment, but I won, in the end, and began to shift back. It was only Seren's face that gave me the strength to do it. If he pulled that trigger, there was nothing in the world that could control my dragon, not magic or fear or even Nana.

"Walk away," I said. I was giving him a chance. "I don't care about you."

"Who are you?"

I was not in the mood to chat. I took a step closer. The gun wobbled.

"Don't come any closer," he said, and I stopped.

Seren was lying still. He looked a fucking mess. His face was barely recognisable, covered with blood on one side from a long cut across his cheek, and covered in vivid purple on the other side, his eye completely swollen shut from the bruise. His lips were cut and crusted with blood and his breath rattled as his chest rose and fell. He was lying back against a wall, not moving at all except to breathe. He looked like someone had thrown a rag doll in the corner and left it there.

"Seren?" I asked.

"I didn't think you'd come."

"You're a fucking idiot then, aren't you?"

He smiled at that. Seren always did think

I had a sense of humour when, actually, I didn't. His lips pulled back in a weak ghost of a smile and I felt my heart stutter. Glimmer hadn't been kidding. I'd never seen a dragon look so fragile and sick before. He looked mere moments from death.

The thought made my dragon prickle.

"Get out," I said, turning my eyes to the man. "Go now."

"I have my orders. He's ours. He doesn't have a clan."

"He's mine," I said, my dragon filling my voice. I must have sounded deranged because the man's eyes widened and his hand shifted on the gun slightly. He was going to pull the trigger.

"He's *my* clan," said Glimmer's voice. I couldn't tell where it was coming from. And then Glimmer slid out of the shadow of the corner, pale and insubstantial as a ghost, and slid his claw across the man's throat.

The gun clattered to the ground and the man's body fell on top of it. Neither Glimmer nor I even looked at him, just headed straight for Seren.

I crouched down beside him and reached out to touch his pale skin. He was cold, like a corpse and his breath was shallow. Only his one good eye glittering as it locked on mine made me sure he was still with me.

Softly, I spoke to him. "Why aren't you

healing, Seren?"

I'd asked him that before. Why did it seem he was always bleeding?

He spoke but his voice was so quiet that I couldn't hear most of the words. His lips barely moved and I only caught snatches.

"... sorry for what I did... wanted you... dreaming but it's..."

"Shh," I soothed. "It's alright now, I'm here. You need to heal, Seren."

When I'd seen Branden slice Seren open, I'd nearly lost it. I'd killed him without a second thought and everything inside me had wanted to wrap Seren in my arms and cradle him, protect him from the outside world. I'd wanted to take him home with me, to be mine, to be my mate. But he'd been slow to heal and he hadn't replied to any of my question, hadn't wanted to come with me. He'd chosen the Somervilles, and look where that had got him.

This time I was not taking no for an answer.

"You're coming with me. I'm taking you home now."

".. nowhere to go... disowned..."

He wasn't making sense and he needed to get warm, to get to a healer. I slid my arm around his shoulders and pulled him to me, gently, so gently, so I didn't jostle his wounds.

"I could have lost you, Seren," I said, and I

nearly sobbed with the words. "I can't lose you, Seren. Not again. Come with me."

Glimmer spoke from a few feet away.

"We need to get him out of here, Dane. Is he-?"

I knew what he wanted to ask. I was wondering it myself. Was he even going to make it?

"He'll be fine," I snapped. "He just needs to get warm. He needs time to heal."

Glimmer said nothing and I dragged my eyes away from Seren to glance at him. He looked guilty and stricken.

"We need to get him to a hospital, Dane. He won't heal by himself. He's not a dragon."

"Of course he is."

"No, Dane, you don't understand. He- he lost his dragon, ok? He can't shift. He can't do magic. He can't heal. He- he won't heal."

I could hear the strain in Glimmer's voice, and I hated it. I didn't want to think about that. It would kill me, I just knew it. If I lost Seren now, my dragon would—

Fuck, I realised suddenly *exactly* what my dragon would do. It would *ruith*.

That feeling of fighting and fighting and fighting until it found Seren, that would come back and overwhelm me, but there would be no Seren to find. A cold practicality came over me. There was no stopping it if it was going to happen, but while Seren was here, and he was alive, and I could hold him in my arms, I was still me. There was still hope.

I stood, lifting Seren as gently as I could in my arms.

"He won't be able to fly like this, and he won't be able to hold on if he rides my dragon. You shift, and carry us both."

It was possibly more sensible for me to shift and for Seren and Glimmer to ride me, since I was by far the biggest of us, but it wasn't like Glimmer's dragon was small and he'd be able to get us to the mainland, at least.

"Right. Let's go outside."

"Not that way," I said. Glimmer had made to walk out of the broken doorway I'd come through and I didn't want Seren to see the mess outside.

"Alright, this way."

We went out an empty window and I saw two lumps in the darkness that looked suspiciously like bodies. It stood to reason. Glimmer had to have got in somehow.

He shifted quickly once we were outside and lay down. He tried to get the best angle for me to climb onto him, but I'd never ridden on another dragon before and it felt unnatural. If it wasn't for the fact that there was absolutely no way I was going to let go of Seren, I'd have switched places with Glimmer. But I *wasn't* letting go of Seren and so I climbed up, awkwardly, trying not to jostle the fragile body in my arms, and finally settled on Glimmer's back.

His head snaked round so he could look at us, check we were secure, and I nodded. I was gripping on with my legs and relying on core strength for balance, holding Seren securely across my lap. It was like cuddling an ice pack.

"Won't be long now, Seren," I murmured. "You're coming home with me. We just need to get you warm."

The irony was that there was nothing on the island to burn. It was all stone and slate and, what little else was there was soaked with sea spray. If Seren had been a dragon, I could have breathed fire over him, just to get him to warm up, but doing that while he was human would kill him. There was nothing I could do and I felt utterly helpless.

As Glimmer took to the air, I concentrated on holding Seren so he was safe and trying to press as much of his body against mine as I could, to give him some of my heat. I kept talking to him in a low voice, just telling him he was going to be fine and that he was coming home with me and he was mine. I said it over and over again and I was almost convinced that his breathing became stronger and less wheezy the more I spoke.

CHAPTER 18: DANE

We flew across the dark sea and the only sign of it below us was the constant noise and the moonlight catching on flashes of white sea foam. I hadn't been aware of how far out the island was, since I hadn't been in my right mind when I'd flown out there. It took a while for Glimmer to fly back and I knew we wouldn't make it all the way back to the Hoskins' castle tonight. Seren might be breathing still – and I was so fucking grateful for that – but he was badly hurt and icy cold and flying in the chill of the night air was not helping. We would be best to find somewhere sheltered to stay.

"We need to get him somewhere warm, Glimmer."

He snorted and I assumed it was agreement. I kept most of my attention on Seren, and kept glancing up and around us only to check we weren't being followed and there were no threats.

Even with a purple face covered in crusted brown blood, Seren was the most beautiful creature I'd ever seen. His eyes were silver. Pure silver. Lord Somerville had pale, pale silver eyes, nearly white, and Glimmer had a dash of blue in his, but Seren's eyes were pure and sharp. He was looking up at me then and I couldn't even tell if he could see me or understand I was there. The wrinkled lines that marred his forehead and creased around his eyes told me he was in a lot of pain and the occasional grimace and soft whimper made my heart ache for him.

He was so weak. How was it possible for Seren to be so weak? He was one of the strongest people I knew. Not just physically – he was a good fighter, though, and he'd even beaten me sometimes – but he had strength of character. He never backed down. Looking at him draped helplessly over my arms was awful.

I lowered my mouth to his head and kissed his hair, barely grazing my lips over it in case he had an injury there. I breathed in and wished I could smell him, not for the first time. When I'd lived in Somerville territory and trained them both, I'd had a near constant obsession with Seren's scent. My dragon had longed for it and I'd found that strange, since it didn't want to smell anyone else and it certainly wouldn't let anyone else smell *me*.

Keeping my mouth close to him, I kept murmuring, "It's alright, Seren, I've got you. You're coming with me now, you're safe. We're going to get you to a healer and get you warm. I won't lose you again, Seren. You're mine."

I felt him shift in my arms and his hand reached up to my wrist and held it. His grip was weak but the fact that he could lift his arm and hold on at all made me want to weep with gratitude. He would be alright. He would.

Glimmer began to fly lower and he circled a large stone building lit with yellow lights. It was a hotel. I didn't like it. I didn't want to be around other people and Seren needed a healer, but I knew warmth was the priority. I let him land in the car park and then I carefully climbed down him and onto the tarmac.

There were only two cars in the car park and the place looked mostly abandoned. We were way out of season, that was for sure. But if they were open, we'd go in. Even if they weren't open, we'd go in. Seren needed shelter.

Glimmer had shifted back and was yanking on his crumpled t-shirt and jeans.

"Where'd you get them?"

He shot me a scathing look. "I picked them up before I left the Honey Pot. And then I dropped them when I landed on the island so I could use all my claws. Didn't you feel me pick them up again as we left?"

I hadn't, so I shook my head.

"Not all of us burst out of our clothes and ripped them to shreds, Dane. And you should be grateful I am so organised, since I'm the one who is going to go in there and get us a room."

He eyed my naked form and I glared.

Glimmer came right up to me and looked into Seren's face. He scanned him carefully, scrutinising him. "I think he's healing," he said. He sounded amazed. On the basis I'd assumed Seren could heal just like any other dragon up until half an hour ago, I wasn't as surprised as Glimmer was about it.

"He's healing," I said, more to persuade myself that it was true than anything else. I needed Seren to heal.

"Wait here a minute. I won't be long."

I didn't even see Glimmer go inside. That was the way with him; he just slipped in and out of shadow and I was never sure if he was there or not. It was an incredible power and I'd never met anyone else with that kind of gift.

"You're going to be ok," I assured Seren. He still had a hold of my wrist as though he could ground himself if he was touching me. At least, that's what I wanted to think.

I tucked us close to the building and tried to use the wall and my own bulk to shield Seren from the wind. It was so cold out. Not if you were dressed for it, not if you were dry, not if you hadn't been out in it all day but Seren was still frighteningly cold and I wanted to warm him up so much.

I heard a door open and looked up. It was a fire escape at the side of the building and Glimmer stuck his head out. I headed over there and, as soon as I stepped inside, I felt the difference in temperature.

Like a lot of old buildings, it was not warm, but it was certainly warmer than outside. There was residual heat and just being out of the wind helped. I followed Glimmer along the corridor and never gave a thought to what people would think if they saw us – a naked man carrying a limp man soaked with blood – and just trusted Glimmer to take us to a room.

He did. It was unremarkable but, again, warmer than the corridor. I liked that.

The first thing I did was to scan the room for anything I didn't want there. I couldn't see anything, couldn't hear anything, couldn't smell anything. There was one large bed taking up most of the room, with a door off to the side for the bathroom and then a row of wardrobe, cupboard, desk and sofa.

I jerked my chin at the bed and said, "Covers."

Glimmer pulled back the duvet and I laid Seren gently on the sheets and covered him back up with the duvet. Then I stood back and looked at him as though just tucking him up in bed would miraculously make him better.

He groaned, maybe because he was adjusting to the new position or maybe it hurt one of his wounds.

"Do you know if there's a healer anywhere near here?"

"No."

Glimmer was already filling the little kettle from the sink in the bathroom and he came back in and put it on. He'd turned the thermostat up as high as it would go.

"Get in, he needs the body heat."

I slid in beside Seren, trying not to jostle him, and gently eased myself up against him. He tried to roll into me but he wasn't strong enough, so I shifted until I was on my side with my arm wrapped around him and he had his chest pressed against mine and was resting his head on my shoulder. Despite the terrible state he was in, it felt so right to have him there. I felt like a complete asshole thinking it when he was in so much pain, but it was the most at peace I'd been in years.

"Do you think he can drink this?" Glimmer held up a cup and steam rose from it. A hot drink would probably do him good but already his breathing was getting deeper.

"I think he's sleeping."

Glimmer looked at me. It was hard to tell

what he was thinking. Maybe that was the angle I was at, since I was laying down and Glimmer was standing, but I'd never had such a hard time reading him before.

"What?"

"Nothing." He walked over and pulled the covers back on the other side of Seren, sliding into the bed and sitting with his back against the headboard. I could feel his legs pressed up against my arm and knew he was trying to share a little more body heat. He sat there, though, looking like he hadn't a care in the world and sipping tea.

"We need to get him a healer."

Glimmer gave me another of those inscrutable looks. "I think Seren has what he needs right now. Just stay there and keep him warm, Dane."

The anger I'd kept at bay once I had Seren in my arms began to seep back into me.

"Glimmer, he needs a healer."

"Trust me, Dane. I don't know any healers here and the ones I know are Somerville healers. They won't come. Stay here for the night and let Seren rest. See what he looks like in the morning."

"He won't—"

I'd been about to say he won't last until morning but the words choked me.

Glimmer's hand reached slowly out to touch Seren's head, like he was giving me time to see what he was doing, and stroked his fingers gently through his hair. He brushed the stray strands away from his face.

"Look at his face, Dane. His bruises are fading."

It was hard to see through the baked blood but Glimmer was right. He was far from healed, but he was better than he was.

"So why did you tell me he had no dragon?"

"He didn't."

I opened my mouth to ask another question but Glimmer cut me off.

"And that's all I'm going to say about it. It's not for me to tell you, it's for him."

I gave a grunt. I wasn't happy about that but I knew Glimmer wouldn't change his mind. He'd spent five years telling me about Seren, even when it was forbidden by Lord Somerville, but he'd never told me about Seren losing his dragon.

"Just tell me when it happened."

"No. He'll tell you when he wakes up."

I gave up and just lay there with Seren tucked against me and listened to his breathing. He sounded fine. There was no wheezing and it wasn't coming in shallow pants any more. A creeping hope stole into my heart. Seren was healing again.

CHAPTER 19: DANE

With every passing hour, Seren looked less sick and bruised and, when I pulled back the covers to check out his chest, I saw that the claw marks across his chest had scabbed over. It was hard to be sure how well they'd healed just yet because his whole front was matted with blood and his shirt was stuck to him but I was sure he was getting better.

My dragon was ecstatic about it. I could hardly keep from purring, I was so happy.

It was bad, I knew, but having Seren lay next to me – pressed right against me – all night was basically the best thing that had ever happened to me and my dragon was content with it. It didn't really care how Seren had got there, it just cared that he was there.

The hours ticked by and I just lay there,

holding him. Beside me, Glimmer watched over us and I got the impression he was looking at us with the same protective fondness that he did his treasure.

As my mind began to calm from the panic it had been in, I slowly started to think again. Seren still may need a healer. Depending on how badly he was hurt still, we could fly home and he could be looked after there. That was my preference. I wanted to get Seren inside Nana's territory, where he was safe from Scaldans and Somervilles and whatever else out there wanted to hurt him. If he wasn't strong enough to make it that far, even holding onto me while I flew and he rode on my back, then we'd either need to wait another day or so or get somewhere else safe, somewhere nearer.

"Where's Laura?" I asked, suddenly aware that she'd been with me at the Honey Pot and I hadn't seen her since. Nana was going to be pissed off that I'd lost her.

Glimmer looked down at me and raised his eyebrows in mild surprise. "I told her not to come."

"Why?"

"I wasn't sure... what you would do. If, you know, Seren..."

He trailed off and I swallowed, trying not to think about the possibility, and looked back down at Seren's face. It had smoothed out and the pain-lines that had formed while he frowned and held himself tightly had gone. His chest rose and fell steadily and I could feel the warmth of his body under the duvet. He was alive. He was healing. There was no need for my dragon to panic.

"Yeah, I don't think I'd handle that well" I said. I couldn't think of anything else to say.

"I told your cousin that Seren was my clan and she wasn't to interfere. I might have scared her a bit but, seriously, I couldn't have her near you. At least I'd be able to take you out if I had to."

It was said with calm practicality and I nodded. Glimmer was extraordinary. There was no way I could beat him, especially if he was on good form.

He smiled. "You never mind when I say stuff like that."

"Stuff like what?"

"That I can beat you."

I shrugged one shoulder – the one Seren wasn't sleeping on. "You can."

"But most people don't like to be told that. You're pretty strong. Not many people can beat you."

"You're one of the ones who can."

"But you were my teacher."

"I just showed you how to access what you already had. Besides, what does that matter? The best teachers want their students to do well. I love it when they learn to beat me."

Glimmer gave a surprised huff of laughter and said, "If you fight me like you did those Scaldans, I might not be able to beat you. I didn't know you could move like that."

"Like what?"

"Just... brutal."

"I was worried," I said. That was all I could think to say. They'd been standing between me and Seren and they'd been trying to kill me, trying to harm Seren, so I'd killed them. I wasn't a monster but my dragon had a different way of looking at the world, certainly where Seren was concerned.

"Yes, I know." He seemed to realise where my thoughts had taken me because, when he next spoke, it was in a lighter tone. Glimmer never did like to be serious for too long. "On the other hand, if you're tactics are always as first-rate as they were today, then I can't imagine I'd have much problem taking you out."

"Ouch."

"Yeah, I'm serious, Dane. You're strong but you ain't smart. When I told you to fly low, I meant for you to stay low the whole time and not charge in like a bloody battering ram."

"I was worried," I said again. It was all I could say to defend myself. What I meant was: I was half out of my mind with fear that I'd never see your cousin again and my dragon was making the decisions and my dragon was pretty keen on just killing everyone to be sure. It didn't sound very good, to be honest.

Glimmer smirked. "At least it worked. Only one guy even got as far as Seren."

"Don't remind me."

I stroked my fingers gently over the patch of skin I could feel below my hand, on Seren's hip, and reminded myself that he was there, he was safe and he was warm.

"What took you so long, anyway? I thought you were right behind me."

"It took me a while to catch up to you. I had to get Seren's hair back first," he said, his fingers going straight to his locket and pressing it against his chest like it was precious.

My dragon shifted uneasily. It didn't like Glimmer having a part of Seren like that.

"And my approach was more... stealthy." He gave that particular smile that meant he'd used his power to shimmer in the shadows and slit people's throats before they even knew he was there. And I didn't want to think about how I knew he had a smile just for that.

We lay in silence for a moment, and I breathed deeply, wanting to inhale Seren's scent but all I got was the slightly musty smell of the hotel room. Glimmer hummed and I looked up at him. He was looking at us in that way again, like we were his treasure.

"Did you mean it, Dane?"

"What?"

"That you're taking Seren home with you?"

"Yes. I want to get him into Hoskins territory as quickly as I can. Nana will be able to protect him from anything."

Glimmer gave a slow nod. "She made quite an impression on Somerville, that's for sure."

I felt a swell of pride. Yep, that was my Nana.

"Dane?"

"Yes?"

"You said he was yours."

"He is mine." The words came out with a growl.

That smirk slid across Glimmer's face again and scrunched his freckles up tight. "That's what I wanted to hear. I'd hate to kill you after everything if you were planning on toying with him."

My throat was suddenly dry, too tight for me to speak, so I shook my head. I wasn't toying with Seren. I wanted him. I wanted him to be my mate. I wanted him to be *mine* forever.

"I'll go and see if I can find a phone we can use. I'll see if I can get a message to your family."

"Thanks, G."

He touched my forehead gently as he slid out of the bed, careful not to jostle Seren, and disappeared into the corridor. When he was gone, I turned my face back to Seren. He looked so peaceful now, sleeping with his head on my shoulder, his chest rising and falling so that it brushed against mine with each breath. There was such a rightness in having him there and I couldn't believe I'd gone my whole life without experiencing it before. It seemed impossible. I couldn't imagine going back to it. Had I never laid in bed with Seren in my arms before? Seriously?

After the rush and fury of last night, this moment felt particularly peaceful and I spent a few moments revelling in it. I became conscious of the feeling and studied it. The sneaking suspicion I'd begun to form when I'd realised that my dragon would *ruith* if it lost Seren became more solid in my mind.

I knew what all dragons did – that a *ruith* was a last act of desperation. Only a dragon who had nothing left to live for would do it, and they'd simply fight and fight and fight until they were killed. It was made difficult by the fact that a dragon in *ruith* was almost unbeatable. I shuddered. I did not want to do it; I didn't want to become that.

I knew I would, though, if I lost Seren. And that told me everything I needed to know.

Before, I hadn't actually *lost* him. My dragon had hated being parted from him but it had been content as long as it had eyes on him. I'd known that Seren was alive and safe and protected inside the Somerville house. It was only when I'd suddenly been confronted with the possibility that Seren was hurt, maybe worse, that I'd felt that rising tide of panic.

My dragon and I agreed: as long as Seren was safe and healthy and happy, we were fine. Even if that wasn't with us, though that would sting, I knew.

If Seren was in danger, if he—

We would *ruith*.

There was only one reason a dragon would do that. In all the history books, all the legends, with all the hundreds of dragons around the world, there was only one reason anybody knew of that a dragon would *ruith* and that was if they lost their fated mate.

Seren was my mate.

With that flash of realisation, I felt winded. I wanted to shake Seren awake and tell him, to ask him if he felt the same, but I didn't. He needed to rest and heal. And I was afraid. Me. Afraid. I wasn't normally afraid of much, but that fear squirmed inside me like a twisting snake in my gut. What would I do if he didn't feel the same? What would happen to me if my mate rejected me?

It wasn't beyond the bounds of reason. He'd dumped me before. I'd assumed he'd grown bored with me or I'd done something wrong. What if I did that again?

On the other hand, it wasn't like he had many options at the moment. As far as I could see, he could either go it alone, come home with me or mate Leicester Scaldan. No. No. He wouldn't do that. He wouldn't. He didn't want to. He'd already refused him once.

But that didn't mean he'd want to mate me, either.

What if I got him home and he found someone else and I had to watch him fall in love —

"I can feel you thinking too hard and it's making you uncomfortable to lie on."

The words were soft and rasped out of his dry throat but they were wonderful. I looked down at Seren's face and saw he was blinking sleepily up at me. My smile slipped onto my face without my permission to see him look at me so sweetly, to see the awareness in his eyes after the haze of pain.

"Sorry," I said. "I'll try to be more comfortable."

"Perhaps I should move."

"No."

I slid my arm further around his middle to keep him there, not that I'd actually stop him if he wanted to get up but it would discourage him. It did. He relaxed back into me and I breathed deeply, wanting to scent him. It was frustrating. At least now I knew why my dragon had always been so cranky about not being able to scent him. It knew we were mates. It had always known.

"What are you thinking about?"

I smiled again. Seren had asked me that so many times. He would stand back and study my face and ask, "What are you thinking?" and look at me as though he were learning to read my expressions like a foreign language.

"I was- thinking about when we go home."

"Oh. I can't do that."

My whole body tensed and my dragon, which had been luxuriating a little smugly in the feeling of having our mate in our arms, snarled in my head as it pushed forward, alert. It was ready to fight about that.

"Where will you go then?"

Seren didn't answer.

That was not good.

CHAPTER 20: SEREN

My body ached but it wasn't in the same way. It no longer felt like I'd been run over by a steam-roller and felt more like the ache after a heavy work-out. Weak and stiff but not necessarily bad.

I might have woken up a few minutes earlier but I'd felt so... happy where I was, and I'd known I was lying pressed against Dane, and so I'd stayed still and just enjoyed the feeling, soaking up the warmth that came off his body like a furnace.

Then he'd begun to tighten up and I'd known he was thinking about something bad. I'd only spoken to interrupt his train of thought. Whatever it was making him tense, I didn't like it. Now I wished I hadn't said anything.

"Where will you go then?"

Wasn't that the question? I didn't have

anywhere to go.

I didn't want to say that. I didn't want to have to beg Dane, either, but I'd rung him for a reason and he'd come to get me from the island—

Wait. What?

I sat up, wincing when the movement jarred my tender ribs and yanked at my skin where it was scabbed.

"You were at the island."

"Yes."

"You- came for me?"

He sat up and moved me, hauling me up to the headboard and propping me against some pillows and then pulling the duvet up over me again and tucking it around my shoulders. Then he settled on the edge of the bed and faced me. I'd let him move me around like a puppet.

Only when he was ready did he look me in the eyes and speak.

"You called me."

"Yes."

I was going to say more but Dane stood and walked into the bathroom and came back with a little plastic cup filled with water. He held it out to me and he almost held the cup to my lips but I took it and he let me.

The water was wonderful. I hadn't realised how dry my throat was and the water seemed to wash away the taste of blood in my mouth.

When I'd finished drinking, he took the cup and placed it on the bedside table.

"Seren, do you remember what I said to you?"

"When?"

"On the island?"

I frowned. That wasn't my best time. I'd had a clear sense of doom, I knew that. I'd been pretty with it, I thought, until Leicester Scaldan cut me open. I'd gone downhill pretty quickly after that. I'd only been aware of the cold and the pain and the red and the empty space inside me.

"Um, no. Sorry."

His face became darker. I could read Dane pretty well and I could tell he was building up to saying something bad. I didn't want to hear it. Was he going to leave me here?"

I blurted out the first question I thought of. "Why did you come to the island? I mean, I know I rang you but that was from the Honey Pot and there's no way you could... wait, how *did* you find me?"

"Glimmer."

"But he didn't know where I was either."

"Are you going to interrupt me all night or let me tell you what happened?"

I thought about it. I wanted to hear Dane talk, yes. There was a nagging fear inside me, though, chewing at the edges of my empty space. I was frightened that he would leave me.

"Seren, don't make that face."

"What face?"

"The one where you try and look like Lord Somerville."

I had a Lord Somerville face? That wasn't good.

Dane leaned closer and I became aware that he was naked. He must have lost his clothes during a shift. How had I been pressed against a naked Dane and not realised it?

He leaned closer and whispered, "Seren, talk to me. Don't shut me out."

"Tell me what happened."

"I'll tell you, if you tell me what happened to get you on that island."

That was fair. "Ok. Are you going to… hold me?"

I was trying to be casual and massively failing. I might as well have thrown myself into his arms and begged him to hold me like a wailing damsel.

To my relief, though, he eased himself up against the headboard and under the duvet and then I was leaning into his chest and his arm was around my shoulder and his head was pressed against mine. It looked like begging worked. The remnants of my pride were about to take a battering because, now I'd discovered that, I'd throw every last scrap of pride away if I could beg Dane to stay exactly like this forever.

"I'll tell you how I found you. Then you tell me how you got there."

I already felt so much better and hearing Dane be so, well, Dane, was doing wonders for me. He was always so clear and so calm.

"Ok."

He told me how he'd found me and I was amazed. "Glimmer really shouldn't have done that."

"Yes, he should."

"No, he could get disowned for that."

"Then he can come home with me, too."

"Oh."

"What do you mean oh?"

"Nothing."

"You meant something, Seren."

"I guess I was wondering what you meant by 'too'."

Dane stilled and there was that tension in his muscles again as he held himself tight.

"Nana said you can come home with me, if you want. Do you want to?"

I twisted round to look into his face.

"Are you serious?"

He looked surly. "It's not like you have anywhere else to go."

"No, I don't, but that- why would your elder take *me* in?"

Dane went from surly to uncomfortable. It was almost an imperceptible change but I'd spent months studying him, trying to learn him inside and out, and I saw it.

"Why wouldn't she?"

"There's nothing in it for her. I don't have a dragon. I don't have magic. She won't get anything from it."

"Why does she need to get something from it?"

"Because she'll end up with a weak clan if she takes in strays and has to expend energy protecting them without getting anything in return. People don't do that. They take in strong dragons and form alliances. That's how strong clans are made."

Ok, so I was now looking at Dane's unimpressed face.

"Are you done?"

"Done with what?"

"Reciting your family motto."

"Fuck you, Dane, I don't have a family."

We stared at each other in shock for a second as those words sunk in. I felt the blood drain from my face. All the same feelings I'd had when I'd been disowned came charging back into my chest and it was hard to breathe.

Dane's palm pressed against my cheek and grounded me and he leaned close, his voice dipping low and far away from the snarky comment of before.

"You have a family, Seren, if you want it. If

you want me. And I don't mean you have to mate me, either. You don't need to mate anyone to come home with me, you just need to trust me. I want you to come home with me, Seren."

"Even though I'm weak?"

"Yes."

"Lady Hoskins won't mind that?"

"No, she won't."

A flicker of something passed over his face but I couldn't identify it.

"Are you lying?"

"No! No, I'm not." He sighed. "I just realised that I think Nana knew something when she sent me to get you back."

"Why *did* she send you to get me?"

"I got your message. I had to ask permission to leave."

"And she let you? Just like that?"

"I guess she knew I was going anyway."

I studied Dane's face, trying to see something in it. I have no idea what I was looking for but I felt I was close to something, some understanding that would help me slot all these pieces in place, but I couldn't identify it.

Staring into Dane's eyes, I felt something stirring inside me. He had the darkest eyes I'd ever seen, the deepest most beautiful grey, nearly black, and they were always warm and kind and calm.

"I can't believe you came to get me."

"You have no idea what I'd do for you, Seren."

We were so close that our breath was mingling and his eyes were all that I could see. Then he pulled away. I'd thought for a moment that he'd been about to kiss me but that was fanciful. He cleared his throat and said, "The first thing we need to do is get you back home. Get you a healer."

He had no idea what he was offering. He was taking me back to the Hoskins castle, to live with him? Could there even *be* anything more perfect than that?

"And you're sure Lady Hoskins will allow that?"

"Yes."

"Even though I'm weak. I can't do anything for her."

"She still wants you there. She'll protect you. We all will. You don't need to earn your place in our family, Seren. Stop thinking you're still a Somerville. You're a Hoskins now."

I felt tears rush up to my eyes and blinked quickly. I turned away, hoping Dane wouldn't notice.

He really had no idea what he was giving me. For a start, I'd get to be in the same place as Dane every day. It was like six years of wishes were coming true all at once. I was definitely not above throwing my pride under a bus at that point.

"I can still do things. Cleaning and stuff like that. I won't be a bother."

There was a little growl in Dane's voice when he responded. "You don't need to earn your keep, Seren. We all do our share. You're one of the family now. You have a right to be there."

Without my permission, I felt my eyes overflow and hot tears streak down my cheeks.

The door opened and Glimmer walked in. I felt my heart soar at the sight of him. It had been so long since I'd seen him.

He raised a quizzical eyebrow at Dane. "You've made him cry already?"

I smiled, hoping my tears would dry up quickly. How embarrassing. I tried to distract Glimmer. "He said I can go to the Hoskins' castle and live with them."

"Naturally. Where else would you go?" He came into the room, shutting the door firmly behind him. He didn't seem surprised by my news, even though *I* was surprised. He was fishing around inside a large bag. "I got you some things. Toiletries and so on. And some clothes. I didn't think you'd want to meet the Hoskins elder for the first time wearing a blood-soaked shirt. And I got some for you too, Dane, but I'm not sure they're going to fit. I got the biggest size there was but you're just so massive."

He shrugged, having done all he could.

"How did you know I would go to the Hoskins' castle?"

He blinked at me and then his eyes slid to Dane. I don't know what he saw there but he gave me the weakest answer he ever had. "Lucky guess?"

Dane coughed. "Thanks, G, I owe you."

"No, you don't. You got Seren back safely."

It was awkward, sitting there while they talked about me like I was a sack of potatoes that had gone missing.

Dane was deliberately studying the wall and I narrowed my eyes at Glimmer. "What do you know?"

He came over and dropped a kiss on my forehead.

"I know I have to get back before they realise I'm missing."

"You really came to save me without his permission?"

"You're my treasure, Seren. I'll always protect you."

That was Glimmer alright. And didn't I just love being called his treasure? I have no idea why it made me feel so right, but between lying in bed with Dane all night and being called Glimmer's treasure, I was just about as content as I could be.

"You won't get in trouble?"

"No. I have my own ways of getting out of

the territory. They don't know I'm gone and I left my phone there so they can't trace me here. You know, you need to learn my phone number so you can call me."

"I don't want to get you in trouble."

"You won't. Learn my number. Dane has it still. Then you'll have two people to call if ever you need help."

Dane growled, "He won't need help. He's coming home with me."

Glimmer smirked. "I don't know, Dane. What if you snore?"

"Fuck you, G."

"No time, Dane. I have to get back. Now I know you're safe."

He began to strip the bed, despite the fact that we were still in it. He took the cover off the duvet and I saw it was smeared with blood but less blood than I'd expect, considering the wounds I'd had the night before. I suppose they must have been healing as we flew here, though how, I have no idea.

"Dane, do you have healing magic?" I asked.

"No."

"Are you sure? I'm sure I was cut last night. Leicester cut me."

"No."

"How was I—?"

I didn't finish because Glimmer stripped

the sheet off the bed, yanking it from under us and tearing it in the process. He tipped us both out of the bed.

"Do you mind?"

"Nope, I don't. I'm just tidying up."

I knew what he meant. He'd take that bedding back to the incinerator and burn it, or he'd make a little bonfire of it before he reached Somerville territory. Either way, all that blood I'd spilled over it would be gone. Glimmer thought of everything.

He put the bundle by the door and then held out his hands. "Those clothes, too."

I began to unbutton my shirt but found it almost impossible to do with the thick blood crusted into the material. It was disgusting.

"Dane, help him, I haven't got all day."

I felt Dane come up behind me and then there was a ripping sound and my shirt fell away from my torso. I managed to strip out of my trousers and boxers before I had to ask Dane to help with those, too, thank goodness. Naked, I handed the clothes to Glimmer, who took them in one arm and hugged me with the other.

"I expect you to ring me as soon as you get back to the castle. Dane has my number."

"I think I left my phone at the Honey Pot."

Glimmer rolled his eyes. "Along with your ripped clothes. I gave the phone to your cousin and told her to look after it. And I just rang that cute little witch there."

"Marcia," I supplied.

"Sure, Marcia. She's lucky she was able to trace you, otherwise Dane- never mind what Dane would do. The point is, it took me a while to get her number and I rang her. I didn't have any of the Hoskins' numbers to hand but she said she'd tell your cousin, Dane, so your family is expecting you home. By the way, I think Marcia has the hots for your cousin and also she's expecting Seren to ring her so she can make sure he's ok. She said something about adopting him."

Glimmer gave a sly smile as he finished and I felt the growl that came from Dane, though I didn't hear it. I had no idea what that was about.

"He doesn't need adopting, he has a family now."

"Yes, and you'd better make him happy, Dane."

Glimmer gave Dane a hard pat on the shoulder as a goodbye and then picked up the whole bundle of clothes and bedding and left.

"I love him but I swear I don't know what he's talking about half the time."

I felt Dane shrug because he'd pressed that close against me that I could feel his body moving. Or had I leaned back against him? Ah, shit, I hope it wasn't that.

"Are you still taking me home with you?"

"Yes. You're mine, Seren. You're coming

home with me."
　　I did not dwell on the delicious shiver that made its way along my body at his words.

CHAPTER 21: SEREN

"You need to get in the bath and wash this blood off you."

I couldn't argue with that, so I followed Dane into the bathroom and let him run the bath, even though I was perfectly capable of doing it myself. He just moved me out of the way and did it for me and I let him. I have no idea why I did that. Then he went out of the room and came back with some toiletries and a what looked to be a blush staining his cheeks.

I looked down at myself. I was naked but dragons generally weren't that shy. *I* certainly wasn't that shy. We learn to be comfortable in our skin at a pretty young age, especially if we need to learn to fight like Glimmer and I had. We spent so much time shifting between human and dragon forms that we barely noticed when we were naked around each other any more. And when Dane had begun to teach us…

Ok, I'd noticed my naked form around Dane, but that was only because I'd had an almost permanent erection around him and it was difficult to hide.

I got suddenly flustered and clambered into the bath while the water was still running. Dane reached out to steady me as I got in and I felt his warm hand gripping my arm. He slid the other hand along my back and lowered me into the water. It was hot and soothing and I lay back and sighed in pleasure.

"Are you comfortable?"

"Yes."

"Is the water too hot?"

"No, it's perfect."

"Just lay there for a while and soak. I want to soak as much of that grunge off as I can before I have to scrub you down. It'll hurt less."

I looked down at my chest again, amazed that it wasn't hurting. I'd spent years – even before my dragon disappeared – not talking much, not telling my family my every passing thought but I'd always had a hard time keeping my mouth shut around Dane. I wanted to tell him everything. I slipped back into that bad habit quickly when I said, "My chest doesn't hurt. I don't think my rib is even broken any more."

"Who broke your rib?"

"Does it matter?"

"Humour me."

"Well, your cousin who tried to kill Morgan broke the first one, but that was healing nicely. He might have just cracked it, Glenwise wasn't sure. And then Leicester Scaldan kicked me pretty hard in the chest before he used his claws, and it definitely felt like he'd broken another one." I took a deep breath, filling my lungs and revelling in the sensation of being able to do that. "It's gone now, though. All better. Are you sure you don't have healing magic?"

"No. But surely your dragon would heal you, even if it won't give you magic?"

I looked down. I didn't want to talk about my dragon leaving me. It made me feel small and weak and ashamed, and I hated those kinds of feelings enough anyway, but especially hated feeling them in front of Dane. I didn't want him to think less of me just because I was... less.

"Seren?"

"It won't heal me. It can't."

"Not at all?"

"No. It's completely gone. Can't shift, can't heal. Can't see or hear or smell with it, either. I'm just plain old human now."

I forced myself to look up at him, meet his eyes. I was daring him to disappoint me.

"Are you still taking me with you?"

"Yes, Seren, you're coming with me." He

said it so confidently that it was hard to argue. We were done with chatting, though, because he said, "I'm going to change the water."

He pulled the plug and, to my surprise, took a flannel and squeezed some shower gel onto it and began to wash my body. He started with my neck and shoulders and worked his way down my arms. I was enjoying the sensation so much that it never even occurred to me to offer to do it. I just let him move me how he wanted and soap up my skin to wash the dirt of the past few days away. He turned on the shower and moved the showerhead over me, rinsing it all away.

"Sit forward."

He did my back and then gently washed my hair. His fingers moving slowly over my scalp were something else. I'd always liked that Dane was so big, and his huge hands could crush me completely if he wanted to, but not now. He was so gentle that I felt like a porcelain doll.

When he'd washed my hair and rinsed it, and I'd closed my eyes so he could wash my face, too, he said, "Lay back."

I was about to do that when I realised I had a problem.

I was hard.

It was so unexpected that I hadn't even considered the possibility. I literally hadn't been hard in five years. I always assumed that my dragon controlled my libido, because I never even got morning wood any more. As I lay in the bath with Dane's large hands on me, though, my dick had filled and it was making it awkward. Why did I have to go and get a sex drive *now* when I'd been enjoying just being touched?

"I can finish," I said. My voice was curt and I hoped Dane would take the hint. He didn't. Dane never did take hints. He sort of trampled through them, especially where I was concerned. Glimmer had always found it hilarious. At least he wasn't here to see this.

"No, I'm doing it."

"I said I don't want you to."

Dane's hand took hold of my chin and forced my head up so I could look into his eyes again. They were dark and intense. He had such beautiful eyes.

"You didn't say that. Is that how you really feel?"

It was hard to know what to say. If I threw him out, he might decide I really wasn't worth the bother – and I really wasn't – and leave me there. Or, if I let him finish and he saw my erection, he might run for the hills anyway.

"Did you like me touching you so far?"

I nodded and I swear his eyes got darker. They were pure black, dark as anything, and I wanted to fall into them and be swallowed by the abyss.

"And now something's changed?"

I nodded again.

"What was it that changed?"

Ah, well, he might as well know now. I wasn't going to be able to hide it for long. "I got hard, ok?"

If I'd thought he would snatch his hand back like he might get cooties, I was wrong. His strong fingers stroked along my jaw and down my neck, and then he was pushing at my shoulder.

"Lay back, I want to finish. I won't do anything else, Seren, I'm just washing you."

That was equal parts relief and disappointment.

I eased back, stiff and awkward. Dane just squeezed more shower gel onto the flannel and began to wash my stomach. My dick was right there, below his hand. I had hardly even thought about sex in five years – it was just another part of me I'd lost, that was all – but I became hyper-aware of my dick right then.

Dane moved the flannel down and over my hips and it was like he was teasing me by not actually touching my dick, and then I wished I hadn't been bitching so hard in my head about him not touching it because he ran the flannel over it and it bobbed, filling with more blood. He moved the flannel back and forth over it and then slipped it underneath to wash my balls. He pushed his other hand against my inner thigh to encourage me to spread my legs and I did, feeling shameless. The material of the flannel was soft and it felt incredible but I wanted Dane's skin on mine.

I needed to do something to take my mind off the sensations he was giving me or I was just going to come all over his hand and then I'd never be able to look him in the eyes again.

"Nobody's ever touched my dick before."

Ah, shit, why did I say that? That was the least cool thing I could have said. And, if I'd been trying to make it less awkward, I'd fucking failed.

Dane didn't even take his eyes off his task. Thankfully – or maybe not, depending on how you viewed it – he moved on and washed my legs.

"I know."

"How do you know?" If I'd been walking through life with a fucking V on my forehead, I was going to be annoyed.

"I know *uasal* save themselves for their mate. That's why I never pushed you to give me anything, even though I wanted you."

"You wanted me?"

"Yes." He said it like it was obvious but it left me reeling.

"You never said. You never—"

I wasn't sure. Had he shown me he wanted me? I had been so besotted with Dane that I'd not been able to tell whether he was into me or not. I'd wanted him. He'd always held himself at a distance, so I'd assumed the desire was one-sided.

"I didn't want to push you to have sex before you were ready to be claimed." He sat back, having washed me from head to toe. "I just assumed *I* was the one you were saving yourself for."

I felt like he'd thrown a bucket of cold water over me. Unwanted erection? That was gone.

"Stand up."

He held me as I stood, making sure I didn't fall. I was feeling strong again and was sure I was moving properly but he still held my upper arm until I was standing on the bathmat, dripping.

He dried me in silence. I didn't even bother to say I could do it, and why? Because I wanted *him* to do it. I'd been in love with Dane Hoskins for six years and if he was willing to touch me now, even in a platonic way, I was completely on board with that.

"Did you really want me?"

He was at my feet, kneeling on the bath mat and rubbing the towel over my calves. It was possibly not the best time to ask, since he had to look up at me and I hoped my dick would stay out of it this time.

"Yes."

"Did you want to claim me?"

"Yes."

"Lord Somerville would never have allowed it."

"No."

He wasn't exactly chatty, which was awkward because I wanted answers. In fact, I wanted one specific answer.

"Do you still want to claim me?"

CHAPTER 22: DANE

I was worried that I was going to lose control if we kept this up. My dragon was nudging me, pushing me to keep my hands on Seren, just to feel him against us. If I'd been able to scent him, I'd have my nose buried in his groin already and be half-way to coming just from that.

Keeping myself in check, I stood and wrapped Seren in a dry towel. I thought it would be better once I couldn't see all his naked flesh on display but a Seren wrapped in a white towel was somehow an erotic sight.

I felt like an idiot for not seeing before that we were fated mates. It had been right there the whole time, staring me in the face, and I'd missed it. It was probably a good thing, I suppose, because if I'd known he was my mate when he dumped me, my dragon might have gone into *ruith* anyway.

Seren hung his head. "Ok. I'm sorry I asked, I won't do it again."

I hated to see him like that. I was so used to Seren being bold and strong and confident. He'd vibrated with power and energy. Seeing him like this was jarring. I wanted to know if it was because he'd been through a series of shocks in the past few days or whether he'd become like this gradually over five years. Why hadn't I gone to him sooner?

Wait. Had he asked me something?

I forced my mind back, fighting my dragon for patience. It was not happy with me at all. As far as my dragon was concerned, we'd just found out the man we'd been in love with for six years was our mate, we'd just got him back and we'd have to be plain stupid to go another minute without claiming him as our own.

I remembered Seren's question.

"Yes, I want to claim you. I'm going to claim you as soon as you let me."

My voice was more like a troll's voice, gravelly and rough with lust and pent-up desire. I stepped into the shower, put the showerhead back on the wall and started the spray, washing myself quickly to get rid of the blood and muck that had been smeared all over me. I hadn't even noticed it until I'd been washing Seren. I had hardly noticed anything but him at all.

It was necessary to wash my cock but it

was hard from the long minutes I'd spent feasting my eyes on Seren's naked body and running my hands all over him. I cleaned it swiftly and tried not to groan as my hand touched it. It was made worse because I hadn't thought of anyone else in six years. All my sexual fantasies had been Seren, and so seeing him spread out before me had taken my mind to places it shouldn't have gone.

After a few moments, I was clean and decided that was as good as it was going to get. I dried myself with the old towel and then stood in front of Seren. He hadn't moved at all.

"You want to claim me?"

I wanted to laugh. We were having the slowest conversation in history.

"Yes. But first you're going to tell me what you want."

"What do you mean?"

I took hold of his shoulders and propelled him into the hotel room. Glimmer had changed the bed while we'd been in the bathroom and I was glad dragons concealed their scent otherwise he'd have smelled my arousal and there were some things I didn't want to traumatise my friends with.

Without looking at his body – which took a huge amount of willpower – I unfastened the towel from around Seren and threw it on the floor. He climbed into bed and I followed him. I might have been tempting fate there but I *had* only just realised we were fated mates and I *had* only just got him back from the brink of death and no way would my dragon allow me to be that far from him. I lay on my side and looked at Seren's beautiful face. The cut had vanished, leaving only a faint pink scar that would fade completely, and the swelling that had squeezed one eye completely shut had gone down. There wasn't even a yellow smear of a bruise to show that it had been there. Now that he was himself again, he was gorgeous and my dragon and I both rejoiced that he was well.

"Now, tell me what you want."

"I don't understand what you mean."

"Do you want me?"

"Um, is that a trick question?"

"No, it's not. I want you, Seren, but I'm not going to claim you against your will. It's your choice. And you can come home and live with us for as long as you like, regardless of what you choose to do about me and you. You're one of Nana's family now and that won't change whether you mate me or not."

"So you'll take me with you no matter what?"

"Yes." I repeated the assurance yet again. I tried not to get irritated that he needed to keep asking the same thing over and over again. It just went to show that he couldn't understand why a dragon clan would help a dragon without some kind of benefit. Apart from the fact that, actually, I did think we were getting something out of the deal – we were getting Seren and I couldn't imagine anything better than that – it bothered me that he'd been brought up in a family where you had to earn your keep or you'd be thrown out. Lord Somerville had literally proven that two days ago when Seren had dared to refuse him what he wanted and the consequence was he was disowned. It stood to reason that Seren was sceptical about Nana taking him in for nothing.

Of course, I also knew something about Nana that Seren didn't, and that was that she knew everything. I had a strong suspicion that Nana had known Seren and I were fated mates. It made sense. She'd allowed me a lot of liberties when I'd been flying off to check on him that she wouldn't have allowed me before. I was going to ask her, and I was going to ask why the hell she hadn't told me.

Still, I didn't want to tell Seren that right now. I wanted him to *choose* to mate me. I wanted him to *want* me. And I didn't want him to mate me just so he could get a clan to protect him.

"So did you always want me? Even five years ago?"

He was lying on his back, looking straight up at the ceiling. I could feel the tension coming off him in waves.

I had decided that honesty was the best policy. Apart from the fact that things could get confusing if I started hedging my answers, I didn't want to lie to my mate. I wanted to be honest. I wanted to know everything so we could make peace with it and move on with our lives together.

It meant my answers were a bit abrupt.

"Yes."

He began to cry again. Before, he'd cried a few tears and I'd been sure they'd been good tears. Tears of relief that he wasn't alone, that he had someone to look out for him. Tears of happiness, maybe, that he was coming home with me. This time, though, it was something else.

They were ugly tears, coming from wrenching sobs, and Seren flung his arm across his face to hide them. I hated that he was hiding from me.

I pushed myself up against him, pressing my chest to his shoulder, and leaned down to whisper, "Tell me what's wrong."

"You wanted me, even back then."

"Is that bad?"

"Yes."

"You didn't want me?"

"That's the problem," he said, choking on a sob. "I *did* want you. I wanted to mate you and leave Lord Somerville and live with you."

"Shit."

"Yeah."

"Why didn't you tell me?"

"Why didn't *you* tell *me*?"

I sighed. He had me there. "Fear, I guess. I didn't want to push you too hard and lose you. I didn't want Lord Somerville to find out how I felt because I'd have been kicked out without you faster than I could say 'family alliance'. I didn't want to find out that you didn't feel the same way."

"I didn't think you were afraid of anything."

"You're an idiot, then, aren't you?"

"Yes. I am."

"Hey, I was joking."

"No, I really am." He pulled his arm away from his face and I saw his wet cheeks and the redness around his eyes. "I could have been with you all this time instead of—"

He sat up, nearly braining me in his haste.

"I can't mate you."

"Why not?"

I leaned up beside him but he was sitting ramrod straight and his voice had become determined.

"I don't have a dragon."

"So?"

"So you can't mate me, are you crazy?"

"No."

"Pft, you are if you think a dragon can

mate a human. What will you get out of it? I told you, I can't even shift, let alone do any magic."

"Seren, I don't want your fucking magic, alright? I want *you*!"

I'd shouted that louder than I intended but he needed to get that through his head right now.

"Even though I'm nothing?"

"You're not nothing, you're perfect. You don't need to do anything other than exist to please me."

"I've never heard of a dragon who mated someone... lesser."

"You're not lesser."

"I'm human."

"You might not want to go around saying that human is lesser once we get home. You're likely to offend Gramps."

"Who's Gramps?"

"He's Nana's mate."

"Why would he be offended?"

"Because he's human."

I saw the genuine shock on Seren's face. His eyes became huge and it occurred to me that he really had been raised in a small world completely controlled by Lord Somerville if the idea of mating a human was beyond belief to him.

"Lady Hoskins is mated to a human?"

"Yes."

"And... nobody minds?"

I growled a bit, but it was playful growling. "Not only does nobody mind, we love it. Everybody loves Gramps. He's the best."

"But- how did she- can she even- and- Lord Somerville said it was impossible!"

"It's definitely possible."

"So, even though I lost my dragon, you could have mated me?"

I didn't like that he was back to talking about 'could have mated' rather than 'will mate'.

"Yes. I can mate you if we both want it."

"And your elder won't mind that?"

I'd seen the hold Lord Somerville had over his household first hand, and I'd seen it again recently when Morgan had mated Lew and had asked again and again whether he was safe from his father. My dragon prickled at the realisation that Seren was still living under his shadow.

"No, she won't. And, even if she did, I would still mate you. You're worth it, Seren."

He gave another sob but, this time, he turned into me and I wrapped my arms around him and held him close while he cried into my neck. I dragged him down so we were flat and tucked him comfortably against me, letting him cry. I'd never seen him cry before today. It was good that he was letting out all those pent-up emotions.

"I can't believe you even want me."

"I want you," I assured him. He had no idea how much.

"And I can't believe how stupid I was to tell you I didn't want to see you again when I lost my dragon."

"Is that why you dumped me?"

"We weren't going out. I'd definitely have remembered that."

"Don't avoid my question."

"Yes, that's why I dumped you. I couldn't see a way- I didn't think you'd want me and I knew I couldn't anger my uncle."

He was rubbing at his wrist as though it hurt, an unconscious movement, and I stilled his hand.

"Did he tell you to do it?"

"Yes. I'm sorry."

"It's not your fault. Neither of us knew."

"Knew what?"

"That we belong together." I rose up and leaned over him, looking down into his beautiful eyes. "I should have told you I love you."

I enjoyed the gasp that he let out far more than I should. I would always remember that, the moment I told him I loved him, and his mixture of surprise and pleasure.

I'd waited long enough. I hadn't wanted to rush him and I hadn't wanted to pressure him and I'd wanted to make sure he wanted me for me and not because he thought he needed to mate me to get the protection my family offered, but I had definitely waited long enough. My patience had stretched to its final breaking point and my dragon was growling constantly in my head, urging me to take him.

    I lowered my head and kissed Seren. It was a perfect kiss. His lips felt amazing against mine and I brushed them together before dipping my tongue into his mouth. Nothing could have prepared me for his taste. With the first swipe of my tongue, I knew, and my dragon knew, that Seren was ours.

CHAPTER 23: SEREN

I was sure Dane was going to kiss me and then, suddenly, he did.

The first brush of his lips made me want to whimper and push myself up to claim his mouth properly, but I was good and waited for what he would give me. And I was more than rewarded. Dane slid his tongue into my mouth and I was engulfed by a feeling so much bigger than me that I was stretched tight by it, filled to bursting. Dane dragged his tongue along mine and it made my body prime with desire, and I let him kiss me for a few moments, enjoying the feeling of him so close to me.

I couldn't stay still for long, though. With each lick of his tongue, I found it harder and harder to stay still until my need burst from me and I pushed back against him. I thrust my tongue into his mouth, wanting to taste him, wanting to be as close to him as it was possible to be, and I got my first proper taste of him.

His flavour burst along my tongue and left tingles along my lips like static electricity. He tasted amazing. It was a flavour I wanted to devour again and again. He tasted- he tasted like he was *mine*.

I jerked back, searching for his eyes. They were dark grey, nearly black, and there was a flicker of his dragon in them. Oh, yeah, he definitely knew.

"You're my mate."

"Yes, we're mates. We're mates," he said and claimed my mouth again. He sounded drunk and I loved it. His body was on top of mine, pressing me into the mattress, the hard muscle of his chest trapping me beneath him, holding me still while he ravaged my mouth. His hand held my neck so he could angle my head and give him the best access and I gladly let him do whatever he wanted to me.

Gradually, I began to lose sense of what was happening. All I knew was that I could taste Dane, that his flavour was everything I'd ever wanted, that he felt so good pressed so closely against me, that his large body was covering mine completely and rubbing against me. He was grinding his hips down and the movement was dragging his erection against my thigh and rubbing my hard dick along his abs, back and forth until I was out of my mind with need.

"God, Dane."

"I want you, Seren. Tell me what you want."

"I want- I want—"

I had no idea what I wanted. I just wanted to keep feeling this good. I'd never had anybody touch me like this. I'd never had anyone's erection pressed against me before. It felt strange. Good, yes, but strange. I don't know if it was just that it felt big against my thigh or whether Dane was above average in that department, but I wasn't going to pull away from him long enough to check.

"Do you want me to suck you off?"

Dane was panting and he pressed his forehead against mine. Having Dane put his mouth on my dick sounded like heaven and even the thought of it was sending me closer to the edge. My dick was so hard. I swear I'd never been so hard before.

"No. I want to see you."

He kissed me again, harder than before. He kissed me like he owned my mouth and he did. I lost myself completely and became just a writhing mess of limbs and desperation under his ministrations. He shifted position above me and I felt his body move up mine slightly as he positioned himself and then his hard dick was pressed against mine. I never thought I'd feel anything so wonderful. I was panting and my heart was thundering. My body was unused to orgasms, unused to arousal or lust, and I couldn't remember ever being this hard, this aroused.

When Dane's hand slid around both our erections, I cried out into his mouth. I was throbbing and leaking pre-come, and he swiped his thumb over the tip and spread the pre-come down my shaft, lubricating it.

Dane tore his mouth from mine, panting, and locked his eyes on mine.

"Fuck, Seren, I want you so bad."

I couldn't answer with words, so I clung to him and thrust my hips up to meet him, sliding my dick through his fist and along his own shaft. The sensations were overwhelming. All the places we touched, all the heat and the hard press of muscle and the slick sweat and the pre-come and the soft skin of his dick and the hard grip of his palm and his harsh breath and his eyes. I fell into those eyes, just like I'd always thought I could. I was swallowed by them and there was nothing except Dane in the world.

"Seren," he grunted, and I felt his thick shaft throb and his hand moved faster. He was giving me everything I'd never known I needed.

With a rush, the gentle tingling in my spine became a bolt of electricity and it shot through me, drawing my balls up hard and sending thick streams of come spurting out of my dick. My orgasm wracked my body and I couldn't do anything but ride out the waves of pleasure as Dane grunted above me and sped up his thrusts, jerking his hand against both our dicks and milking more and more come from me.

He went tense as he came and, just as I was starting to think my orgasm was waning, Dane climaxed on top of me and I found another burst of pleasure. I felt him come. The sudden tightness of his body and the hot liquid that poured over my dick were wonderful. I wanted to cling to him and never let go of that moment.

When he flopped back down on top of me, though, I realised he had more to give because he kissed me slowly and gently, and it was just as perfect as everything else he'd given me.

"Are you happy, Seren?"

"That you're my mate? Yes."

"Good."

"Are *you* happy?"

The haze of pleasure and contentment faded a bit and left me worried. After all, he didn't get much out of having me as his mate.

"So fucking happy. I can't believe I'm this blessed."

I kissed him again, letting my tongue explore his mouth in a leisurely way, and revelled in the taste of him in my mouth.

"Let me up, I'll get that flannel to wipe us

down."

I didn't want to let him go so I scrambled out of bed with him, touching him all the time, getting in the way far more than I helped, and we got to the bathroom and wiped ourselves down. I wiped Dane's chest and stomach and bit back a groan at the sight of his hard abs and the dark happy trail that cut through them. He'd bulked up over the years, and he'd been big enough to begin with. I ran my hands over his chest and shoulders and down his arms. The strong muscle felt so good underneath my palms and I wanted to kiss every inch of him.

"You're driving me crazy," he said. I smiled. I'd never thought I'd get to touch him like this.

"I can't believe you're my mate." Then I thought to ask, "How long have you known?"

"About an hour."

"Seriously?"

"Yeah, I never said I was smart."

"Hey, I'm smart and I didn't figure it out."

I loved seeing Dane smile. It made his eyes shine and it always made my heart beat faster.

"At least we know now. And I know why my dragon has been such a dick for the past five years."

"Your dragon's not a dick," I said, smoothing my hand over his peck and resting it over his heart. I could feel the steady beat of it under my palm.

"Don't say stuff like that. You're giving my dragon permission to keep being a dick."

"I told you, it's not a dick. Stop being a dick to your dragon."

He smiled and his eyes shone and he dragged my body against his. He kissed me and spoke against my lips, brushing our mouths together deliciously.

"It's been close to the surface for years. I could never understand why. I think it knew we were mates. It always wanted to be close to you and I had to fight it to stay away."

"See, your dragon's not a dick at all! It's smarter than both of us. I can't believe you've controlled it like that for five years."

He cringed.

"What? Tell me."

"I didn't always control it. I talked to Glimmer a lot so he could tell me you were ok, and sometimes," he cringed again and I got the impression that 'sometimes' was an understatement, "I would sneak into Somerville territory just to set eyes on you."

"You broke into my uncle's estate?"

"Yes."

"Wow, you're good."

He smashed his lips against mine briefly. "I told you, stop giving my dragon permission to be a dick."

I was feeling light and happy, much more myself than I had been in years, stronger, more confident, and I kissed Dane back.

"I think your dragon is by far the most romantic of the two of you. You could learn from it."

"Oh, I will. But I warn you now: it wants to claim you. It's not happy that I haven't claimed you yet."

I pushed away from Dane, briefly feeling the pang of loss because my own dragon should have been inside me, telling me that Dane was my mate, urging me to claim him. I shoved the feeling down. I wanted to be claimed by Dane.

"I knew your dragon was the smarter of the two of you."

CHAPTER 24: DANE

At least now I'd got off once, I should be able to last long enough to actually claim Seren. He was looking more like himself every minute, that pink scar fading from his cheek and the dark bruise that marred his chest had gone, along with the tenderness of his ribs that made him wince even without realising it.

I wanted to claim him so he'd be mine forever. Then I could take him back home and show him off to my family and wrap him in my arms and hold him tight, protect him and love him for the rest of our lives.

I didn't see why I couldn't do just that.

"Get on the bed."

He walked into the bedroom and climbed onto the bed without a second's hesitation. That was a surprise, even though it shouldn't have been. I'd assumed that a *uasal* who'd saved his virginity for his mate would be shy about sex but I should have known better. I should have known *Seren* better than that.

There was a sureness to his movements and he always did things with a single-mindedness that I admired. Back when I'd been teaching him, I'd been amazed by his tirelessness when he wanted to learn something new. I guess he wanted to be claimed.

My dragon was shivering with the anticipation of finally, finally claiming our mate. I tried to stay in control. I needed to make this good for Seren.

I stood at the foot of the bed and looked up Seren's long, lean body to his face. Despite my release just a few minutes ago, my body was responding to him. I'd never seen anyone so gorgeous. My dragon pushed at me, wanting to get its teeth into Seren's neck and mark him permanently, but I stayed where I was for a moment and just looked my fill.

Seren looked back at me and I have to admit I got a bit of a kick out of the way his silver eyes darkened as he dragged them down my body. To have my mate look at me like that gave me a feeling of rightness I hadn't experienced before.

I crawled up the bed, dropping kisses along his body on my way up to his face, where I claimed his mouth in a long, deep kiss. By the time I was done kissing him, I was pressed against his body, trapping him beneath me and rubbing myself on him, hard and aching and desperate.

"Are you sure this is what you want?"

"Yes, I want you to claim me. I've wanted it for so long, Dane, I promise."

Hearing him say that broke the last of my restraint. I surged up and demanded, "Lift your legs."

He pulled his knees up to his chest, exposing himself to me and I caught my first sight of his pretty pink hole. I had no restraint left so I dived in, licking a long stripe over it and ending at his balls, sucking them into my mouth one at a time. Seren moaned and the sound spurred me on.

I dipped back down to his hole and licked it, running my tongue over the wrinkled flesh and kissing it, sucking, nipping at it and, finally, pushing my tongue inside him. I was inside Seren. His muscles clamped down on my tongue and I kept up my assault, licking and spearing my tongue inside him.

By the time he was whimpering and repeating my name like the dirtiest mantra, I was so far gone in my lust that I barely knew what I was doing. All I knew was that Seren's taste was amazing and his moaning was the most erotic sound and I needed to be in the tight heat of his channel right now.

I gave one last long lick inside him, making him buck his hips, and I pulled back, kneeling between his open legs.

"Hurry up and claim me," he said. He sounded wrecked.

I leaned over him and kissed him, letting him taste himself on my tongue, getting more of his flavour in my mouth. My dick was so hard it was starting to throb and I pulled my groin back so I wasn't tempted to rub against his hard stomach. I knew that, if I did, I'd blow.

"Just a little longer," I said, pecking kisses along his lips and jaw and neck. Reaching under the pillow, I felt around for the bottle I'd stashed there earlier. When I pulled it out, Seren raised his eyebrows.

"You always carry lube everywhere?"

"No, but you should be glad we have it. I wouldn't be able to claim you otherwise."

"Just use spit."

"No, we're not doing that. I won't hurt you. Beside," I said, clicking open the cap and squeezing some onto my fingers, rubbing it around to warm it up. "We have lube."

"Yeah, but *how* do we have lube?"

I smiled. It sounded like Seren was jealous. I must be an awful person because I loved that.

"Glimmer bought it with the other toiletries. Either he knew we were going to need it or he's going to get home and find he forgot his lube."

"I don't want to think about my cousin using lube right now."

"No? How about you think about *us* using it?"

I slid my fingers along his crack and over his hole before dipping one slick finger inside him. My tongue had loosened him up a little but it was going to take a while to get him ready.

"You're tight."

"Do it quickly, I don't mind."

"No."

He huffed and I laughed into his mouth as I kissed him. Impatient Seren was one of my favourites.

"How long has it been since you did this?"

"You *know* I've never done this before."

"But toys? Fingers?"

He shrugged. "Not for five years."

I paused and he gave a grunt of displeasure and pushed his hips down harder onto my finger.

"You haven't done this for five years? Why not?"

"I thought my dragon took my sex-drive with it. I haven't wanted to."

"But you want to now?"

He looked down at his groin and my eyes followed his to his hard dick standing up from his pubic hair, flushed and leaking. Yeah, he wanted it.

I slid my finger all the way in, spreading the lube around and added another finger. The stretch was tight and I went slow, determined not to hurt him. Tiny frown lines appeared around his eyes and I slid my fingers slowly in and out until they disappeared and he was relaxed again, and then I figured he'd earned a reward and so I crooked my fingers forward and searched for his prostate.

He yelped and bucked up off the bed completely. I did it again, and again, loving the sounds he made as the pleasure assaulted him, loving the way his body moved as it sought more from me. I was going to make him come just like that, with my fingers buried in him and watching him like a show, but he ordered me to claim him.

"Do it now. I want you to claim me. Don't make me wait any longer, Dane."

I couldn't resist him. I went quickly, adding a third finger and more lube and loosened him as carefully as possible, and then I smeared lube over my own dick and had to take deep breaths to stop myself from blowing as my hand moved over my sensitive flesh. I had a big cock and it was harder than it had ever been, filled with blood and purple with want. My balls were so heavy that they were starting to get painful.

I positioned myself over Seren, draping my body over his. I wanted to be able to touch him everywhere. We kissed and I nudged the head of my cock against his entrance before pushing inside.

Even though I meant to take it slowly, I

couldn't. I pushed in further and further until I was sliding into him in one long, slow thrust. When I was fully seated, with my balls pressed firmly against his ass, I managed to regain enough control to pause.

Looking into his eyes, I asked, "Are you ok?"

"Yes. Keep going, please. I want you."

The tightness of his channel pressed against me in the most wonderful way and I felt every inch of my dick worked as I slid in and out of him.

I wanted to stay buried in him for years, to make up for not having had him for years, but my body was betraying me. The pleasure was beginning to overwhelm me and my balls were drawing up tight. I could feel Seren's dick, trapped between us, rubbing against my abdomen every time I thrust inside him. I could feel the wetness, the sticky pre-come that was smeared all over me, and I wanted to reach between us and take it in my hand and wring out his orgasm, but I couldn't bring myself to stop moving exactly the way I was. I pistoned in and out of him, pressing him close to me with my arms under his shoulders, kissing him in a desperate, sloppy, delicious way. I couldn't bear to do anything that would end this moment.

Seren suddenly broke our kiss to cry out and the sound of my name, said in that way – with

Seren in ecstasy – filled me with a different sort of pleasure, one that was deeper than the physical pleasure that wracked me then.

The hard cock pressed against my stomach throbbed and I felt the hot semen spill over me. I kept thrusting, chasing my own orgasm, so close, so very close, and the slick glide of Seren's still throbbing cock through his own come was somehow perfect and sexy.

I pressed my lips against Seren's throat, right where I was going to bite him, and lost myself to the pleasure of Seren's body.

My cock was about to explode and my balls were drawn so tight against me, and I felt the first wave of my orgasm crash over me. And then I felt the bite. I couldn't work out what it was at first, since I was blind with lust and lost in my orgasm. I was only aware of the sharp sting in my neck, and then the roll of pleasure that radiated out from that spot, making my whole body judder and my balls empty out the last of my come, squeezing it out in a burst of feeling so bright and intense that it hurt as much as it brought pleasure.

The feeling wracked my whole body and I couldn't do anything but spurt my come inside Seren and cling to him.

His slick tongue licked softly at my neck and I found that soothed me.

"Claim me," he said.

My dragon pushed up inside me, filling me, making my teeth lengthen and it locked its eyes on the pale stretch of Seren's neck. This was what it had wanted. This was what it had been waiting for, all this time.

I buried my face back in his neck and inhaled. I'd never caught Seren's scent before but I caught a faint trace of it then and my dragon rumbled loudly inside my head, drowning out everything except the word *mate*. He smelled like heaven.

When I struck, sinking my teeth into his neck, right where it joined his shoulder, I was washed away on another tide of pleasure. My dick spurted the very last of my come – and how I still had any left inside me, I don't know – and I felt Seren's dick do the same, pressed between our stomachs and spilling more of his seed between us.

Coming back to myself was a slow process and I licked at his mating mark, tasting his blood, and smelling his scent for the first time. I couldn't bear to take my nose away from his skin but just breathed and breathed. Claiming him had bonded us and I could scent him, even when he concealed it.

"Dane?"

I didn't want to move but there was something in Seren's voice that reached inside me and took hold of my heart. Something was wrong.

CHAPTER 25: SEREN

I didn't know what to do. I felt... I felt complete.

It was like all the pieces that had been missing from me had been slotted into place. I was filled with my dragon and Dane and the two of them together made me feel perfect. Whole.

I couldn't remember when my dragon had come back to me. Dane had been working my body like a master and I hadn't been able to think of anything except him and the feeling of his skin against mine and his tongue and fingers and dick inside me. It had been everything I'd ever wanted, more than I'd ever imagined. The sheer amount of pleasure had become unbearable and I'd felt my orgasm swelling inside me, but something else, too, my dragon, beginning to fill me again, breathing back into the empty space it had left behind.

When I'd come, I hadn't even thought. With my mind taking a break from reality and my dragon freshly returned, larger than life, feeling suddenly overwhelmingly *present*, it had taken control. I'd bitten Dane.

I'd claimed him. Before he even claimed me.

He was still on top of me, still inside me, and his face was pressed into my neck where his claiming bite was. He was heavy and pliant and sated, but what was he going to do when he realised I'd claimed him?

"Dane?"

He lifted his head and our eyes met. His were dark and suddenly hard. Oh shit, he was going to be angry.

"What is it?"

"My dragon," I began, but I couldn't say anything else. My whole throat closed up.

To my surprise, Dane pressed his lips against mine and it was sweet and tender. He didn't seem angry at all, in fact.

I winced as he slid out of me and I felt the sticky mess between us, between my legs and our stomachs.

I smelled it, too. Stronger than before. I smelled it with my dragon's keen sense and it was like taking a deep breath.

My legs were stiff as I lowered them and

Dane sat up.

"You bit me."

My throat was still tight, so I nodded instead of talking.

"You claimed me."

Again, I nodded.

"Your dragon- did it come back?"

"Yes."

The smile he gave was bright and overwhelming. I felt it in my very soul. He was wrapped around me and his lips rained kisses down over my mating mark, my cheek, my lips.

"My dragon came back," I said, sounding slow and amazed. "It came back. How did it come back?"

"Maybe it wanted to claim me," said Dane. His voice was muffled slightly because his mouth was still pressed against my neck. It was like he didn't want to take his lips off me in case I vanished. Every now and again, I felt the flick of his tongue brush against my skin and I have to admit I liked it, this feeling of being savoured, of being precious.

"I didn't know I would do that. I didn't have a dragon; I didn't know I *could*."

"But you wanted to, right?"

I twisted to look at him, forcing him to take his mouth off my shoulder to look me in the eyes.

"Are you angry about that?"

"Why would I be angry that you claimed me?" His smile blinded me again. "I *wanted* to be claimed by you, Seren."

"But *you* were supposed to claim *me*."

"And I did." He looked smug and, I have to admit, it suited him. Perhaps smug was the wrong word. Content, perhaps. "I claimed you and you're mine forever. And your dragon came back. You claimed me and I'm yours forever."

That sounded wonderful but it wasn't what I'd been told before.

"You're ok with having my claiming mark on your neck?"

His hand went up to feel the wound. It had already closed up and, unlike every other wound, it scarred instead of healing straight over. His fingers found each round tooth-mark and he was still smiling. He jumped out of bed and strode over to the mirror that hung behind the desk, examining himself carefully. I got a great deal of satisfaction from seeing that mark on him and, for the first time in years, I felt my dragon in me and sharing with me. It gave a little rumble in my head, a little like a purr, and I realised it was admiring the mark on our mate.

Dane turned back to look at me and I could actually *see* the love in his eyes.

"I love it. I wanted to be claimed by you, Seren. I've wanted that for years. I want to wear your mark on my neck so the whole world knows who I belong to."

My dragon surged up in me, sudden and overwhelming. We liked the idea of Dane belonging to us. I felt my dragon start to take over me. It had been so long since it had been a part of me that I'd forgotten the feeling and I couldn't remember how to control it or work with it.

The sound of Dane's laughter made me focus through the surge of power in my body and I looked at him.

"You like that, don't you? Me belonging to you?"

I nodded.

He walked back to the bed and crawled up it so he was straddling my legs and leaning into my space.

"What did you think it meant to be mates? Did you expect the claiming to only work one way?"

"Yes. I didn't have a dragon."

"I'd still belong to you, though, wouldn't I?"

"But that's not... how it works."

He growled, a mixture of playfulness and warning. "It is with you and me. You're mine. I'm yours. Get used to it."

Oh, I could get used to that, alright.

We kissed again and I dragged Dane down on top of me. The squelch of our come made me wrinkle my nose and Dane licked over his mating mark, leaving the skin of my neck tingling.

"Come on, we need to wash that off."

He dragged me up and I was reminded of our training, when he'd been teaching me to fight. He was always filled with energy and he'd dragged me around all over the place, fighting and flying and learning and working magic together. Now he bundled me into the bath again and climbed straight in after me. We washed each other, running our hands over each other's body with care, revelling in the freedom to touch. I'd seen Dane naked plenty of times before, when he'd shifted, but I'd never been able to touch. I toyed with his nipples and pressed my fingertips into the hard planes of his shoulders, feeling the strength he had in them. His big hands ran over my entire body in long, sweeping movements and my dragon grew so big inside me that I was worried it would burst out through my skin.

"You look like you're about to shift."

"I can't control it. It likes being touched by you. I've forgotten how to- to live with my dragon."

"You'll remember. Don't worry about it, it'll come back to you. There's no rush."

I felt the dark hum of my magic just out of reach. I didn't try to grab it. This feeling of power was too new to me, overwhelming me. I couldn't even remember living with such power before. It felt like my dragon had grown, in the intervening years, and now it was bigger and stronger and I'd have to battle it harder if I wanted to use it.

When scales broke out over my skin, Dane shut off the shower and lifted me up, holding me pressed against him and carried me into the bedroom. He held me close and I struggled to control my shift. Even when I'd been learning how to do it the first time around, I hadn't felt like this.

"It's alright, Seren. Let go. You can shift – there's room in here, if you want to."

"I'm not supposed to."

"Says who?"

"My uncle. We're only supposed to do it when we're fighting. He says shifting is dangerous."

"It's not." Dane spat out the words and his scent changed ever so slightly. I could smell the anger coming off him, and that's when I realised I could scent Dane.

I lost control of my dragon.

It surged up inside me, filling me, more than filling that empty space where it should have been all this time, and burst out of me. Dane stepped back and my body grew and grew until I was curled around the bed, trying to fit in the hotel room and not knock out the window or something. It was a good job I was slim – most *uasal* dragons were.

I shoved my snout right up against Dane, breathing in deeply. He smelled incredible. It was hot and musky, and the scent made my whole body shiver, sending ripples down my scales to my tail.

"Fuck, Seren, I'd forgotten how beautiful you are as a dragon."

The rumble that came out of me was beyond my control. I liked Dane calling me beautiful. My dragon lifted its head, snorting, and then stuck its face back against Dane's neck and breathed deeply. Among the heat and musk, I could smell his pleasure and happiness, and a hint of desire.

If ever there was a good reason for me to control my dragon, that was it. I forced it down, learning the edges of it, finding a way of talking to it inside. I told it that if we shifted back, Dane could kiss us again, and it liked that idea enough to hand my body back over to me.

I was barely human again before I was on Dane, wrapping my arms and legs around him and fusing our mouths together. He laughed as he kissed me and I loved the rumble of it in his chest and the pressure of his large hands gripping my ass.

Before I knew where I was, I was flat on my back on the bed and Dane was sucking my dick to the back of his throat. I don't even know how I managed to get hard again after the energy it had taken to come so many times just a short while ago, but I did. I bucked my hips up into his mouth and he swallowed around me. His mouth was hot and wet and his tongue massaged my length and he sucked hard and I was coming again in no time.

Dane began to jerk himself off but I pulled him up the bed, using my newfound strength, and pushed him onto his back. I went straight for his dick. It was hard and there was one bead of pre-come at his tip, which I licked off. It was the essence of Dane, distilled into one taste, and I licked and licked every time a new drop swelled up over his slit. He was leaking constantly and breathing hard, his fists clenched in the bedding.

"Seren, fuck, do something."

"I'm enjoying myself."

He groaned loudly and the sound was so right. I'd never given anyone a blow job before but I knew the basic premise and I was loving the taste of Dane so much that I could have just sucked and sucked until I'd swallowed everything he had to give. When he came in my mouth, I swallowed and took the next shot and the next, letting it fill my mouth and tasting him. It was divine.

By the time we were lying side by side, gently kissing and sharing our tastes, I felt drunk. It made me loose-lipped.

"I missed you. I missed being with you."

His arm tightened around me, pressing me harder against his chest. "I missed you, too. So much. I couldn't bear to be away from you."

"I'm so sorry I dumped you. I don't know how you can forgive me for that."

"There's nothing to forgive, Seren."

"I could have killed us both. If we'd known we were mates and I'd done that, our dragons would *ruith*."

"We didn't know."

"But if we had—"

"If you *had* known we were mates, would you have let me go?"

"No."

I felt him smile and breathed in his scent. It was strong and happy.

"See. We belong together. Now we know that, and now we're together."

I thought he was letting me away with that far too easily. Maybe he was just a much better person that me, because I don't think I'd have forgiven me that easily. It just went to show how wonderful Dane really was. I was going to do everything I could to show him that I loved him. I'd spend my whole life trying to deserve his love.

With that thought, I closed my eyes. I was sated and sleepy, all my energy wrung out of me, and I drifted into sleep. I was half-aware of everything, of Dane's body against mine, his lips on my skin, his whispered words, "You're mine, Seren. You're coming home with me."

For the first time in years – maybe forever – I felt content. I was loved and I was safe. I'd never felt anything like it before.

CHAPTER 26: DANE

I felt Seren stir next to me and gave a soft moan, tugging him tighter into my body and trying to tell him that I wanted to sleep a bit longer with him there. He moved again, though, sitting up in the bed and I smelled the trace of tension and awareness in his scent, though it was faint. I was thankful for that – I'd never known Seren to be afraid before two days ago and I hadn't liked it. On the other hand, a dragon alone in the world was vulnerable, and one without the ability to shift was practically handing himself over to the dragon-hunters, so he'd had very good reason to be afraid.

He looked down at me. "What can you hear?"

"Nothing."

"Your smell changed. Fear."

"Just thinking, that's all."

"Well don't think, listen."

He tilted his head and began to climb slowly out of bed. I let my eyes follow his long, lean form as it prowled around the room. He moved with surety again, strength and grace. He was more himself and I was glad of it – I wanted my mate to be confident, to show the world what he could do and believe in his own worth.

"What are you listening for?"

"I don't know."

The sun was streaming in the window. We'd spent the morning mating and enjoying each other's bodies and then we'd slept through into the afternoon. I couldn't hear anything out of the ordinary. If I strained my ears, I could hear a couple of footsteps at the other end of the hotel and the occasional car passing on the nearby road.

I studied Seren. He was wary. After being so weak for so long, he had grown used to trying to protect himself, worrying that he would be hurt or squashed or disowned. It would take a while for him to fully understand that he was protected.

But, then, out here in the middle of nowhere, he wasn't protected. Not by my family, he wasn't.

"Let's get going. We can reach home before it gets dark."

Darkness wasn't that much of an issue for a dragon and, now that Seren had his dragon back, he would be able to see and hear and smell any danger around him. At least he wouldn't be clinging to my back, blind and afraid.

"Do you feel strong enough to fly yet or do you want to ride me?"

He didn't even make a joke about riding me, which just went to show that he was spooked by something.

"I'll fly."

I climbed out of bed and went across to him, wrapping him in my arms and looking down into his silver eyes.

"I love you, Seren."

The tension actually melted away from him right before my eyes. It wasn't gone completely but I was pleased that I could soothe him like that.

"Have you been taking lessons from your dragon in romance?"

"Maybe."

"Keep taking the lessons."

He kissed me briefly – and it was far too brief – before asking, "Are we taking anything with us?"

"Just the clothes. The rest we can leave here."

He began to bundle up the clothes Glimmer had bought him and I felt a trickle of unease flow through me. Something really had spooked him. He wanted to go right away.

"Seren, what can you feel?"

"I don't know, alright? I'm not- it's been a long time since I had a dragon and I can't work out what exactly it is that's bothering me. I'm not sure if I can hear it as such but there's something right on the edge of my senses. My dragon doesn't like it and neither do I."

That was good enough for me.

"We'll fly together. If you get tired, let me know and we'll land so you can shift back and ride me the rest of the way. Don't try and be a hero, either, Seren." I knew from experience that he often pushed himself too far and exhausted himself rather than admit he was tired. "If you get tired, stop. I want you to be able to fly quickly if you need to."

We both knew what I meant. I meant I wanted him to be able to flee if he needed to.

"I will, I promise."

We got ready to leave and slipped out of the door into the hotel corridor. I wasn't sure whether Glimmer had paid for the room, persuaded someone to let us sneak in or whether he'd just moved from shadow to shadow and taken the key to a room as far away from the rest of the guests as possible. I suspected it was probably the latter, so I didn't really want to be caught sneaking out. Especially since I was naked.

We must have looked quite the sight, creeping down the corridor with our clothes bundled up and pressed against our chests. I went first and led Seren to the fire exit Glimmer had used to get us in the day before.

Outside, I glanced around to check there was nobody in sight and then I shifted. Behind me, I felt Seren shift as well and then his large body pressing up against mine – still small in comparison – and he rubbed his head along my sharp cheek and down my neck. I snorted in satisfaction. It felt right to have him there beside me.

In the daylight, he was even more beautiful than I remembered. His silver scales glistened in the sunlight and, when he moved, they rippled like water.

I might have stared at him all day, just marvelling at his beauty, but he nudged me and I saw his front claw curl around the bundle of clothes, holding it securely and then his shoulders bunched, his whole body tensed like a spring and he pushed off with his back legs and his huge wings beat down, forcing the air down and lifting his huge form into the sky.

I let him gain enough height and then I took off after him. My dragon was enjoying the feeling of flying. I hadn't been able to do that for years. Mostly, when I'd been flying, it had been because I'd shifted in a panic and had streaked off to see if Seren was alright, just to set eyes on him and reassure my dragon that he was alive and well. I'd always flown with the thought of reaching Seren in my mind and I hadn't enjoyed the feeling of freedom that it brought.

Now, I could very nearly enjoy it. As soon as we got into Nana's territory, I was going to relax and revel in the experience of flying beside my mate but, until then, I'd enjoy it a little, even if I did keep my senses open and alert for danger.

I have to admit, I didn't really expect any trouble. I was flying, scanning the horizon and the ground beneath us, but it hadn't really occurred to me that anyone would deliberately come after us. The sort of mercenaries and scum who killed dragons when they found one alone were chancers, stumbling across an opportunity and taking it. They wouldn't seek us out. They wouldn't have tried it with either me or Seren, not now he could shift, and they definitely wouldn't have tried anything with the two of us together. I hadn't heard of any *ridire* in the area in years and I assumed we'd be able to fly fast enough to get away.

My only real concern was the Somervilles. Clans who disowned a dragon could decide to come after them and kill them. I didn't want any of the young Somervilles to take it into their head to try and impress Lord Somerville by bringing Seren's head back on a plate. Not that I was really concerned they'd manage it. I'd fucking flay them alive if they tried it.

No, as we flew together and I felt the cool air on my scales and looked around me with the keen senses of my dragon, I wasn't afraid. The only thing that made me nervous at all was the constant low-level anxiety I could feel radiating from Seren. It turned his scent slightly sour, and my dragon wanted to cover him completely and wrap its wings around his body and breathe warmth over him to soothe him and reassure him. I tried to work out whether he knew something I didn't – which was possible, since he had a different way of sensing the world around him than I did, especially as a dragon – or whether he was simply overwhelmed by his dragon and the damage his body had taken in the past few days and the emotional toll of being disowned and kidnapped and then finding his mate. That was bound to make anyone skittish, right?

I flew higher, soaring over Seren's long form and shadowing him. It felt comfortable. It meant I could see him and I knew nothing would get to him before I could – I could have myself wrapped around him, protecting him, in an instant.

He flew hard and we were making good time but, after perhaps half an hour, he began to slow. I noticed that I was overtaking him and having to drop back. I gave a snort and his silver head tipped up to me briefly before focusing back on his flight. He was still tense and I could see him scanning constantly.

I wasn't happy with that. If he really was worried, if something was going to come after us, I needed him to be able to flee at a moment's notice and being too tired to fly or fight was going to make him vulnerable.

I snorted again, dipping down in front of him, guiding him down towards the ground. He knew what I was doing – we'd done it before, when I'd been training him and Glimmer – and he followed.

When I landed, I shifted back and waited for him to do the same. He stood before me, all pale skin and panting. He'd tired himself out.

"I told you not to wear yourself out. What will you do now if you need to fly quickly?"

"I can manage."

"No, you can't. We've got another hour to go yet before we're even in Hoskins' territory. You're not flying again."

"We need to get—"

"You'll ride on my back."

He blinked. "What?"

"You'll ride on my back."

"You mean just sitting there as a human?"

"Yes. What's wrong with that?"

"Nothing!"

He was not good at subtle.

"Seren, what's wrong with it?"

"I just… feel funny about it, that's all."

"You don't want to?"

He shifted from foot to foot and looked down at the ground. "It's not that exactly."

"Then what is it?"

"I'm scared, alright? I don't know what my dragon's going to do if it gets on your back. I feel like it will... I don't *know!* Blow up or something?"

"You think your dragon might blow up?"

"Maybe. Is that possible?"

"I've never heard of it."

"But don't you feel weird about it? Someone on your back?"

"No. I've given piggy-back rides to the kids before. And I rode on Glimmer's back."

Seren glowered. "I don't like that."

"It was necessary." He pouted and I stepped forward to wrap my arms around him. "I didn't like it but it was the only way to get off that island. At least, it was the only way to do it without letting go of you."

"I think that helped, you know. I think my dragon was healing me because it was touching you. Maybe. I don't know. I don't know if it had been coming back to the surface to be close to you."

"You're still not sure about it, are you?"

"I just feel like there's too much dragon inside me. I don't know if it always felt this way and I've forgotten what it was like or whether it's stronger now. I don't know if I can control it."

"I'm here, Seren. I'll help you. Get on my back and see what it's like. You can't fly the rest of the way alone and tire yourself out."

He narrowed his eyes at me and I let him think about it. It wasn't like I would make him ride me, but I couldn't see a faster way of getting both of us to safety if he was weak. He wasn't used to flying. He wasn't used to having his dragon at all.

That was still weird to think about. My own dragon had been so close to the surface for years, a constant simmering presence just below my skin, but Seren's had gone the other way. Disappeared. I couldn't even imagine what it would feel like to suddenly lose half of myself. I would feel so empty inside.

"Alright."

He looked at me expectantly but I shook my head. "Put your clothes on. You'll get cold as a human."

I watched him dress and then gave him one last kiss before shifting. I was going to kiss him at every opportunity.

Crouching down, I waited for Seren to climb on my back. He hesitated and I thought for a moment that he wasn't going to do it after all. Then he put his hands on my scales and hauled himself up my back until he was sitting astride me.

"You're too fucking big. I can't even get my legs around you." I turned my neck so I could look at him and he snapped, "Don't look at me like that."

That made me smile, even with my dragon jaw, and he shuffled forward until he was sitting on my shoulders with one leg either side of my neck.

"That's better."

There was a wabble in his voice, though. He really didn't want to be there. I was hurt that my mate didn't want to be on me, but I was more hurt that he had to do something he didn't want. If we'd just been flying around for leisure, I wouldn't have asked him to do it but I wanted to get us both to safety. Once we were in Hoskins' territory, I'd let him down and we could take our time getting to the castle.

When I'd given piggy-back rides to the kids, I'd never taken off the ground. It meant I didn't know how to do it without throwing him around up there. In the end, I had to just give it a go.

Unfurling my wings and crouching down, I pushed off hard and I felt Seren tip forward and wrap his arms around my neck. He stayed like that as I took to the sky and flew towards home. I felt bad for thinking it but I liked having Seren on me like that. He was a weight on my shoulders, just where I wanted him to be, and his body was warm where it was pressed against my neck. My scales were thick and hard, armour, and so I couldn't feel it but I was sure I heard him press a kiss to them.

We flew in silence. I was concentrating on getting home so it surprised me when, after ten minutes or so, he spoke.

"I love you, Dane."

I gave a rumble of approval. I thought that was all but he carried on.

"I like riding you. It feels... natural. I can't explain it."

Nana had said something about that, when Lew had mated Morgan. Something about a *uasal* warrior riding their *curaidh* mate and becoming more powerful. Perhaps that was it. Seren wasn't used to power any more.

"I've loved you for years, Dane. I'm so sorry I let you go. I didn't think you'd want me if I was broken. And I couldn't ask you to mate me, not if I didn't have a dragon. I couldn't let you be stuck with a weak mate forever. I can't believe you came for me, after all this time. I thought you'd have forgotten me by now. I thought it was only my own heart I was breaking when I said I never wanted to see you again. I missed you so much. I never felt whole unless you were with me. I can't lose you now, Dane. I love you too much."

All the words I'd wanted to hear came

pouring out of Seren's mouth as we flew. He spoke the words into my neck and it was only my dragon's hearing that allowed me to pick them up at all. That was Seren, alright. It didn't surprise me that the only way he felt able to tell me about his feelings was when I couldn't look him in the eye, and when I couldn't say anything back.

"I love you, Dane," he whispered. "You're wonderful. I swear I'll be a good mate. I'll do anything to stay with you."

I gave a huff. I didn't like where that was going. It was much too close to him thinking he needed to earn his place in my family and he didn't. That wasn't what family was. I loved him. That made him family.

He went silent again and I flew hard. I was going pretty fast, wanting to get home.

Suddenly Seren sat up. His weight shifted on me and my neck went cold from where he'd been plastered to it.

"Can you feel that?"

I checked in with my senses. I couldn't hear anything out of the ordinary, scanned my eyes along the ground and the horizon, took a deep breath to smell the air and the only thing that was unusual was the sourness of Seren's scent. He was alert again.

"How far out are we from your territory?"

I couldn't answer since my dragon jaws couldn't form words. I didn't really need to answer. The fact that he was asking showed that Seren was much more afraid than he was letting on. I'd learned years ago to listen to Seren's instincts. He had a knack for sensing things, particularly malicious intentions.

As I flew, I strained my eyes and ears, I tried to open my senses and let my dragon warn me about any danger we might be heading towards, but I felt nothing for minutes and minutes.

It was only when I heard the first beat of a wing behind me that I realised we could really be in danger. I twisted my head round, sure I was travelling too fast to be followed. I couldn't remember ever flying that fast before. But we weren't being followed. The beat of wings wasn't coming from behind us, it was coming from in front. They'd been waiting for us.

CHAPTER 27: SEREN

I saw them rise up from behind the treeline of the nearby woods where they'd been concealed. That would explain why my dragon had been low-level humming for hours. It had made my nerves jangle but it had been so long since I'd been able to feel my dragon that I'd lost the ability to interpret what it was telling me. From the look of those dragons, it had probably been telling me that we were flying into an ambush. Too late now to wish I'd understood it.

There were six dragons in total and all of them had shimmery silver scales, marking them as *uasal*. *Curaidh* warriors like Dane were bigger and thick with muscle, but they were dull grey. In fact, the only *curaidh* warrior I'd ever seen who could take my breath away in dragon form was Dane. He was dark grey, with charcoal accents along the ridges of his back and the spikes of his tail. Not only was he beautiful, he was a warrior, too. I felt it in the shift of his scales beneath me the second he saw them.

I began to calculate. We were outnumbered, sure, but both Dane and I were strong. They'd be expecting Dane to be strong. Would they be expecting it from me?

Flying on Dane's back had rejuvenated me. Not only had I needed a rest, but I felt filled with energy, more and more powerful with each movement of Dane's body underneath me. It had taken me a long time to settle into the feeling as we'd flown. I'd been trying to trace the source of it but, in the end, I'd given up and just concentrated on the sensation of *something* flowing through me. I was overwhelmed by freedom and happiness and love, and I'd had to tell him. And, strangely, when I did, I felt him respond. He couldn't say anything but I knew he was agreeing with me, that my big tough *curaidh* warrior had been waiting to hear me say three tiny little words.

No way was I going to let go now I'd finally claimed him.

One of the dragons sank down to the ground and shifted into human form. It was Leicester Scaldan.

"Seren, I see you've got yourself a bodyguard."

He paused, as though he expected me to

respond. I didn't. I wasn't going to dignify that with an answer. Dane was more than a bodyguard; he was my *mate*. I wanted to scream it, but I didn't think Leicester deserved to hear it. I'd do my screaming with the people who mattered.

"*Curaidh*, I have no interest in you. Give me Seren and I'll let you go."

All this time, Dane had kept flying. We could hear Leicester from that distance but we were too far away for me to even think of using any kind of magic. We were getting swiftly nearer, though. Nearer and nearer and I could see the five other dragons starting to fly towards us. They were taking up assault positions; one in front, two behind that, the final two behind that. It was a strong formation, I had to admit. It meant they would come at us in waves. They had to assume they could take us because we were so badly outnumbered.

They underestimated both of us.

Below us, in the distance, Leicester sneered. "Seren, you don't have a clan. You need me."

That was it. Dane roared. And the sound was filled with fury and possessiveness. It was hot as hell. Inappropriate as it was, I couldn't help the smile that slid onto my face at the sound. I belonged to Dane. Nobody could take me from him.

The fastest of the five dragons was nearly

on us. Dane let it get so close I could see the silver if its eyes and then he twisted his body, rolling, and slashed with both his front claws as he flew past. I felt the hard lash of his tail follow, getting in a final blow as we passed it.

The next two came at us together. I'd become comfortable on Dane's back and I wasn't afraid of falling off. I sensed his movement a fraction of a second before he made it and kept my body on his shoulders even when he twisted and bucked.

My magic had never been very showy. That had always disappointed Lord Somerville, I knew, but he'd found it useful enough to consider me for the next Guardian. If I hadn't lost my dragon, I might have had a chance, even against Glimmer, and that was because my magic was defensive. I might not be the best fighter but I could protect what I wanted protecting. My uncle had planned for me to protect his treasure, and I had. Now, I planned to protect my mate.

Leicester was still in human form on the ground, which I found strange. It made him open to attack and so he had to have a reason. That made me nervous. I also wasn't sure whether he knew I was a dragon again or not and, if not, I didn't want to spoil the surprise that would be and give away any advantage we might have, so I worked my magic as subtly as possible around Dane, whispering my magic out along his scales and hardening it until it had flowed all over his body and solidified, like he'd been dipped in liquid silver. I knew nobody would be able to see that magic.

I was concentrating so much on working my magic around him that I didn't follow what he was doing. I felt his body move, even spinning completely, rearing up in the air and gaining height, making me cling on by my legs and throw my body forward like I was riding a bucking horse, but he was aware of me, I was sure, and he kept me stable and steady. I heard him snarl and roar and rip, heard his teeth tearing at the other dragons, felt their claws scrape along the hard shell of my spell and was glad, when we emerged from the battle, to feel my spell was still solid and hadn't ripped. That meant Dane was unharmed. The two thuds of bodies hitting the ground were proof that the other two dragons were not so fine.

"He can't pay you, *curaidh*. Which clan are you? Let us talk. I'm prepared to be very generous."

I huffed. The last time Leicester Scaldan had said that, he'd offered to claim me or leave me to die. Call me bitter but I was not over that yet.

Dane kept flying. He was gaining height and it was a race between him and the last two dragons to get the highest. That was one of the first things he'd taught us. The dragon who has the high ground has the advantage.

The other two were fast, being smaller, and Dane had been dragged down by gravity and two attacks.

"Come on," I said, willing him on. I knew he could do it.

I wasn't expecting what he actually did.

His body suddenly streamlined, his neck was out and his body was long and he shot down towards Leicester like an arrow. All I could do was hold on, flinging myself flat against his neck and trying not to strangle him and trying not to fall. He lost height so quickly, the rush of wind and the blur of the ground made me reel. I wasn't the only one he surprised.

I just managed to glimpse Leicester shifting back into dragon form as Dane flew towards him and he barely managed to cover himself with scales before Dane was on him. He'd expected to be left out of the fight, for some reason. Or perhaps he'd assumed that Dane would get to him last. That had been a mistake.

The fight was brutal. I clung on and Dane's huge body rolled and bucked and writhed and I felt the claws and the teeth trying to break through my spells, but nothing got through.

The other two dragons had realised they'd been left out of the fight and they dropped towards us, too. I caught sight of them above me as Dane lunged for Leicester's neck with his huge jaws and tore into him with his teeth.

"The other two are coming," I said. I didn't want him being taken by surprise.

It was only then that I realised I'd poured my magic over Dane, thick and defensive, but I hadn't wrapped it around myself. I felt the dip of my stomach as I realised how stupid that was. I'd left myself totally exposed, and in human form, too. I was about as squashy as I could be and the two dragons streaking towards us had their jaws open and their claws out, reaching for me like an eagle about to pluck a rabbit from the ground.

Dane reared up. His whole body lifted and he faced the two newcomers, meeting their snapping teeth with his own and slashing at them with his own claws and he managed to lash one of them across the face with his tail, too. I found myself in a sort of cocoon of Dane's scales, his long, broad back beneath me, his thick neck at my front and his thick wings swooping up at my sides, creating a perfect protective shield around me.

I should have known my mate would protect me above himself. Lifting his wings like that left his chest open and Leicester slashed at it. I felt the first crack in my spell, just a little scrape, peeling a sliver of it away with his sharp claws.

Quickly, I poured out more magic, wrapping it around both of us. My dragon wasn't pushing at me to get out and fight, which was a surprise. With three dragons around us, fighting us, I should have been shifting already. In dragon form, I was bigger and stronger and had thick scales. I might even be as big as those two other Scaldans, though not as big as Leicester and nowhere near as big as Dane. Still, bigger than I was now and definitely with more scales. But my dragon wasn't pushing for it. It was fully awake, fully engaged, pressing forward in eagerness and alertness, but it was more of an intense interest than a desire to break out. My dragon should have been going mad to protect me but it wasn't. I was already protected.

I smiled. I didn't even think about it, I just beamed at what I had just realised: my dragon felt completely safe on Dane's back, so safe, in fact, that it wasn't even thinking about protecting me itself; it was trusting Dane to do that.

A small chuckle escaped me, even when Dane twisted and screeched in fury as Leicester lunged for me. He didn't even get close. Dane protected me. He always would.

I lost track of what happened. I had to keep my arms around Dane's neck and my legs gripping on to his shoulders and that meant my face was pressed into his neck, feeling the rough texture of his scales against my cheek. He was a twisting, writhing, snarling force, all scales and muscle and teeth and claws. I just closed my eyes and poured my magic out over the two of us, willing us to be safe. My dragon was happy that we were doing that but it wanted more. I felt it pressing for something else, but it wasn't to get out. I didn't know what it wanted, all I knew was that I was safe on Dane's back and I needed to keep working my magic to keep that shell around Dane and stop those sharp teeth and claws from slicing into his flesh.

The other three dragons were snarling and biting and huffing and squealing when they were hit. I could kind of tell that they were being wounded by the sounds, one by one, as the fury I felt radiating from Dane battered against them.

At last, Dane went still. His wings lowered and his back rose and fell with his panting breath and I looked up. Two dragons were at his feet, unmoving and bloodied, and Leicester Scaldan was in human form, standing a hundred metres away and covered head to toe in blood. I only hoped it was all his own and none of it Dane's.

"Give him up."

Dane snarled. It was a very clear answer.

It was basically his dragon's way of saying, "Fuck off." Because dragons were articulate.

"Do it now and I'll overlook this. If you don't, I'll kill you and your entire clan. You don't want to be responsible for that."

Dane's response was a low rumble of a growl. It was still a 'no'.

"I will slaughter everyone you care about."

Leicester wasn't getting it, was he? How many ways did Dane have to tell him to shove it before he got the idea?

"And I'll take back that bitch and fix him."

Ouch. That was not a flattering description of me. Perhaps that was why my dragon began to rumble in my head, making my whole body vibrate with... something. Power. Magic.

"This is your last chance to give him back before I kill you for taking what's mine."

That was too much for me. I couldn't keep my mouth shut any longer.

"I'm Dane's."

It felt so good to say it. My dragon loved to hear it. It was *right*. I was *his*.

Dane roared and I could discern the satisfaction and the pride that slipped out as an undertone to the anger and possessiveness of that roar. It made me feel like I belonged.

Leicester's face contorted.

"A *curaidh*? You allowed yourself to be possessed by a *curaidh*?"

Looked like Leicester thought very much along the same lines as my uncle. There were standards, and *curaidh* didn't meet them. It was like he thought we were different species or something.

"I don't want you if you've been sullied."

For a stupid moment, I thought he'd just

leave. Like that would ever happen. I don't know why the thought occurred to me but there I was, assuming he would just leave if he no longer wanted me. But Leicester Scaldan was nothing if not a dickhead and I'd apparently offended his delicate sensibilities by mating someone who wasn't a *uasal*. I genuinely think he wouldn't have reacted so badly if I'd mated someone he approved of.

Because I'd had my senses so open to feel the magic I'd been working, and before that I'd been searching everywhere I could to see if I could spot whatever it was that was making me nervous, I felt the magic before I saw it.

Leicester was older than me by some years and he was powerful in his own right. He – and his two flunkies – might not have been a physical match for Dane but, now that Leicester knew that, he wasn't going to try and fight Dane with muscle. He was going to fight with magic.

Shit.

CHAPTER 28: DANE

I was not happy. My dragon was angry and scared that Seren would get hurt and that made me… less reasonable than I could have been.

Perhaps if I'd been able to stop growling at Leicester Scaldan and shift back to human, we could have talked. Maybe we could have gone our separate ways.

Even as I thought it, I knew that wouldn't happen. This man kidnapped Seren and was going to force him to mate him. No. No way. My whole being revolted at the very idea. He'd beaten Seren. Left him to die. Left him alone and afraid and hurt and freezing to death.

The rumble in my chest grew louder. I was going to tear Leicester apart and I was going to enjoy every fucking second of it. He deserved it. He'd touched my mate. He'd hurt Seren. Now I'd hurt him.

It was that simple.

Surging forward, I took to the air and beat my wings, streaking towards Leicester. He was in human form, weak, stupid. I could take him.

I hadn't counted on him using magic. I saw it, just a second before it struck me in the face. It was like a dark cloud, if that cloud hit with the force of an armoured truck driving into me at full speed. I was wrapped in black smoke that I could actually feel pressing against my skin. It stopped my wings flapping and my chest from expanding enough to breathe, and I dropped to the ground.

Seren. If it could nearly crush me, what would it do to Seren?

Fighting the thick black magic, I twisted my neck and shoved my head back to see Seren. He was still on my back, still breathing, though it was more laboured than before.

I gave a small whine, asking him if he was ok. I could flee if he needed me to.

"It's alright, Dane. I've got you."

He had me? Who had *him*?

The smile that slid onto Seren's face was beautiful and confident and just a little bit evil. If I hadn't been fighting for my life and worried about getting him to safety, I would definitely be hard just at the sight of it. Fuck, Seren was everything.

I felt it again then, that tingling sensation

across my skin, like Seren's hands stroking across my scales and soothing me. I'd felt it when we saw the Scaldans and I felt it when I was fighting but I'd never felt it before and I could only guess what it was. On the basis that I'd been fighting like an animal with brute strength and righteous anger on my side, I should have been covered in wounds. Even though I'd been stronger and I'd *needed* to win that fight, I should have been hurt. I'd felt their teeth scrape along my scales and their claws slash at my underbelly when I raised my wings instinctively – the stupidest instinct I'd ever had, since it left me exposed, except my body and my dragon knew better than me and it knew that keeping Seren safe was all that mattered – and I should have at least bled but I hadn't. I didn't have a single scratch on me.

That was magic if ever I'd seen it.

Now I felt it again, warring with the pressure that the black cloud was putting on me, clamping itself around me like it wanted to squeeze me like a boa constrictor.

The stroking sensation won. The black cloud grew thicker around us until I couldn't actually see through it, could only make out vague shapes and that was only because my dragon could sense heat. But it stopped pressing down on me. The pressure eased and I could breathe. I kept watching Seren, listening to his breath in and out, and listened to make sure Leicester didn't move.

"Shit, Dane, I feel- I feel too full."

What? Too full of what? Was Leicester doing something to him?

My dragon pushed up. Leicester was *still* hurting Seren and it needed to stop. I needed to stop it. Now.

When I charged forward, I did it suddenly. We shot out of the cloud of magic and into daylight and it was blinding and the sudden ability to breathe easily crashed in on me and I was across the open space to Leicester in a heartbeat. I might have laughed at the sheer astonishment on his face if I'd been in a less murderous mood, but this bastard had hurt Seren and I was fucking furious.

With a snarl that seemed to rise up from the centre of my belly, I tore into him. He just managed to get one hand up as I lunged and the thick black smoke surrounded him, and all I got was a bite of his arm. I snapped my teeth closed around it, severing it from his body, and let it fall from my mouth. Wasn't like I wanted to eat it.

He screamed. My dragon prickled with satisfaction at the sound. We wanted to hear him scream. Had he made Seren scream? Had he felt like this when he was slicing Seren open?

I kind of lost it then. Just the thought of what he'd done made me blind with rage and I tore through the black smoke to get to Leicester. I didn't care that it was thick magic and it pushed against me, all I knew was that, if I could get through it, I could hurt Leicester again. I kept going.

The black smoke tried to thicken but I was beating it.

Leicester screamed, "Wait, wait," like he thought I would stop. Had Seren asked him to stop? Well, he had another thing coming if he thought I would. He'd been prepared to do barbaric things – *had* done them – and he would pay.

Finally, I managed to claw my way through the black smoke that wound around him, fighting me off. It seemed like it was alive but it was just magic and for all that it pushed against me and tried to wrap around Leicester protectively, it never managed to wrap around either of us again and every pathetic attack glanced harmlessly off my scales.

The last thing Leicester Scaldan did was look into my dragon's eyes as I lunged for him. The taste of him was bitter and vile, acidic, and I spat his body from my mouth. I hoped he took that image of me to hell with him.

Just to make sure he was totally gone, I sat back on my haunches and used my claws, pressing down on his body with one forearm and ripping his head off with the other. He was definitely dead after that.

I took to the air and circled back around,

scanning the ground for the other Scaldans. Two of them were still in dragon form. That meant they were alive, since dragons reverted to human form when they died. I glided down to land beside them.

They looked ok from where I was standing. The ground around them was soaked with blood but their wounds had begun to heal already.

Looking back at Seren, I tried to ask what he wanted me to do. I could kill them if it would make him feel safer.

"Let me talk to them," he said.

I did not want him getting off my back. If nothing else, I wanted to protect him. Now that I'd grown used to having him there in just the short time he'd ridden me, I felt… powerful with him there. Like he trusted me.

He made no move to slide off my back and I was glad.

"Can you wake them up?"

I used my tail to tap each of them across the face until they stirred and then I stepped back. No point in standing too near.

They both cringed back when they saw us. They didn't make any move to fight, for which I was grateful. It was not the done thing, to continue to fight once you've been defeated. It was bad form. Generally speaking, if you lost a fight and the dragon you were fighting let you live, you honoured their generosity by fucking off when they told you to. It was a sort of trade, I suppose. I could have slit their throats when they were unconscious, but I didn't. They owed me.

Seren asked, "Are you part of the Scaldan clan?"

They nodded, still in dragon form. That was to be expected. They would feel more vulnerable as humans standing before us.

"Are you here with Lord Scaldan's blessing?"

Ok, I wouldn't have thought to ask that. Both dragons shuffled, they made eye contact, and then, reluctantly, one of them began to shift.

"What do you mean?" she asked.

"Are you here at Leicester's bidding or Lord Scaldan's?"

She cocked her head. "I... assumed it was Lord Scaldan."

"Do you know why Leicester kidnapped me?"

"Leicester? He said *this* dragon kidnapped you," and nodded at me, still standing in dragon form with Seren settled on top of me.

I felt Seren shake his head. "Leicester tried to claim me against my will."

The woman was frowning now. "He said you were his mate. He said you'd been taken by someone. We weren't expecting it to be a *curaidh*. We assumed it was one of your old clan who wanted you back."

I hoped Seren didn't mention Glimmer. No need for him to get into trouble over this.

"No, it wasn't. It was my mate."

I couldn't help it, I fucking glowed with pride when Seren said that.

"You are Seren, right?"

"Yes."

"And you were disowned by Lord Somerville?"

"Yes."

Her eyes scanned us, taking in our positions.

"Were you disowned because this is your mate?"

"Long story but, pretty much, yeah."

She frowned. "Somerville's so old-fashioned. We didn't know that. Wait, you say Leicester tried to claim you?"

"Yes. As soon as I was disowned."

"That's not right. Lord Scaldan would never have allowed that."

"Well Leicester brought you here to kill my mate and claim me. Don't know what he thought he was doing."

The dragon behind her started to shift. It looked like they were feeling pretty confident I wouldn't rip their throats out. She was smaller than the first woman and stepped up so she was standing slightly behind her, a little nervous, hanging back. Strange, since I was almost positive she'd fought like a demon in the air.

She hardly looked Seren in the eyes when she spoke.

"Leicester's not been himself lately."

Her companion turned to look down at her.

"He wouldn't do something like this, though."

The smaller woman shrugged. "He wants to be the head of the family."

Seren interrupted and they both jumped, like they'd forgotten we were there.

"Wanted. He wanted to be head of the family. He doesn't want anything now; he's dead."

"You say he wanted to claim you against your will?"

"Yes."

I stopped growling, not even knowing when I'd started. I really hated that thought.

Both of them studied me and then the smaller one nodded. "Are you letting us go?"

"Yes."

"We're going home. Can we take the bodies with us?"

"Yes."

"Lord Scaldan might want to talk to you. We can tell him what we know but I get the feeling there's more we missed. Am I right?"

She could say that. Missed him kidnapping Seren and torturing him. I reigned in my growl again.

Seren, though, sounded completely calm as he said, "Yes, there is."

"Which clan are you now?"

That was when he hesitated. I gave a huff and he said, "Hoskins. I'm a Hoskins now."

"Can we tell Lord Scaldan to contact your elder?"

He hesitated again. I gave a nod. The first woman said, "Thanks," and put her arm around the smaller woman. That was it. We were done. Leicester was dead and these two weren't a threat any longer. I wanted to get us both home.

I took to the air, gaining height and gliding for long distances in the thermals, flapping my wings only occasionally. I admit, I was tired. Not exhausted, considering the fight I'd been in, but tired enough that I was content to glide.

Neither of us made a sound and I kept my ears open for Seren's steady breaths. We flew miles like that until we began to near Nana's territory and then Seren said, "Can you feel that?"

My heart jolted. Shit, what was it this time?

I spun around, searching for what had disturbed him, but saw nothing.

"Are we near your territory, Dane?"

I dipped my head in a nod.

"That explains it. I can feel something. Must be your protections." There were a few moments of silence and then Seren asked, "Will they let me in?"

I snorted. Of course they'd let him in. He was my mate. He was a Hoskins now.

We drew nearer to the boundary and I felt Seren become nervous. I'd intended to just fly us straight over it and get as far into Hoskins territory as I could but I couldn't stand Seren feeling like that, so I drifted lower and lower until I landed. I shivered slightly to tell him to get off me and he slid to the ground.

Before he even had the chance to get his feet steady beneath him, I wrapped myself around him, my long neck winding around his torso and my shoulder pressed against his chest and I shifted back, sliding my arms around him and pressing him close to my naked body.

"I love you, Seren."

He nodded, pressing himself harder against me like he wanted to burrow inside me.

I leaned back a little to look down at him. "Are you hurt?"

I couldn't smell any blood on him and he'd never cried out in pain during the fight, but I wanted to check.

"No, I'm fine. You protected me."

"Yes, I meant to talk to you about that. I think, really, *you* protected *me*, didn't you?"

He shrugged.

"Seren," I warned. "Don't dismiss me. That was your magic protecting me, wasn't it?"

"Yes."

"Why did you never tell me you could do that?"

"Because my unc- Lord Somerville told me not to. He said nobody outside the family should know what we can do. Although, even most of my family don't know I can do that. It's not very showy."

"Powerful, though. Those dragons were clawing at me and I never felt a thing."

"It's never been *that* good before. I've never made it *that* strong. It was riding you. I felt... too full of power. Like I had to let it out or burst."

I stroked a hand down his cheek, loving that I was able to do that.

"We'll talk about your power later, if that's ok. I want to know more about it. And we can experiment, if you like."

"If your elder agrees to let me stay."

He still wasn't sure about that, was he? My first instinct was to tell him again that Nana would let him stay but, since he hadn't believed me yet, and since his whole experience with his old family told him it was impossible, it would have been pointless. I needed to prove it.

"Come on, let's get inside the territory.

Then I'll fly us back to the castle."

I took his hand and walked along the edge of the field I'd landed in. Hoskins land was mostly fields and rocks and a towering cliff with the sea below it. We walked together, and I breathed in deeply just to get Seren's scent in my nostrils.

The territory was marked with protections. I could feel them, just, and only because I'd trained myself to identify them. Magic was not my strong point and really the only thing I could do was identify when someone else had it. I'd felt it in Seren but it had been a calm kind of magic, laying low and innocent. I should have made him show me before. I should have done a lot of things before, and then perhaps we wouldn't have spent five years apart.

My dragon huffed inside me, the closest thing to a pout a dragon got, and I let go of Seren's hand to wrap my arm around his shoulder, pulling him so close against me that we bumped limbs awkwardly as we walked. I didn't care, I just wanted him close.

He hesitated as we crossed the boundary but nothing happened. Seren turned to stare at it for a while and then he looked up at me and I saw the amazement on his face that he was inside Hoskins land, with me, and I finally gave in to the urge to kiss him.

Once my lips were on his, I lost track of everything, as I'd known I would. I let myself go completely, now we were safe, now nothing could reach us to harm us, and I dragged Seren's body against mine and kissed and kissed him, dipping my tongue into his mouth to taste him and moaning at his flavour, until we were both out of breath and had to break apart just to gulp down some air.

I reached for him again, basically intending to kiss him and rub against his delicious body until we both came, but he darted back.

"Your family can see us."

"They won't care."

"I care. I want to hear Lady Hoskins tell me I can stay."

My heart ached for him that he could hardly comprehend unconditional love because he'd never been given it.

"Alright. We'll get back to the castle. But, I warn you, once Nana says we're good to stay, I'm going to ravish you."

Seren grinned. "That's what you think."

It was cute, that he was even thinking of pretending we wouldn't be going at it like rabbits for the foreseeable future. I, for one, wanted to touch him constantly, just to remind myself he was there and mine. He jerked his chin. "Are we walking or are you shifting?"

I began to shift and Seren leaned forward to whisper in my ear. "If your elder lets me stay, Dane, *I'm* going to ravish *you*."

I'd never shifted into my dragon form with a hard-on before and I felt totally fucking exposed and a little embarrassed as he climbed on my back again and settled against my shoulders, his hands stroking my neck and making sure I stayed aroused. I took to the air with my dick hanging thick and erect between my legs and, fuck, I needed to calm down before I got within sight of the castle. No way could I fly home waving my erection below me like a rudder.

CHAPTER 29: SEREN

I let the feel of Dane's body settle me. It felt natural to ride him and I couldn't believe we'd never done this before. It wasn't the done thing, of course, to ride someone's dragon but it hadn't occurred to me to shift as well so we could both fly together. I wanted to ride Dane. I liked the feel of his warm scales beneath my legs and I enjoyed the feel of them beneath my fingers, too, as I ran my hand over his neck. I didn't think I'd ever get tired of touching Dane.

I felt my dragon inside me, warning me that we were approaching magic again and I looked up. I hadn't even realised that I'd had my eyes on Dane for the whole time instead of the territory around me. That was stupid.

Dane didn't falter and so I knew there was nothing to worry about. I still reached out, though, and brushed my magic over theirs to feel what it was like. More protections. They were thick and solid, like the thick grey walls of the castle I could see atop the hill. Everything about it screamed *curaidh*. It was solid and squat, huge. Made for comfort and endurance rather than beauty. I liked it immediately. This was where Dane had grown up. This was where he lived. It was where I'd live, if Lady Hoskins allowed me to.

I felt uneasy at the thought and tried to shove it aside. I didn't want Dane to sense it. I didn't want him to know I was afraid. It was just that I couldn't see any reason why Lady Hoskins would let me stay except that Dane wanted it. Maybe that would be enough. Maybe he was right and she'd allow his mate to stay just to make him happy. I could work to pay for my accommodation. I could get a job or clean the castle or run errands for her or take on a job, like Rhod had become Lord Somerville's PA or Glenwise had become medic, to earn their keep. Of course, not even my own family had thought I'd be any good at those jobs or I'd have been doing them already. The only thing my un- Lord Somerville had thought I'd be good at was guarding his treasure. And he'd been right.

I gave a nod. I could use my magic to protect her treasure, if she had any. Or to protect her territory. I'd earn my keep. She wouldn't regret letting me stay.

I'd do anything to stay with my mate.

As we got nearer to the castle, I could see faces appearing at the windows. More and more faces. Some of them were there for a few minutes and then left and others stayed pressed against the glass as we flew towards it.

One window burst open.

"Uncle Dane! Who's that? Why is he riding you? You never fly when *we* ride you!"

Beneath me, Dane snorted and I noticed his scent change. It was a constant tickle in my nose, an awareness of him, but it was also incredible and made me want to hump against him even when he was flying, so I'd pushed that awareness aside. Now, though, I took a deep breath and inhaled him. He smelled… content. Happy. Proud. All the good things.

Ok, it looked like Dane was not only pleased to be home but he wanted to show off his family and his castle to me. I could go with that.

"Hello!"

The voice shouted again and I identified it as coming from a little girl, maybe ten years old. She was hanging out the window to see us better and there was a little boy practically on top of her, climbing up to get a look as well.

"Hannah, Ed, get inside!"

"But Uncle Dane is back! And he bought us someone."

Another face appeared in the window and took a good look at us. I kept my expression neutral, which was just about the best I could manage, and then that shrill little voice said, "He looks like Uncle Morgan."

I whipped my head round to look at them.

Morgan. I'd forgotten he was here. I hadn't thought about anything except Dane all day and I couldn't believe I hadn't considered it.

"Is Morgan healed?" I asked. He should be healed. If he had his dragon. Surely he had his dragon?

The adult face – a young man with the dark hair of the *curaidhs* but not much of the traditional bulk – met my eyes and gasped, slamming the window shut. The glass cracked. He'd shut it too hard.

I wasn't sure where Dane would land. I just had to hold on and wait for him to choose a place. He circled the castle once, and it was like he was showing me it from every angle, or maybe he was showing me to all those faces pressed against the windows.

Eventually, he rose up and landed on the roof. I slipped off his back and he shifted. Before I had the chance to say anything, he was wrapped around me again and I was engulfed in his strong embrace. I had no idea when I'd become the sort of person who wanted cuddles but I absolutely did. I hadn't had them before and I hadn't realised how amazing they were, especially when they were from Dane. Maybe *only* from Dane. I didn't want anyone else's hands on me. That would be weird and horrible.

"Is Morgan healed, Dane?"

His voice was muffled against my skin but, since he said, "Yes, he is," and since I liked that he had his mouth on me, on my neck, I didn't mind that one bit.

"Good."

He stayed where he was for a while, seemingly content to just breathe in my scent and hold me. I was ok with that, too. But his elder would know we were here. She would be waiting.

"Aren't we going to go and ask Lady Hoskins if I can stay?"

"No. We're going to go downstairs so I can introduce you to Nana and Gramps. I only landed here because I can't fit through the windows in dragon form. I leave some clothes up here. I dropped the last lot when we started fighting."

When he let go of me, I wanted to pout.

Instead, I watched him walk to a large gardening box and open it up. It was waterproof and it had a stack of blankets and clothes folded neatly inside. He yanked on a pair of jogging bottoms and a t-shirt.

"Stop looking at me like that or I'm going to get hard again and I only just got my dick to go down."

I smirked. I couldn't help it. I liked that Dane got hard for me. I wanted him to find me sexy. Of course I did, why wouldn't I?

My eyes strayed to the mating mark on his neck and I felt a deep rumble of satisfaction inside me.

"Come on."

He took my hand and led me across the roof and through the door, down a spiral staircase into a corridor and then along several corridors and down another flight of stairs. He took me straight to one room and I knew it had to be the elder's office.

I stood upright.

Shit, she was going to hate me for hurting Dane.

She was going to throw me out and then I really would be without a clan, only for real this time.

Dane knocked and a sharp voice called out, "Come in."

He pushed open the door and went inside. It was not an office. It was a lounge with two pretty floral couches and several low coffee tables, and a desk in the corner and chairs by the large windows. My eyes flickered over all that before settling on Lady Hoskins. She was tiny but she radiated power and protectiveness. If there was one thing I could identify, it was that. Protection was my talent, after all.

I met her eyes briefly, just to see what they were like before dropping my gaze. I shouldn't have looked – Lord Somerville hated it when we made eye contact – but I'd wanted to see. They were black and deep and brimmed with power.

"Dane. Seren."

Ok, she knew who I was then.

"Lady Hoskins," I said, keeping my eyes lowered.

"Nana, I got him."

"I can see that."

She didn't sound thrilled. On the other hand, she hadn't sliced me open, either, so I was taking that as a good sign. With my eyes lowered, though, it was hard to see what was happening. I reached out with my magic, like I always had with Lord Somerville, since it was a subtle magic, so subtle and unremarkable that he didn't notice it unless I layered it up or he was looking for it. I felt the protective power that was wrapped around the elder, and then something else. Someone else in the room. They were just as wrapped in power as she was but, from just that one quick touch, I was sure it was her power.

I couldn't help it. I needed to know who else was in the room. It could have been anyone. I wasn't going to stand there with my eyes lowered and wait to be killed.

I looked up at the window where the person was standing and saw it was a man. He was silver-haired and smiling softly at us and, as soon as I noticed him, I realised that I could scent him, too. He was human. That must be Lady Hoskins' mate.

I lowered my eyes again quickly, hoping she wouldn't take offense at my looking.

"Seren?"

Dane's voice soothed and thrilled me.

"Seren, this is Nana."

Her sharp voice was clear and commanding. I could see why Lord Somerville feared her, even if he refused to say that.

"I don't require you to keep your eyes lowered, Seren. You'll learn that my family works in a very different way from Lord Somerville's."

Unsure, I raised my eyes. She was looking directly at me and I almost flinched.

The human spoke and Dane jumped, only slightly, like he hadn't realised he was there.

"It's so good to meet you at last. We're glad you came."

He walked over and Dane lifted his other arm – one hand was still holding mine tightly – and the human walked into his embrace.

It was strange to have the human so close to me. I could see that Dane adored him. But he hadn't seen him?

I slowly reached out with my magic again and just brushed the edge of that power that was wrapped around him. Ah, that explained it. It concealed him. Only a little, only until he spoke, but it was a little layer of protection that the elder could wrap around her mate. I understood that. I still had a thin layer of magic wrapped around Dane, too. No way was I letting him walk around without that.

The human pulled back from Dane and studied me. I felt like a bug under a microscope. Then he smiled. "I'm so glad you found each other. Welcome to the family, Seren."

I didn't know what to say to that. He sounded sincere. On the other hand, it wasn't his choice. My glaze slipped to the elder.

"We're glad you're here, Seren."

"But—"

Ah, shit, I hadn't meant to speak. And Lady Hoskins raised her eyebrows at me because I was a fucking idiot who always messed up.

"What is it, Seren?"

She still didn't sound mad but then Lord Somerville never sounded mad, either. He'd never been more calm than when he dismissed me from his clan and his life and left me alone in the world, so maybe Lady Hoskins being calm didn't mean anything.

Dane slid his hand around my shoulder and dragged me into his side.

"Seren, I told you: you're family now. You're my mate."

The human gave a gasp and said, "You claimed him already?"

I looked over, not sure whether that was bad or not. The elder should probably have approved it, no matter what Dane had said at the time.

The human carried on. "And you didn't tell us? I'll *never* get your mating party ready for tonight."

Dane chuckled. "Seriously, Gramps? You're still calling it that?"

The human huffed and I swear I saw Lady Hoskins' lips quirk.

"Regardless, we need to celebrate."

"You can have a mating party for them tomorrow, John."

"But Edith, I've been waiting to meet Seren for *years*."

"Tomorrow, John. Tonight, they're going to tell me what happened and we're going to make sure everyone's safe."

He mumbled, "I suppose that's logical. Even if it's not as romantic."

"Safety is always romantic," she said. "Besides, I think Seren needs to hear a few things before we do anything else."

Call me a cynic but I didn't think that would be a good thing.

I was surprised when she gestured at the couch and said, "Sit down. I've called Lew and Morgan. They'll be here soon."

I sat next to Dane, who pulled me into his

side again. I was glad, though I'd never have said it.

"Morgan's been worried about you, Seren. He felt so guilty that you were injured protecting him."

I lowered my eyes reflexively. "A dragon protects his own, Lady Hoskins."

The human had settled on the couch opposite me and I could feel his eyes on me. "Morgan's yours, is he?"

I glanced up. There were things I was willing to let go and things I wasn't. For all that I laughed at Glimmer with his 'you're my treasure' stuff, I secretly loved that I *was* his treasure, and, actually, I totally got what he meant. I might have lost my dragon but I had been in line to be Guardian. A dragon is nothing if not protective of the things he loved and I'd had my power wrapped around Morgan for years – since his birth – and so I looked the human in the eyes and said, "Yes."

There was a gasp from outside the door and it swung open to reveal Morgan standing there, eyes wide and hand covering his mouth.

Behind him, a *curaidh* stood with his hand on Morgan's shoulder and a smile on his lips.

CHAPTER 30: DANE

Morgan was just about the only one who was surprised to hear that Seren thought he was his to protect. Dragons were like that. Seren had taken his duty of protecting his family seriously. Seriously enough to throw himself between Brendan and Morgan when Brendan had been wielding a knife, despite the fact that Seren hadn't had a dragon to protect him or heal him. Fuck, I realised all over again how very close Seren had come to dying that day and my arm tightened around him.

Morgan and Lew came into the room and Seren stood. I was right behind him because I hadn't got over that feeling of how precious he was and I wasn't about to let him out of my embrace.

Morgan glanced at me. I saw the familiar unease, which he'd always had when he looked at me and I was aware that it was because I was so big and intimidating, and also because I had been a complete dick to him. It wasn't his fault he looked like Lord Somerville, who had kept me away from Seren and then nearly killed him. It wasn't his fault he looked a little like Seren, either, when I'd wanted Seren so badly and found Morgan both an inadequate and painful reminder.

Ok, I'll admit that biting someone in half in front of him hadn't helped, either, but Brendan had been about to kill Seren, so I didn't regret it.

"Seren, are you healed?"

"Yes, I'm healed now. I've got my dragon back."

Morgan frowned. "What do you mean 'got it back'?"

"Ah," said Seren, and I could feel him wish he hadn't said anything. I wrapped my arms around his waist and pulled him against me. He fit so fucking perfectly, tucked against my chest.

Behind me, Nana said, "Sit *down*, Lew, you're looming."

I have no idea why she always said that to Lew, especially since I was taller than he was, but I found it funny nonetheless that Lew dropped instantly onto the sofa.

Gramps came and sat next to me on the sofa and Lew and Morgan sat next to Nana. Morgan looked a little happier, nestled between Nana and Lew, like he finally thought he was safe. I had to admit, there was almost nobody better protected at that moment than he was.

Then I remembered him using his magic on me. In my opinion, he didn't really need protection from someone else. He had that covered himself.

"Your nose looks better," I said to Lew.

He grinned. "Yeah. It's my own fault. Nana totally told me off for not being able to block you but, seriously, you were strong that day."

"Sorry," I said.

"No need to apologise, Dane. I knew what you needed."

"No, I mean for all of it. For the last five years."

Lew kept smiling at me and I wondered again how he could be so easy-going after all the things he must have seen as a soldier.

"I've only been back for four, so don't worry about it. Besides, I think I get it now. If Lord Somerville had kept Morgan from me, I think I'd have been like that, too."

It struck me then that Lord Somerville had kept me away from my mate. He'd hurt my mate. That was why I'd felt so angry all the time.

"Fuck," I breathed. "Lew, do you know how close I was to a *ruith*?"

He shook his head and that smile fell off his face. "I can't imagine. I don't want to imagine.

But you've got your mate now, Dane. He's right beside you and he's safe."

Just the thought of it must have scared him because he put his arm around Morgan automatically.

My dragon was starting to get panicked just at the thought of it and Nana must have sensed it, because she said, "Now you know why you could look me in the eyes, Dane. I knew you were closer to a *ruith* then than you'd ever been."

Seren's voice sounded wrecked when he cried, "I'm sorry, Dane, I'm so sorry."

I was fierce when I replied. "It wasn't your fault. It was Lord Somerville. He kept you from me. He told you lies. He took your dragon."

Morgan gasped again. It was more emotion than I'd ever seen from him and it soothed me a little because the more animated he became, the less he looked like his father. "Is that what happened?"

Seren nodded.

"But... how? How is that possible? You mean you didn't have a dragon at all?"

"No."

"Is that why you weren't healing?"

"Yes."

"You could have been killed. Why did you save me from Brendan?"

"You're my baby cousin, that's why. If I'd had my dragon, he wouldn't even have been able to cut you in the first place."

"How did he take your dragon?"

Seren shrugged. "I don't know. I just know that he said he was sending Dane away and I'd never see him again. I lost my dragon."

"How?" insisted Morgan.

"I don't know. It just left me. I felt it go."

Nana gave a small cough. "I think that, perhaps, it was protecting you."

"It refused to heal me when it left. We could have died. It was unnatural for it to leave me to die."

I remembered his broken body, so pale and cold and bleeding, and had to hold onto him tighter.

"Yes," said Nana. "But if it had stayed and you'd been separated from your mate, you'd have gone into *ruith*. The only way it could stop that was to disappear and hope you never realised Dane was your fated mate. It was protecting you, from yourself."

I turned slowly to look at Nana.

She met my eyes. Her dragon was not in them and I could hold her gaze.

"Nana, you knew? Why didn't you tell me? You *knew* Seren was my mate?"

"No, I didn't. I suspected he was. And everything you did subsequently confirmed it."

I felt my dragon stir, anger spreading through me. "Why didn't you tell me?"

"Because the only thing stopping you from doing exactly the same was the fact that you didn't know. Be honest, Dane: if you'd known Seren was your mate and you'd lost him, what would you have done?"

"*Ruith*," I admitted. I'd felt it, even without knowing he was my mate.

"I couldn't allow that. We all know there's no coming back from it. You'd have been killed, and you'd have done untold damage before you were. I couldn't tell you."

There was silence for a moment as we all absorbed that, and then Gramps spoke up from beside me. He always did know how to settle me after Nana had made my stomach twist into knots.

"She was trying to get Lord Somerville to see reason, Dane. Invited Morgan here to train and look how well that turned out."

Lew spluttered, "I don't think it went as smoothly as all that, Gramps."

He tutted. "I don't know. We got Morgan out of the deal. And now we've got Seren, too. I think we did very well out of it."

I agreed whole-heartedly.

Gramps clapped his hands. "Right, now that's over, we can start arranging your mating party. You'll want to meet everyone, Seren."

I looked down at my mate and found him looking not as thrilled as I'd expected.

"What's the matter?"

His eyes slid towards Nana.

"Lady Hoskins," he began, but Nana gave a little wave of her hands.

"None of that. We don't do that here. Talk to Morgan and he'll tell you how we do things here. You can call me Nana, now you're family."

"And I'm Gramps," said Gramps, sounding proud of that fact. I suppose he was. He was the best Gramps and he had a soft spot for me.

"Thank you, Lad- Nana. I'll make sure you don't regret taking me into your clan. Now I have my dragon back, all my power is at your service. I'll work hard."

"Seren," I said. "I told you, you don't need to earn your keep."

"But I can. I might not be the best fighter but I can still do some things. I can help your clan protect your territory, Lad- Nana."

Nana's eyes were surprisingly soft when she said, "You're family now, Seren. You don't need to earn your place here. You belong. But if you want to help protect our family, we'll be pleased to let you do that."

Gramps leaned around me and took Seren's hand in his. "All you need to do is love our boy the way he deserves, and we know you do that already."

My heart was so full, I wasn't sure how it could contain all the love I felt pouring into it.

The mood was shattered by a knock at the door.

"Come in," said Nana.

Prince opened the door and peeped in, still standing in the hallway.

Nana sighed. "I said come in, Prince."

"My cousin, Prince," I murmured into Seren's hair by way of an introduction.

He stepped into the room but he looked ready to bolt.

"What is it?"

"Um, I just, you wanted to know if anything, um, broke?"

I bit my cheek so I wouldn't snigger. Prince made it sound like things broke all by themselves, but we all knew that was him. He couldn't help it. He just attracted accidents.

"What broke?"

"The, um, window? It cracked when it shut." He cringed.

Nana nodded. "Show me which one and I'll order a replacement. She glanced back at us and said, "The rest of the evening is your own. I'll keep everyone away from you for tonight."

I was grateful for that. I could feel the emotions swirling around Seren. His scent was a confusing, heady mix of confusion and worry and happiness and love and amusement. I called after Prince before he left, "Hey, Prince, you haven't met Seren yet."

He poked his head back into the room and

smiled. He had a brilliant smile, did Prince. He had this little gap between his two front teeth that was cute as fuck.

Prince walked over to us with his hand out, ready to shake Seren's hand. Just as he said, "Pleased to meet you," he tripped over nothing and face-planted the arm of the sofa.

He hauled himself up and covered his face with his hands. "Ah, shit, I didn't mean to get blood on your sofa, Nana."

She sighed again. "Never mind, I'll clear it up. You come with me before you do any more damage."

Prince blushed and I frowned. "Hey, Prince." He looked back at me, the blood from his lip already drying as it healed. "If you can stop Hannah and Ed getting to me tonight, I'll give you that training you want."

The smile burst across his face again and he left.

Before she disappeared out the door, Nana turned back to Seren. "One last thing: would you like Lord Somerville informed of your whereabouts?"

"No, thank you, La- Nana. It's no longer his concern."

She nodded. "Very well."

Gramps followed Nana out the door with just a last squeeze of my shoulder because he never liked being away from her for too long. I

understood that now, more than ever.
 It left just me and Seren, and Lew and Morgan in the room.

CHAPTER 31: SEREN

Whoever that Prince was, I could tell at once that he was special to Dane. I expected to feel jealousy curl inside me but I didn't. I wasn't particularly the jealous type. Possessive, perhaps. Protective, definitely. Jealous, not so much. Just because someone belonged to me, didn't mean they didn't belong to others as well. And I got a good vibe off Prince. I got the feeling I'd end up liking him.

I turned back to Morgan and his mate. I felt better now La-Nana had said I could stay. It was official.

That didn't mean I didn't have questions.

I started with, "Does she really allow her clan to look her in the eyes?"

Morgan gave the smallest smile. It was weird, to see him do it. He'd never really gone in for facial expressions before. He'd basically been a cardboard cut-out of my unc- Lord Somerville. I liked the smile, though.

"Yes. And her mate is human."

"Yes, I noticed."

"And she lets everyone call her Nana."

"Yes."

"And we don't dress for dinner."

"No?"

"And we all eat together, not just the elders and warriors."

"Really?"

"And the children play these games."

"Huh."

"And Lew's training me to fight."

I'd basically got an excited babble about everything Morgan apparently found important. I'd have to ask for more details later. But...

"Lew's your mate?"

I slid my eyes across to him. He was leaning back on the couch, looking content, and he had his hand proprietarily on Morgan's leg. He noticed my gaze but didn't move.

I let my voice dip a little into that creepy coldness as I said, "I don't suppose anyone's told him yet what happens if he hurts you?"

He actually sat up then. I wanted to laugh because he looked astonished.

Dane actually did laugh. "You sound just like G. And, just so you know, Lew can whoop my arse at fighting so you're on your own if you want to beat him up."

"I'll think of something," I said.

Morgan let out a tiny huff that sounded like it might be laughter. "Actually, Gramps told him not to hurt me already. Not that Lew would. But it was nice that he was looking out for me."

"The human threatened the *curaidh* warrior?" Morgan nodded. I turned to Dane. "Is this your cousin who was in the Fife Army?"

"That's the one."

I smiled, remembering Dane telling me and Glimmer about him. I'd been impressed, but Glimmer had shimmered into darkness and said, "I'd love to meet him some day," in just that tone that said, actually, he'd love to *fight* him some day and Dane and I had laughed so hard together that we'd turned towards each other and breathed in each other's breath.

Dane's hand on my knee told me that he was remembering the same thing.

"You say he's teaching you to fight?"

Morgan nodded.

That seemed stupid to me. Dane was the best teacher in the country. Even my u- Lord Somerville admitted that. Hence he'd hired Dane to train me and Glimmer. Lord Somerville liked getting the best.

Lew said, "Actually, Dane is going to teach him a bit. When we've covered basics. No rush."

I nodded. That made sense. No point in

Dane doing that. He specialised in bringing out the best in people. He'd brought out all that power in Glimmer that even Glimmer hadn't known was there. And he'd brought it out in me, too.

"I can help you get a handle on your magic, if you want. I don't know if there's anyone here to teach you that."

Morgan looked about as astonished as his mate.

"What?" I asked, warily. Had I overstepped some boundary?

"You- you're going to help me?"

"Yes, why not?"

"Because I left you. And I- I ignored you. For years. I just ignored you because talking to you made Lord Somerville mad and I didn't want him to notice me. I'm sorry, Seren. I should have been braver than that."

"Hey," I said, slipping off the couch and kneeling in front of Morgan. "I knew what was happening, alright? I never minded. In fact, I preferred it if it kept you out of his sights."

Lew growled low and I heard Dane's growl follow a split second later. Seemed neither of them was that fond of Lord Somerville.

Morgan sniffed tearfully. I'd literally never seen anyone else cry before. We learned not to, certainly not where others could see. I'd allowed Dane to see me cry and that was the first

I'd cried since I'd been a child.

"And I didn't even know you'd lost your dragon. I could have told Lew. He could have helped."

It was sweet that Morgan thought his mate could have helped when he absolutely couldn't have, but I didn't correct Morgan. Instead, I said, "Hey, we've got another chance now. To start over. I'll train you to use your magic and you can tell me all the weird things the Hoskinses do so I don't mess up."

He gave a wobbly laugh and I took that as a win. My baby cousin was finally breaking out of his shell in this clan and I was all for that.

While I was there, with him in my sights, I sent a thin trickle of power out to cover him, wrap him in protections. When I'd lost my dragon, most of my protections had vanished unless I'd made them deep enough that they stood independent. The ones around Morgan had vanished completely after five years. The only thing that annoyed me was that, if I'd had my dragon a week ago, and my protections had still been in place, then that *curaidh*'s blade would have glanced harmlessly off him and he wouldn't have been injured at all.

Lew stood and I backed up, standing. His elder had been right. He loomed.

"We can talk later. Why don't you let Dane show you to your room?"

I blinked at him. My room? As in, separate from Dane's?

Dane was standing beside me in an instant, with his arms wrapped around me, and he said, "You're not leaving my sight, Seren. Come to my room with me and spend the night? We'll be busy tomorrow, I guarantee it. Gramps wants to throw us a mating party and he won't listen to reason about how weird that sounds."

I snorted. "Ok then."

I gave a little wave to Morgan as I left the elder's rooms and followed Dane through the corridors. When we got to his door, he paused outside it and cocked his head.

Inside the room, there were shuffling noises and the odd burst of giggles.

Dane pressed a finger to his lips and went into the room. He said, a bit louder and clearer than necessary, "Alone at last!" His eyes swept the room and landed on a shoe poking out from underneath it. "Why don't we sit on the bed?"

He went over and sat down heavily and then bounced up and down on it. "This doesn't feel right," he declared. "Something must be wrong with my mattress! Let me take a look at it."

He knelt beside the bed and I got a warm, squishy feeling inside when he gave a huge gasp of surprise. I also got a rather nice view of his ass as he reached under the bed and locked his hands onto two ankles and carefully pulled out two wriggling children. He stood, with his hand still around their ankles so they dangled upside down. My mate was strong.

He lifted one child up higher. "This is Hannah," he said, and then lifted the other one up. "And this is Ed."

They giggled and wriggled and eventually Dane lowered them onto the bed so they could right themselves.

"What are you doing in my room?"

"We wanted to see your new friend!"

"You've been gone *ages*, Uncle Dane."

"Why don't you fly when *we* ride your dragon?"

"Who is he anyway?"

Dane straightened up and said, "This is Seren. He's my mate."

There was a lot of squealing again and Dane stood still while the two of them clambered all over his bed to get higher so they could see his neck and examine his mating bite.

"Do you think it's pretty?" he asked.

"Yes."

"No."

"No?"

Hannah shrugged. "I don't like biting. Did it hurt?"

I swear Dane blushed but it was so faint that I couldn't be sure. "No, it didn't hurt. It doesn't hurt when it's your fated mate."

I thought they'd leave – I was totally unfamiliar with children, had never had anything to do with them, except Morgan and Alfie, and then my role had been limited to wrapping my magic around them and sneaking them chocolate when I could and sometimes Alfie would steal into my room at night to cuddle when he had a nightmare, but that was it, really.

They didn't leave. I was summoned forward and Dane totally indulged them as he let them examine my mating mark as well and that squishy feeling in my stomach grew as I saw how light Dane looked and how easy his movements were and how filled with love and happiness his face was. This, *this* was exactly what Dane had wanted all along and it was how he was supposed to live. I vowed then, silently, to myself, that I would do anything to make him happy.

When I'd been poked and prodded in the neck by his... niece and nephew?... Dane finally got rid of them. I had to admit, they were kind of cute.

Just before they left, he dropped to one knee and whispered, "Hey, don't tell anyone you were here, alright? Nobody else has met Seren yet and I don't want them to be jealous."

"Ok," they whispered – really loudly. Seriously, how was their whisper louder than their talking voices?

Then they left. Dane shut the door and waited until their footsteps had faded and then he locked it.

"Don't tell anyone?" I asked.

He shrugged, trying for nonchalance and totally failing. I knew him better than that. "I didn't want Prince to find out they'd got in. Then he'd think he'd failed."

"Oh, yeah, I remember. You want to tell me about Prince?"

Dane smiled smugly. "Are you jealous?"

"No, but I can tell he's special to you."

If I'd thought I'd lived, I had been mistaken, because seeing Dane Hoskins pout was the cutest thing ever.

"Not even a little jealous?"

I checked inside. Nope. My dragon and I were both absolutely fine with it. I was torn between indulging Dane by saying I was, and telling him the truth just to keep that pout on his face.

"If I say I'm jealous, will you tell me?"

The pout fell off him quickly. "You're not really jealous, are you? I swear there's nothing between me and Prince. We're related. I think. Probably. Maybe second cousins?"

Chuckling, I walked across to Dane and pressed my whole front against him. "No, I'm not really jealous. I don't do jealousy. You're mine. And as long as we both agree on that, I don't mind who else you love." I pecked a kiss to his lips. "Of course, if you ever sleep with anyone else, I won't be jealous. I'll just kill them."

His arms wound around me tightly and pulled me harder against him. "Fuck, that shouldn't be hot but it is."

I was glad he thought so. Didn't stop it being true.

Dane's lips pressed against mine and his tongue slipped out to run along the seam of my lips. I opened up to let him in and sucked on his tongue. After the jangling nerves that had forced me up and out of that hotel room, and the subsequent fight, and then the fear that his elder would throw me out, I finally allowed myself to relax. I wanted Dane. I wanted his body every way I could have it and I wanted to stay locked in his arms and I wanted to taste him and scent him and finally we were free to do that.

I growled, pushing Dane back hard against the door, holding his body there and attacking his mouth. I wanted his taste in my mouth. I wanted his body pressed against mine.

"Fuck, Seren," he panted, and I rolled my hips against him. I could feel his thick erection growing bigger and it began to dig into me. He tried to buck his hips but I pushed harder and held him still. He groaned and the sound was pure lust.

I wanted him, and I was going to have him.

CHAPTER 32: DANE

Seren had me pinned against the door and I couldn't move. I'd never thought that being trapped and held like that could be a turn-on but, judging by the way my dick was pressing against his hip and twitching excitedly, it really was.

I pushed back, so desperate for Seren's mouth that I couldn't just wait, but he pushed harder and, when he did press his lips to mine, he owned me completely. His hand angled my head so he could thrust his tongue deeper into my mouth and a groan rose up inside me from my very soul. Having Seren do whatever he wanted to me was my new favourite thing.

I don't know how long he kissed me for, only that my whole body felt alive and needy and my dick was leaking so hard it was soaking my trousers. His taste was incredible and the way he ran his tongue along mine, and explored every part of my mouth, made me want to beg, if only I could have brought myself to tear my mouth from his to do it.

By the time he broke our kiss, I was right on the edge of coming and the feel of his lean body pressing against me and his muscles holding me and the way he rolled his hips to grind his erection against my thigh was making my brain short circuit.

"Seren, please," I gasped, dragging breath into my body again.

"Don't worry, Dane, I've got you. I'm going to take care of you."

Fuck, that sounded incredible. I didn't even care what he meant, as long as I had his hands on me somehow. Even if I just had his attention, I think I could live my life in complete satisfaction just from knowing that his eyes were on me.

I might have whimpered, but I wasn't sure.

Seren smirked and grabbed the front of my t-shirt, dragging me across the room to our bed. He pushed me against it and I toppled backwards, landing with a little bounce.

He'd stripped my jogging bottoms off before I'd even realised what he was doing and all I was aware of was the way the waistband caught against my dick and dragged against it before it sprang free and slapped my stomach. Seren yanked my t-shirt over my head and I was naked again, laying in front of him, completely at his mercy.

The way his eyes devoured me made my cock throb. Had I thought I could live my life just with Seren's eyes on me? No way would I manage that, not if the intensity I saw in his silver eyes was anything to go by. They were filled with lust and possession and, underneath it all, the same love I'd seen in them before. I felt so stupid that I'd never realised that was love. He'd looked at me with that expression almost from the start.

Watching him strip out of his clothes was both divine and torture. His skin was so smooth and his limbs the perfect balance between slender and muscled. The way he moved, though, that did it for me more than anything. He never took his eyes off me and he moved with the same single-mindedness as a predator. My cock dripped more pre-come onto my belly.

Seren smiled, wolfish and satisfied.

"You enjoying the view?"

I was nearly beyond words but I managed to force a, "Yes," out of my throat. It came out deep and gravelly and it made Seren smirk harder.

"Point to where your lube is."

I pointed to the drawer across the room and he went to it, only taking his eyes off me to reach inside the drawer and bring out the bottle.

I was sprawled in the middle of the bed and, if I'd been thinking properly, I would have moved over so he could lay down beside me and I could start to work him open, but all my brain power was needed to feel and not come at the sight of my mate, naked and marked by my mating bite.

When Seren crawled up the bed, I assumed he would straddle me and let me work him open like that. Clearly he wanted to be in charge of this round. But when he reached my knees, he hooked his hands under them and lifted and my ass was suddenly in the air and spread open as he bent my knees back towards my chest.

I didn't have time to do anything before he ducked his head and licked a long stripe up my crack and I nearly shot my load. Only the surprise and unfamiliarity kept me from losing it.

"Seren!"

He lifted his head.

"Do you need me to stop?"

I hesitated for a second. I'd never bottomed before. I'd never submitted to anyone else before, allowed them to take charge. I'd never felt I was missing out. Now, though, I *wanted* to feel this, I *wanted* him to take charge, I wanted to experience everything he was going to give me. And I trusted him. I trusted him with everything.

"No, keep going. I want you."

He smirked again and licked a stripe up my

aching dick.

"You'll get me. Trust me."

"I do."

He gave a muffled moan as he dove back down to my ass and the way he began to eat it was desperate and greedy and absolute heaven. I'd never expected it to feel this way but, even as my mind began to short out from the pleasure, I knew it was the fact that it was *Seren*'s mouth on me that was making it so good.

I don't even know when he added his first finger inside my hole. I was totally gone on the feel of his hot, slick tongue as it licked at my hole and pushed inside little by little. I only noticed the second finger because it stretched me harder and stung, just a little, but it was enough to bring me back to awareness after teetering on the edge of my orgasm for so long. Fuck, when I did come, I was going to blow so hard after enduring such a build-up.

Despite my inexperience, I never worried about it hurting. If there was one thing I knew about my mate, it was that he would take care of me. I didn't even need to say anything; all I had to do was lay there and feel and moan with the overwhelming pleasure and Seren read me like a book. Everything he did drove me higher, nothing felt wrong, nothing felt taboo. There was only pleasure and Seren's touch and his mouth and his scent, thick with arousal and love.

When he settled between my legs and brushed the head of his dick against my slick hole, I managed to speak one word, and it was all I could say, but it encompassed everything.

"*Seren.*"

The look on his face was pure amazement and he said, "I love you, Dane," just as he slid inside me.

I'd never been possessed in such a way. I was filled with my mate and the closeness was something I'd never been able to anticipate. We were joined in the most intimate way as he made me his completely.

"Fuck, Daaaane, you feel so good."

He moved inside me, slowly at first, even though I could see from the tension in his shoulders and the sweat running down his skin that he was holding back. He eased in and out of me in long, slow strokes, and the sensation was too much.

I grunted, too close, wanting to warn him, but completely unable to form words.

"I got you," he said, and he shifted position, sliding into me at a different angle, and again, and again. I wanted to touch my cock so badly but I was holding my knees and Seren had one hand braced on the bed and the other on mine with our fingers linked, and I wasn't going to let go of him, that was for sure.

Then he slid into me at a new angle and

I felt his dick brush up against something inside me that broke me completely. I let out a roar that shredded my throat and Seren pushed into me again and again, sliding against that same spot as the pleasure became too much and my balls tightened hard and I came like a fire hose.

There was nothing except the pleasure wracking my body and the feel of Seren inside me. My ass clenched and I felt Seren's dick throb and his hot seed fill me. That. I wanted that every day. I was Seren's and he was mine. It was all I was capable of thinking in that moment.

By the time I came to my senses, Seren was lying beside me with his head on my shoulder and one hand stroking gently over my chest and stomach, tracing the dips between my muscles. I was clean and my legs had been stretched out flat to the bed, uncramping them, and a blanket was draped over my lower half to keep me warm.

I turned my head and saw Seren's face, inches from mine. He grinned. Smug bastard. I loved it.

"I take it we can do that again?"

The smile slid onto my face against my will. "We can do anything you want."

He snuggled closer to me, leaning more on my chest. I managed to get my arms to work and wrapped them around him, pulling him as close as he could get.

"Just let me know when you're ready," he

mumbled.

He sounded sleepy.

"You sure? You're not going to take a nap on me instead?"

"Maybe. But I'll wake up for you."

I tightened my arms. "No need. I'll be here when you wake up."

His breathing was already changing, sliding into sleep, but I heard him ask, "You sure?"

"I'm sure, Seren. I'll always be here for you. We belong together."

His last word before he fell asleep on my chest, exactly where he should be, was, "Mates."

CHAPTER 33: DANE

By morning, we were both sore but perfectly sated. I couldn't even comprehend how I'd managed to live five years without Seren in my life. Just having him beside me made me feel whole in a way I hadn't realised I was missing, and my dragon had finally calmed down enough to be reasonable. It was satisfied that Seren was really here and that he was staying and he was ours. For the first time in years, I wasn't battling against it.

To be honest, having Seren right beside me was a massive help in that. Before, my dragon had wanted to set its eyes on Seren, just to check he was ok, and I'd had to fight against the shift even though all I really wanted to do was go and see Seren anyway. My dragon hadn't understood why we couldn't watch him constantly if we both wanted to. Now, I understood that urge. I also thought that maybe I'd listen to my dragon a bit more in future, since it was hard to remember why we couldn't have just gone to the Somervilles and taken Seren away from them. It had seemed impossible at the time. And if Seren had still been one of Lord Somerville's family then it would almost certainly have sparked a war, especially after the stunt we pulled by taking Morgan, but still. My dragon knew what it was doing where Seren was concerned.

    I kept him right by my side all morning, from the moment we went downstairs to grab breakfast. I talked to him, showing him how things worked in our family. Every time he asked a question like, "So you're saying I can come into the kitchen any time I want?" and, "You mean I get to choose what I wear?" it made me angry. It reminded me of how he'd lived all his life. Every time he asked something so sweetly, I rewarded him with a kiss. Ok, I might have done that anyway but it was definitely as good a reason as any. I wanted him to feel loved. And if I got to put my mouth on him, however briefly, all the better.

    By lunchtime, I had put my mouth on him too much. I'd been kissing his lips and his shoulder and his neck all morning and worked myself up. He seemed surprised when I dragged him upstairs and into our room, and then he seemed even more surprised when I threw him on the bed and finally got my mouth on his dick. I sucked it right into my throat and came just from a couple of strokes of my own hand and the heady taste of Seren's seed in my mouth and the way he shouted my name when he came.

I kissed my way back up his body, pleased that he responded so beautifully to me.

"Come on," he said. "We should go back downstairs and help."

"We can't," I said.

"Why not?"

"Because Gramps has banished us."

Seren sat up. His scent changed to panic and he said, "But... they said I could stay."

Fuck, I'd been careless. "No, I didn't mean that. We can stay. They want us to stay. That's the point," I insisted. His expression told me he didn't believe me. "Gramps is thrilled that you're here, Seren, I promise. Didn't I tell you he was going to throw us a mating party? I didn't mean we were disowned, I meant he wanted us out of the way so he could arrange the party without us seeing it."

His whole body slumped back and I couldn't resist dragging him against me so I could hold him.

"Sorry," he mumbled.

"Don't be sorry. I phrased it badly. It was stupid of me."

He smacked my arm. "Hey, don't call yourself stupid."

I chuckled. "If you say so." Nosing at his

ear and pressing little nips and kisses to it, I asked, "So what do you want to do all afternoon if we're not allowed downstairs?"

What I meant by that was 'do you want to fuck me or me to fuck you?' Apparently, I hadn't actually said that, though, because Seren climbed off the bed and yanked his trousers up.

"Let's go flying. I want you to show me your territory."

Ok, so that was a change of plan. "Or we could stay all naked up here?" I suggested.

Seren leaned on the bed, bringing his face close to mine. I thought he was going to kiss me.

"No. Let's go out. I wasn't paying attention yesterday and I want to see what we're dealing with."

"Dealing with?"

I couldn't think properly when Seren was that close to me.

"Yes. I said I'd help protect your territory and I meant it, but I need to see it first."

Groaning, I tried grabbing hold of him. "Seren, you don't need to earn your keep. And you certainly don't need to do it now."

He pouted. It was hot as fuck to see him so confident again after witnessing the way he'd become just a shell of himself. That's what swayed me. I climbed off the bed, muttering.

"Alright, if you insist. But we're spending a whole day naked in our room soon."

The sultry way he looked at me made me flush. "If you say so."

I did. I did say so.

I nearly forgot what we were doing but Seren kept me on track. He got me cleaned up and in fresh clothes and took me up to the roof where I folded the clothes into the supply box and shifted. I'd assumed he would shift as well but he just raised his eyebrows at me and I realised he intended to ride me. I crouched down and he swung up onto my shoulders. The shiver that ran through me felt *right*. It was like Seren was meant to be on my back, that I was meant to feel his weight and his warmth and his hands stroking over my scales. Everything felt right and I took to the air feeling lighter than I ever had.

We were way out of hearing of the family when he first spoke.

"I like your Gramps."

I gave a nod. That was good. Everyone liked Gramps.

"And I like your Nana, even if she is the head of the family. And Lew, I think he's good for Morgan, isn't he?"

I nodded again. They were good for each other. Even I could see that. Lew was built to be protective – it was why he'd become a soldier, to protect the weak – and I could see he totally got off on the adoring way Morgan looked up at him. It was cute.

"Does Prince have a mate?"

I shook my head.

"Is he straight? Gay? Bi? Pan?"

I huffed. He was listing things too quickly for me to answer.

Above me, Seren laughed. "Alright, I'll leave it. But if a gorgeous man/woman/dragon/sexy beast turns up wanting to mate him, I'm going to set your precious Prince up and gift-wrap the lube."

Turns out, a dragon can laugh in dragon form. Unfortunately, they can't laugh and fly at the same time. We dipped and dropped ten feet, and I tried to keep us in the air while my body was weak with laughter. Before we stumbled to the ground, I managed to get my wings working properly again and I spent the afternoon flying Seren round the territory.

We went slowly, lazily, and Seren stopped me sometimes and made me double back so he could look at something, or he got me to land and shift back so we could walk along together, hand in hand. I was never sure why he chose those particular places but I suspected that at least some of them were because they were pretty.

When I flew along the cliff, I felt Seren tense above me and I dipped away from it and landed in the field.

"What's wrong?"

"Nothing!"

"What is it, Seren?"

"Urgh, it's so stupid."

"No, it isn't."

He glared. "You don't even know what it is."

"I don't need to. I know it's not stupid. Tell me what's wrong."

He chewed his lip for a second, thinking, and then it burst out of him. "I've never been this close to the sea before, ok? Only when Glimmer flew us off the island and I didn't really see it then. I wasn't paying attention to the view."

I already had my hands on his cheeks, looking into his eyes.

"What do you think of the sea?"

"It's bigger than I realised."

I was really struggling not to laugh at him but that would be terrible of me. It wasn't his fault he'd never seen the sea before. I was kind of angry about it, actually. He'd never been out of Somerville territory.

"Do you want to go down and see it close up?"

"No. Not yet."

I was surprised by that. The Seren I knew – before we'd been parted – had been almost dangerously adventurous. He'd wanted to try everything new.

"I won't let you get hurt, you know that, right?"

He smiled. "I know that. I'm not afraid of the sea, not with you here, but I want to see the rest of your borders before it gets dark. Just to see the whole territory."

That explained it. The only thing that could stop Seren from charging recklessly into something was if he was already focused on something else. Once he started something, he wanted to see it through.

"Alright, we'll keep going."

I shifted and Seren climbed back onto my shoulders and we completed our lap of the entire territory just as dusk was falling.

"Just in time," I said, taking Seren's hand and leading him downstairs. I could hear noises from the west rooms and knew everyone would be waiting for us. I could smell the excitement and nerves in my mate's scent and I clutched his hand tighter.

When we walked into the room, everyone cheered and I saw a banner strung out across the back wall that said '*Happy mating*'. I met Gramps' eyes and he sniggered. He'd been saving that for me, I was sure.

Nana was standing at the front of the crowd, with Gramps beside her. She raised her glass and everyone behind her did the same.

"Welcome to the family, Seren. It's good to have you here at last."

Gramps gave a little sob and wiped his

eyes. Nana turned to him at once.

"It's alright, Edith, really. I'm just so happy they're finally here together."

I led Seren into the room and then hugged Nana and Gramps at the same time, one arm around each of them.

"It's good to have you back," Nana said as she pushed back from my embrace. I nodded. I knew she didn't just mean having me home. It was good to *be* back. Back to myself again and not half out of my mind, fighting my dragon constantly. I tugged Seren into my side, feeling I'd been separated from him too long. All of thirty seconds.

"This is like the parties that Glimmer and I used to have."

"Yeah? I didn't think you'd ever been to a party like this one before."

"Maybe not exactly. It was only me and Glimmer. He snuck into my room at night and we'd hide under the blankets and talk and sometimes I managed to get a bar of chocolate for us."

I growled playfully. "You're not to hide under the blankets with anyone but me now."

A flash of sadness passed across Seren's face but it was gone in an instant.

"Seren? That a problem?"

"No. No, it's not. I just realised I won't see Glimmer again."

There was nothing I could say to that. He

wouldn't. Not unless Lord Somerville changed his mind and that seemed unlikely.

"Um, can I borrow your phone for a minute?"

"Sure."

I handed it over. I'd already programmed his thumb-print into it so he could access it whenever he wanted to.

"Thanks."

He slipped away and I let him go. There was only one person who Seren would call, other than me, and I was just fine with him talking to G as much as he needed. Whatever it was he wanted to say to him, it wasn't much, because he was back after only a couple of minutes. He looked happier, though, and I could smell the relief on him.

"Everything ok?"

"Yes. Everyone's fine. I- I just had to check."

"You can check as often as you like."

I spent the rest of the evening introducing Seren to people and kept him pulled tightly against me. Having him there with my family was the best feeling.

Even having Hannah and Ed tell me off – again – for not letting them ride me when I was flying didn't dampen my spirits and I just passed that buck straight up the food chain with a quick, "I'll fly you as soon as Nana says it's ok."

They ran off straight away to go and pester her and I didn't even feel bad about it.

The only thing that I didn't like at all was when a stranger arrived in the middle of my Mating Party – and shit, I hadn't meant to think of it in those words, Gramps had completely messed with my mind – and Nana introduced him to everyone.

"This is Darren Rockfell. He's here as a security consultant and he'll be staying for a few weeks."

I took a deep breath, smelling him. He was a gargoyle. That made sense. Gargoyles were experts in home security. It kind of went with the whole guarding-buildings-and-turning-into-stone thing. I'd met gargoyles before and had become quite friendly with one woman. It wasn't him that bothered me, or the fact that he was a gargoyle. It was the condescending look he gave Prince when there was a huge crash behind me and I turned to see Prince clutching one single champaign glass while a tray and a dozen more glasses lay shattered at his feet. Darren turned away from Prince like he couldn't even bear to give him the time of day and I saw the humiliation in Prince's eyes before he carefully placed the only surviving glass on the nearest table and then fled from the room.

Seren's arm tightened around me and I looked down. He was frowning, and I followed his line of sight to the gargoyle. It looked like my mate wasn't happy either. This Darren had better watch out.

NEXT IN SERIES

Find out what Prince thinks about far-too-sexy, put-together older men in the next book in the DRAGON'S MATE series.

Gargoyles are born to protect things. If there's anything left to protect once Prince has broken it all.

Sign up to Hope's newsletter to make sure you don't miss it.

https://hopebennettauthor.com/newsletter/

OTHER BOOKS BY HOPE

FAMILY OF FIRE (Dragon's Mate book 1)

If you haven't already read FAMILY OF FIRE then check it out now!

It's the first in this DRAGON'S MATE series and is Lew and Morgan's story. Just like HEART OF FIRE, it can be read as a standalone.

Lew is a warrior dragon shifter and, when his family agrees to train a noble dragon, he expects he'll hate it. He doesn't expect Morgan to be quite as sexy and sweet as he is. This is not what he signed up for, but there's no going back now. Lew and Morgan will just have to find a way to get along, and then they'll have to find a way to accept what their dragons are telling them: that they are fated mates. If they want to stay together, they'll need to learn to be honest with each other or their families will tear them apart.

THE ASSISTANT CRISIS
(Magician's Luck 1)

A series of M/M Romances with a sprinkling of magic. Clueless magicians, surly assistants, steamy interludes and a happy ever after. Book 1 can be read as a standalone so get it now.

Al is the most respected magician in Britain. But he's clueless when it comes to love. Therefore, when he finds himself with an assistant, and that assistant is gorgeous, clever, strangely sweet and *bossy*, he's at a complete loss. Join Al as he tries to show Sean that he's the best assistant he could wish for. And if Sean decides to show Al that they can be more than that, then who is he to complain?

THE FAMILY MISFORTUNE
(Magician's Luck 2)

The second in the series. There's just as much magic, Sean is just as sweet and Al is just as clueless!

Al is happier with Sean than he's ever been but he knows it can't last. When his family start asking questions and Al realises that they're going to scare Sean away, he'll do anything to stop that from happening. But how long can he keep Sean away from his family? And will Sean, perhaps, notice that?

A NEW NORMAL CHRISTMAS
(Standalone)

My first Christmas story, written especially for December 2020. It proves that love can be found, even in the hardest of times and a little Christmas magic can go a long way.

Bart has spent the past three Christmases with his neighbour, GG. But this year she's gone and Bart is worried that he'll never see her grandson again. Danny has been crushing hard on his grandma's neighbour and he knows this Christmas is the last chance he'll get to persuade Bart to give them a chance. He's going all in, because Bart needs to realise that he's had family all along.

WISH FROM THE HEART
(Bric-a-brac Love 1)

A standalone story about a prickly genie, an adorable master, three wishes and a happily ever after.

Jordan has been trapped in his bottle for years and he knows just what to expect when a young man buys him, with no idea what it is he's just bought – a genie, actual magic. He knows the drill. But his new master, Pat, turns out to be not what he expected at all and Jordan is in danger of giving him far more than three wishes. He might just give Pat his heart.

ABOUT HOPE

Hope is a M/M Romance and Fantasy author. She is an absolute believer in true love, head over heels for a happy ending and always on board for a sprinkling of magic in her stories!

If she's not curled up with a good book, she's out hiking. At least, she tells people it's hiking but really it's just walking with sensible shoes on. She loves to reach the countryside when she can.

Hope embraces the British stereotype by being addicted to tea, glorious tea. She drinks it from mugs and doesn't understand why anyone would try to talk to her before she's had her first one of the day. Let's just say that mornings aren't her time to shine.

Where she really shines is in her writing. Sign up to Hope's newsletter at https://hopebennettauthor.com/newsletter/_to get updates on her latest releases.

Printed in Great Britain
by Amazon